Double Deceit

By Palma Harcourt

PALMA HARCOURT

Double Deceit

A Crime Club Book
DOUBLEDAY
New York London Toronto Sydney Auckland

A CRIME CLUB BOOK
PUBLISHED BY DOUBLEDAY
a division of Bantam Doubleday Dell Publishing Group, Inc.
666 Fifth Avenue, New York, New York 10103

DOUBLEDAY and the portrayal of a man
with a gun are trademarks of Doubleday,
a division of Bantam Doubleday Dell
Publishing Group, Inc.

Library of Congress Cataloging-in-Publication Data
ISBN 0-385-41770-5
Copyright © 1990 by Palma Harcourt

All Rights Reserved
July 1991
Printed in the United States of America
First Edition in the United States of America
10 9 8 7 6 5 4 3 2 1

For Veronica

PROLOGUE

The stable doors had been left partly open and a light wind blowing in disturbed the straw on the floor and caused the body that was hanging from a rope thrown over a rafter to rotate very slowly. It turned first to the right, then to the left, and the rafter creaked.

Beneath the dangling feet of his master lay a dog, a Cairn terrier. He had tried to jump and sniff at the elegant pair of hand-made boots above him, but he was too small to reach them, and had finally abandoned his efforts. From time to time he whimpered softly. Otherwise the stables were silent. The horses they had once housed were long gone, and nowadays they served partly as garages and partly for storage.

But outside a blackbird sang. It was seven o'clock of a May morning, the dew still heavy on the lawns of Fauvel Hall.

Fauvel had been built by one Alfred John Mourne in 1768. It was a plain, grey stone house, distinguished mainly by its largely unspoilt simplicity—a simplicity which had resisted the attempts of a long line of Mournes to extend and modernize. Always a "desirable residence," by the last quarter of the twentieth century it had become a house to be envied, for itself, for its ten acres of grounds and gardens, and for its proximity to London.

Yet until recently the Mournes had never been an eminent or important family. Since Alfred John, who had been an astute businessman in the terms of his period, and had married well, they had produced successful soldiers, lawyers, diplomats, politicians and civil servants, who had received the honours due to them. These honours had been comparatively minor, no more than an occasional knighthood.

Five generations after Alfred John, the incumbent of Fauvel had been David Mourne, a direct descendant of its builder. David had married twice, first to a Sophia Alford who predeceased him, but by whom he had one son, Peter David, and secondly to Elizabeth Grey, who outlived him and gave him two children before he died in 1937, a boy and a girl called John and Helen.

It was the next owner of Fauvel, Peter David, who had broken the family's pattern of modest though remunerative achievement. His current entry in *Who's Who* scarcely did him justice. He had had a long and distinguished political career, culminating in the post of Secretary of State for Foreign and Commonwealth Affairs. Indeed, at one point he had seemed a likely candidate to become Prime Minister, but the vicissitudes of politics had intervened.

Instead, he had retired a year ago in his seventies after a major heart attack, to become the first Viscount Mourne of Fauvel, honoured and respected in retirement in both Houses of Parliament, and a confidant of the Prime Minister.

Thus it was Peter who had made the family name famous, and it was the same Peter, Viscount Mourne, who was now hanging by his neck in the stables at Fauvel Hall.

For most of his life Peter Mourne had made a habit of rising early, for he was one of those fortunate individuals who needed little sleep. Even in his retirement and after his coronary, he had not changed his habit.

Today, as usual, he had risen at five-thirty, slipped out of bed without waking Carmela, his wife, and gone into the adjoining dressing-room. Here, with his customary rapidity, he had showered, shaved and dressed in the clothes laid out the night before by Simpson, his houseman.

Twenty minutes later he was in the big stone-flagged kitchen, bending to pat the Cairn who had leapt from his basket and was nuzzling himself against his master's legs.

The Cairn gave an excited yelp. Then he watched and waited, wagging his tail furiously. He knew the morning ritual as well as his master did. It seldom varied when they were at Fauvel.

Charlie's wants attended to, his bowl filled with fresh water and a handful of dog biscuits tossed on to the floor, Peter Mourne made himself a mug of instant coffee and sat at the kitchen table to drink it. He was not a big man, not more than five feet nine, and lightly built, but he still held himself upright and there was about him that certain air which implied that he was accustomed to a life of privilege, safe in the assurance that whatever he requested would be carried out promptly and efficiently. Perhaps it was the excellent tailoring of his jacket and breeches, carefully cut to disguise his small paunch; or maybe it was his expensive watch, his cuff-links and signet ring with the Mourne crest. Certainly it was not his face.

For Peter Mourne's features were not memorable. True, he had the Mournes' long thin nose, rather patrician and arrogant, but his mouth was narrow and, in old age, set in peevish lines. His eyes were a greenish brown, neither large nor small. In short it was a nondescript face, but the jaw line was firm, and the skin still healthy.

Having finished his coffee, he swilled out the mug and left it on the draining board. Then he whistled to the Cairn. The route of their morning walk was well established. The man and the dog did not leave the house by the main kitchen door, but instead moved along a passage, past doors leading to strange and now largely unused rooms—the pantry, the bottling room, the utility room, the cold store. To the dog they meant nothing except intriguing smells. The man was oblivious of them. He was deep in thought, and his thoughts, to judge from his frown, were not altogether pleasant.

Automatically he unbolted and unlocked a side door and Charlie shot past him into the open. It was a beautiful morning, the faintest hint of cloud striping the sky in the west, though at this early hour the sun had not yet risen, and the breeze was chill. However, Peter Mourne didn't seem to notice the cold. He strode off after the Cairn, as if hoping that the air and exercise would clear his mind.

Their daily walk invariably took them across the lawn, past the rose garden to the shrubbery, and then in a wide circle through the orchard to return via the stables to the house. This arrangement enabled Mourne to avoid the security guard and his Doberman.

The Prime Minister had insisted that Mourne should have protection, in spite of the latter's protests that once he had retired it was unnecessary. There had never been any trouble at Fauvel. A high wall surrounded the grounds, and at night the gates at the end of the drive were locked. But it had been impossible to gainsay the PM, and the best Mourne had been able to do was to come to agreements with the various guards that they should be as unobtrusive as possible.

Apart from the fact that Peter Mourne appeared unusually preoccupied, today was no different from any other. As was his wont he walked briskly, pausing occasionally to inspect a young camellia bud or to throw a stick for Charlie. By the time he reached the stone archway that led into the stable yard he was feeling refreshed and considerably more cheerful.

The Cairn darted ahead. He disappeared through a stable door, both halves of which were standing open, and did not reappear. Peter Mourne, who had followed him into the yard, frowned at the sight of the open door. No one should have been in the stables at this hour of the morning, but Charlie had not barked. Whoever was there—if anyone was—had to be someone he knew and accepted.

Unaware of any danger Mourne went across to investigate. As he stepped from the light into the deep gloom of the stable he was momentarily unable to see. Then he realized that Charlie was being held in the arms of a man whom he too recognized at once.

"Hello," said Mourne in surprise. "What on earth are you doing here so early?"

They were the last words he was to utter.

As Peter Mourne stepped forward into the stable the men who had been waiting to kill him took him from the rear. One pulled a thick soft textile gag across his mouth, while the other dragged back his arms, effectively rendering him almost helpless. Nevertheless, Mourne did his best. He kicked out hard behind him, and a blow must have landed because he heard a muffled curse. But it was merely a token resistance. There were two of them, half his age, and they were professionals. He had no hope.

At least it took but a short time to hang him. All was ready: the rope with its running noose secured to the rafter, the stool beneath, conveniently found in a corner of the stable, and carefully placed later in a position to which a would-be suicide could easily have kicked it.

But the third man, who was having difficulty holding on to a squirming Charlie, was impatient. "Hurry!" he said. "Hurry!"

The others ignored him. They knew their jobs. And within minutes Peter Mourne's body fell with a sickening jolt and his neck broke. At the same instant, almost as if he were aware of what had befallen his master, the Cairn stopped struggling and uttered a plaintive cry.

A swift check to make sure that Mourne was dead, a brief inspection of the stable, and the killers went the way they had come. Though there was time to spare before the security guard would reach the stable yard on his round, nevertheless they moved swiftly.

The two who had actually hanged Peter Mourne climbed over the high wall surrounding Fauvel Hall with ease, using the nylon ladder they had brought with them. Once on the other side they walked quietly along the lane for some twenty yards until they came to a gap in the hedge opposite. Behind it was their means of transport—a motor-cycle—and soon, anonymous under their statutory crash helmets, they were speeding towards London.

The other man, having seen them safely over the wall and heard the noise of the departing motor-bike, returned to the Hall and let himself in by the kitchen door. He was Simpson, the Mournes' houseman.

Carmela Mourne had been awake at five-thirty when her husband rose from his bed carefully, so as not to disturb her. She had feigned sleep, for she had passed a bad night and had no wish to talk. There was nothing more to say. They had discussed the situation far into the night, and had decided that nothing could be done; to deny rumours only fuelled gossip. But it was impossible not to worry.

After Peter had left their bedroom she pictured him dressing, going downstairs to greet Charlie, drinking his coffee, and setting out on his morning walk. She thought of him with affection. Over the years they had been through a lot of crises together, and she loved him dearly. It infuriated her that in their old age they should suddenly have become the target of malice—unexpected, hurtful malice.

Viscountess Mourne was small, with a neat, well-proportioned body. She had never been pretty, but now seventy, always impeccably groomed, and with all the aids that money could buy, she was undoubtedly handsome. Born Carmela Drelano, in Spain, it was very many years since she had lived in her native country. But she possessed the vibrant personality that is so often popularly associated with Spanish women, and there had been many who had envied Peter Mourne his wife.

On this particular morning, after a poor night, she must have drifted into sleep again, because she was startled when there was a sharp tap on the bedroom door. She sat up, and glanced instinctively at the clock on the night table beside her. The time was fifteen minutes to eight, too early for the coffee and toast which comprised her daily breakfast. Nevertheless, here was Mrs. Compton, the cook-housekeeper, with the tray.

"Are you awake, my lady?" Mrs. Compton asked.

"Yes!" said Carmela, and thought the woman must be stupid not to see in the light from the window that she was already sitting up and pulling on her bed jacket. And why had she brought only coffee? There was the pot on the tray, with a cup and saucer, but not toast. "Mrs. Compton, is something wrong?"

"Yes, my lady. I'm afraid there is."

Mrs. Compton put down the tray in its usual place and automatically went to draw the curtains. There had been some argument in the kitchen about who should break the news to Lady Mourne, and whether or not they should wait for the doctor or the police, but there had really been no doubt that Mrs. Compton must be the unwilling bearer of bad tidings. Now she didn't know how to begin.

"For heaven's sake," said Carmela impatiently. "What is it?"

"It's Lord Mourne, my lady. I'm so sorry to have to tell you, but—the security guard found him. He was in one of the stables. Dead."

"In a stable?"

Even as she asked it, Carmela realized how ludicrous her question was. What did it matter where Peter had died? What mattered was that he was dead, that he had died alone, without her beside him. Biting her bottom lip to restrain her tears, she began to get out of bed.

"My lady, I think you'd better stay here until the doctor—"

"Where have they put him?"

"Lord Mourne? He—he's still in the stable. The security guard said he mustn't be moved until the police—"

"Nonsense! Of course he must be brought into the house. Immediately! What can that fool guard be thinking of? The police are only a formality." Carmela was working herself into a temper. Later she would grieve for Peter. Now she must be practical and cope with the situation. "Well, what is it, woman? Why are you standing there, staring at me? Go and tell that guard what must be done. Lord Mourne should be put in the—the—"

But Mrs. Compton didn't appreciate being addressed as "woman," and she felt herself to be in a false position. She interrupted her mistress, speaking with unintentional brutality.

"Lord Mourne can't be moved, my lady. He didn't die natural. He hanged hisself, or so it seems."

Very slowly Carmela Mourne, who had been about to put on a silk peignoir before going to the bathroom, sank down on the side of the bed and let the robe slide to the floor. Hanged hisself, she repeated under her breath, unconsciously using Mrs. Compton's phrase. No! No! She didn't believe it. She wouldn't believe it. But the alternative was frightening.

She found herself staring into a mirror at a face that she failed to recognize as her own. The ribbon with which she tied back her long silver-grey hair at night had become loose and the hair, once so black, hung around her shoulders. Her dark-brown eyes were wild, as if seeing ghosts. Her mouth was slack. She might have been some mad creature, like those men and women she had seen wandering among the ruins of bombed-out houses in Madrid during the Spanish Civil War. Then she had despised them, wondering why they made so little effort. Then she had been young. Now—

Carmela, Viscountess Mourne, got back into bed. If there was one trait she didn't lack it was courage. She took a deep breath, squared her shoulders, and bowed her head in a gesture somehow reminiscent of royalty. "Thank you, Mrs. Compton," she said in a steady tone. "Would you please pour me a cup of coffee? As you advise, I shall stay here until the doctor comes."

CHAPTER ONE

Mark Ryle strode swiftly from his unobtrusive office at the top of Cork Street, through the Burlington Arcade and down Duke of York Street to St. James's Square and the Army and Navy Club, where he was to lunch with his uncle, Brigadier Richard Ryle, DSO, MC, retired. Reaching his destination, he ran up the steps and went through the large glass doors. He glanced at his watch and saw that he was on time. This was a relief; the Brigadier believed in punctuality. Indeed, the old man was already in the hall, at this time crowded with members awaiting their guests.

They shook hands—an unusual gesture for them. The two men were not given to outward signs of affection, though the bonds between them were deep since Dick Ryle and his wife had taken the twelve-year-old Mark into their home when his parents had been killed in a light aircraft accident. But this occasion was special, for they had not met each other for some months, as Mark had been abroad.

"Good to see you, my boy," said the Brigadier. "How are you? You're looking absolutely fine—much too brown for this time of year."

"I *am* fine, thanks. I've been in the Middle East, which accounts for the tan."

"A successful trip?"

"It's hard to tell, but at least I managed to avoid getting kidnapped."

"I'm glad of that," was the laconic response. "That's saved your aunt and myself a lot of worry. Let's go and get a drink. It may be a bit less crowded in the upstairs bar."

As he followed the tall, lean figure in its dark-grey suit and Guards' tie up the broad stairs to the first floor, Mark thought—not for the first time—how lucky he had been to have such relations, relations who would effectively adopt a small boy just when their own family had grown up. It had never occurred to him that, once the initial shock had worn off, Dick Ryle and his wife might have considered that it was they who were lucky.

Mark Ryle was a modest man, in spite of his achievements. At seventeen he had won an open scholarship to Oxford, where he had taken a First Class degree in politics, philosophy, and economics. When he left the university he had refused several excellent job offers, and had spent two years travelling. He had an ear for languages, which he enjoyed, and by this time he spoke five fluently, if not always grammatically. He was fit, too; he needed to be. His squash was first-class, and his golf handicap was in single figures.

Attractive, with dark hair and grey eyes, Mark Ryle had seemed to have the world at his feet. His contemporaries had expected him to rise effortlessly to the top of whatever field he chose. They were duly surprised when, by the age of thirty-three, he appeared to have settled for making a career as a political columnist for a comparatively unimportant weekly magazine, and as a freelance journalist and author. He claimed, when asked, that the job saved him from the rat race, and gave him the freedom he craved to write and travel.

To some extent this was the truth. He had always been a loner, and he had deliberately decided upon his present way of life, and pulled the necessary strings to achieve it. His views might have been different if an early love affair had not ended miserably, if he had married and had children. But the relationship hadn't turned out that way and, though he never lacked girlfriends, none of them had ever again been of sufficient importance for him to contemplate marriage. The nature of his real work militated against any such step, too.

"You're deep in thought, Mark," said Dick Ryle, putting down the drinks he had brought from the bar, and settling himself on the banquette beside his nephew. "I can't believe the view from the window is so absorbing."

"It's had its moments," Mark said briefly. His companion understood him; some years ago a bomb thrown through a large plate-glass window on the ground floor had wrecked the smoking-room. More recently the Iranian Embassy directly across the square had been under siege, and a policewoman killed. "But no. I must admit my mind wasn't on the view." He changed the subject. "How are you, and Aunt Penny?"

Dick Ryle smiled at the way in which Mark had avoided his unspoken question, but he made no comment and didn't press the point. He was one of the few people who were aware that Mark's seemingly unimpressive occupation was a cover for intelligence activities that were sometimes unrewarding, always demanding, and often dangerous. Instead, he answered Mark.

"We're both in good form, thanks, but Penny complains bitterly that ever since her seventieth birthday she's beginning to feel old."

Mark laughed. "I imagine that doesn't make her go slow at all."

"Not that one would notice. Naturally, she wants to know when you're coming down to see us."

"I can't promise," Mark said with a rueful shrug. It was one of the drawbacks of his work that it played havoc with any social life. "I'll phone."

The Brigadier nodded. He got to his feet and collected their glasses. "Let me get us the other half, then we'll go into lunch," he said.

It was not until they had eaten and were having coffee in the smoking-room that Brigadier Ryle broached the subject that had been at the back of his mind throughout the meal. By this time the main lunchtime crush had disappeared, and they had found a corner table where there was no fear of their conversation being overheard. Nevertheless, Dick Ryle kept his voice low.

"Mark, you've been back in the UK only a few days, so I imagine you've not yet caught up with London gossip."

"No. Don't tell me there's another scandal brewing."

"Possibly. There's a strange rumour going around at the moment about Peter Mourne, Viscount Mourne as he now is, the last Foreign Secretary. You know him?"

"I can't say that I'm more than acquainted with Lord Mourne, but when I'm home I often have a meal with John and Colette." John, Peter Mourne's half-brother and his wife, Colette, had been very kind to Mark Ryle, ever since their son, Hugh, had taken him home from school one half-term holiday, and introduced him as his best friend.

"I keep in touch with Hugh, of course," Mark continued. "At present he's a First Secretary at our embassy in Madrid. And Helen Mourne, John's sister, sometimes asks me to a meal—usually when she wants a spare man. So I do see a certain amount of the family."

Mark spoke with a studied casualness which he guessed failed to deceive his uncle. But he didn't want to talk about the final member of the Mourne family—Jeanne, daughter of Colette and John and sister of Hugh. He had read of her engagement to the Honourable Simon Maufant, MP, in a week-old copy of *The Times* while he was abroad, and he had told himself that it was no concern of his. He had thought of writing, but somehow hadn't got around to it; the letter was too difficult to draft. When the time came he would send a present, and make sure he was out of the country for the wedding. She wouldn't mind.

Mark went on quickly, "Anyway, what is it about the Viscount? I'd have thought he was beyond reproach—a pillar of the Establishment!" Mark was amused. "What on earth is he supposed to have done? Cheated on his income tax, or been found running a chain of brothels on the quiet?"

"It's no joke, Mark. The story is that he's a Soviet agent, and has been one for years. Another Philby or, to be more up to date, another Sir Percy Dart." Dick Ryle was referring to Percival Dart, Eton and Oxford, head of one of the most secret Government research establishments, adviser to the Prime Minister, friend of Royalty, who had been tried as a Soviet agent a couple of years ago and was at present serving a life sentence in jail. The case had rocked the British Establishment and the British public, as well as the entire Western alliance.

"What? But that's absurd. It's nonsense to suggest—"

"I'm afraid it's gone way beyond an absurdity by this time." There was an edge to Dick Ryle's voice. To Mark's surprise it was clear that the old man took the matter very seriously indeed, and he was not prone to exaggeration, especially where gossip was concerned. "You know how these things can grow, Mark. A whisper here and a whisper there. It's becoming unpleasant."

Mark still shook his head in disbelief. "And what's Mourne doing about it?"

"Ignoring the whole thing, as far as I can make out," said the Brigadier.

"I see," said Mark thoughtfully. "I suppose there's no reason for him to take action. After all, he's no longer in office. He's got nothing to lose, and no one in his right mind would believe such nonsense."

"As I say, to my knowledge Mourne's ignored the gossip so far, but there *is* a limit. One of our supposedly witty columnists made a crack about it yesterday in one of the tabloids. Admittedly, it would have meant little, except to those already in the know, but soon it could be open season in the media."

"There's such a thing as libel. Mourne could sue."

"I don't think it's reached that stage yet, but he may have to—though I often think going to law about this sort of thing does more harm than good." Dick Ryle was bitter. "A public apology, a large out-of-court settlement that the injured party donates to charity as a superior gesture. But the damage isn't undone. On the contrary, it's multiplied by the publicity given to the affair. It's a dreadful truism that mud sticks."

"And this kind of mud, if it were to stick to Peter Mourne—ex-Foreign Secretary, close friend of the Prime Minister, recipient of Royal favours and acquainted with innumerable highly-placed foreigners—could cause havoc in a great many places. There can't be many secrets he isn't privy to," said Mark quickly, and thought his comment might prove something of an understatement. "I see your point. Are the authorities taking any line?"

"Not that I know of, but it's a question in the House they must be afraid of. The Opposition might well try to make something of it. Or some fool of an MP might take it upon himself to name Mourne under the cloak of privilege."

"You think it's a possibility?" said Mark.

"Yes, I do!" replied Dick Ryle sharply.

Mark waited while the old man—Mourne's contemporary, he reminded himself—slowly stirred the dregs of his milkless, sugarless coffee. The silence lengthened.

At last Mark said, "I suppose no one has any idea who originated the story?" And when the Brigadier shook his head, he continued, "It's never easy to demonstrate a negative, but if it could be shown that someone had started it out of spite it might die a natural death."

"I doubt if that's likely—to be able to point a finger at a single culprit, I mean, Mark. I think we'll just have to hope that because it's such a preposterous story it won't be given any credit."

As the two Ryles left the smoking-room they were greeted by a buzz of noisy and excited voices from a group of men clustered around the Teletext monitor.

"Something's happened," Dick Ryle said without much interest. "Probably another scare on the Stock Exchange."

"Or a bomb somewhere," said Mark casually.

Then they heard the word Mourne mentioned on the fringes of the small crowd, and simultaneously they moved towards the set.

An acquaintance of the Brigadier turned to him, as they tried to see the screen, and said, "It's Peter Mourne, Dick. He's dead."

"Hanged himself," said someone else. "In the stables of his house. What a way to go! Personally I'd choose a bottle of whisky and some sleeping pills. Much less painful."

While Dick Ryle pushed his way to the front of the group so as to read the bleak statement for himself, Mark stood to one side and listened to the various comments. Most were routine; surprise seemed to be the most common reaction, followed by frequent expressions of regret. There were references to Mourne's heart condition, and some suggestions that he might have been otherwise ill. But Mark heard one man, someone whom he knew to be a senior official at the Ministry of Defence, mutter to another, "Stand by! This could really open a can of worms."

He repeated the remark to his uncle as they left the club and strolled along Pall Mall towards Trafalgar Square. Dick Ryle nodded soberly.

"I'm afraid the man's right," he said. "This could be nasty. There could be a heap of reasons why Mourne no longer chose to live; his suicide doesn't necessarily suggest his guilt. But there's no doubt that a hell of a lot of people will believe it substantiates these damned rumours."

"Can anything be done, except wait for the cloud of suspicion to settle?"

"Not unless his doctor swears he was suffering from senile dementia or inoperable bowel cancer or something that might provide a plausible explanation. And even then, there'd be plenty who'd claim it was a whitewash. I can think of—" Dick Ryle left the sentence unfinished.

For a few moments the two men walked in silence, Mark slowing his pace a little to accommodate his uncle. As was only to be expected, their thoughts were not dissimilar.

Then Mark said, "Apart from any rumours, the suicide of such an eminent character will be bound to cause a stir."

"Yes. The media are going to have a field day."

"It's not going to be very pleasant for the family, either. Worst for Lady Mourne, of course—but the rest will suffer too. It'll be a trying time for all the Mournes—except perhaps Helen. She's certainly one who won't grieve for her half-brother. They've never got on together, though heaven knows why."

"There's no law to say one must love one's relations."

"No, but one does, if one's lucky." Mark grinned. He had stopped walking, and was signalling to a taxi. "I'm sorry but I must get on. I've got to go across the river for the afternoon. Can I drop you somewhere?"

Dick Ryle shook his head. "I understand." He knew that Mark's office in Mayfair was connected with the SIS, and he assumed that his nephew was about to visit Century House, its headquarters on the south bank of the Thames. "I've some shopping to do."

"Okay. Then many thanks for the lunch. My love to Aunt Penny."

Dick Ryle gave a wave of his hand as Mark's taxi drew away from the kerb, and was lost in a line of traffic. He had indeed noticed Mark's earlier omission of any reference to Jeanne Mourne, and it grieved him to think that Mark still cared for Hugh's sister. He regretted their break-up. He had liked Jeanne. As he turned to walk up Lower Regent Street he wondered if she would be happy with the aggressive, ambitious Simon Maufant, who saw himself as a future Cabinet Minister at the very least. Somehow he doubted it. But he was more concerned about Mark—and the possible outcome of the rumours about Peter Mourne.

For his part, Mark Ryle was not concerned about himself. Nor was he really concerned about Jeanne, who worked as an interior decorator in Paris, and anyway now had a fiancé to look after her. Hugh, too, was well established in the Foreign Office—probably too well established for any scandal to affect his career—and certainly the acerbic Helen could cope. What worried Mark most was the thought of John and Colette Mourne.

Apart presumably from Lady Mourne, whom he scarcely knew and for whom he felt no particular affection, John and Colette were likely to be among those most affected by Peter Mourne's suicide, and the scandal that might be precipitated. Though they had never been close to Peter and Carmela, Colette was French and had a strong sense of family; she would insist on giving every support to the widow. And John, though only Peter's half-brother, was still his closest blood-relation.

These were the personal aspects of the matter. The public angles, Mark was fully aware, could be far more important. He found no reassurance in the billboard by the newspaper stall on the corner where his taxi had deposited him. In block capitals it read: "MOURNE'S MYSTERY DEATH."

And, as he paid his fare, the driver said, "Between you and me, one of my passengers told me that old geezer was a Red."

Mark hesitated, startled. Then he said non-committally, "People'll say anything, won't they?"

CHAPTER TWO

John Mourne came out of Court Three at the Old Bailey. At sixty-two, his appearance, except for the long Mourne nose, was not particularly distinguished, but he had an unblemished reputation for integrity. Then he saw his clerk hurrying along the corridor towards him, and he knew instinctively that here was bad news.

"Mr. Mourne, sir!"

"Hello, Lander. What brings you over here?"

"I wanted to catch you, sir, in case you preferred to go straight home without coming back to Chambers. It's Lord Mourne. I don't know if you've heard, but I'm afraid he's dead."

"Yes, I had heard. Someone told me as I was going into court that it had been on the news. But thank you for coming across, Lander. Of course, it's a great pity, but it's not exactly unexpected. He wasn't a young man and he'd had one bad coronary."

Lander interrupted him. "I'm afraid that's not all, sir. I'm sorry, but it seems that Lord Mourne took his own life. He—he was found hanged."

"That I hadn't heard. Damnation!" said John Mourne.

It was a moment before he collected himself, and made a more conventional response. Lander, who had been looking shocked, bowed his balding head and offered condolences.

"It's very sad for the family, sir, when things like this happen."

"Sad" was hardly the word John would have chosen in the present circumstances. Some much stronger adjective was needed, he felt. Though by nature he was a kind man, "bloody annoying" came unbidden into his mind. He wondered if Lander had heard the rumours about the late Viscount. Never by so much as a flick of an eyebrow had he implied any knowledge of them, but it was more than likely that he had—little gossip escaped the attention of barristers' clerks in the closed world of the Inns of Court.

"Thanks again, Lander, I'll do as you suggest and go straight home," said John Mourne quickly. "Take my briefcase, will you? Unfortunately, I dare say there'll be plenty for me to do. Lady Mourne has no children, and I'm Lord Mourne's nearest relative."

John unlocked his Volvo, started the engine, and sat thinking. He supposed that he should be overwhelmed by horror that Peter had committed suicide, but he wasn't. His immediate reaction had been anger that Peter, by his own fool action, should have given credence to the absurd rumours that had started to circulate. He knew this feeling was neither rational nor fair. He was a little ashamed of it, and he admitted to himself that his remark to Lander implying that he might be about to assume responsibility for Peter's affairs had been, in a sense, a sop to his own conscience.

Nevertheless, John Mourne continued to curse under his breath as he set out for home. Traffic was heavy. There were long delays at junctions. The journey to Hampstead seemed unending. He tried the radio, but the first words he heard were those of someone commenting on the surprising death of Viscount Mourne. This was only the beginning, John knew, and as the speaker made some inaccurate remark about Peter Mourne's career, he turned the set off in disgust.

His thoughts, however, remained centred on Peter. In fact, they had shared the same father, but little else. He had known Peter less well than he knew many of his personal, though unrelated, friends and colleagues. The ten-year gap in their ages had made all the difference. He had still been in the nursery, and Helen scarcely born, when Peter was sent away to boarding school, and even in the holidays they hadn't seen much of him, for Peter was a solitary child who appeared to show a measure of affection for little Helen, but for no one else.

Suddenly John felt a rush of sympathy for his half-brother, and yet—He recalled the day of the "great row." He had been nine, home from his first year at prep school. Helen, two years younger, didn't yet go to school, but instead had a governess. It was 1937, and they were looking forward to the summer holidays, three weeks to be spent by the sea, the rest at Fauvel Hall.

The row had started over lunch, though later no one could remember precisely who or what had precipitated it. But for some reason Peter, who was expected to go up to Oxford that autumn, had chosen this moment to announce that he had no intention of wasting his time at any university. The *Spectator* had recently accepted an article he had submitted, and he proposed to do his best to become a journalist.

The ensuing argument had been bitter, and it was probably because of this bitterness that Peter had not been swayed by references to undergraduate journalism and the bright prospects that might eventually accompany a degree. The root of the matter, of course, was that David Mourne, essentially a late Victorian, regarded journalism (unless perhaps one were the editor of *The Times)* as a disreputable trade rather than a profession.

In the end, matters had reached such a pitch that Peter had slammed out of the room, packed a bag, and left the house. At first his father had tended to regard this move as a childish tantrum, but when Peter failed to reappear that day, or the next, or the next, action had to be taken. The authorities had treated the matter with some seriousness and searches and inquiries had spread across southern England. The notoriety that was involved had proved hard for the parents to bear, and the pressure was only eased when after some months a friend reported that a friend of his had come across Peter operating with some success as a freelance journalist on the fringes of the Spanish Civil War.

Nevertheless, no member of the family was to hear directly from Peter for several years, and the Mournes could never again be regarded as truly united.

John and Colette Mourne lived in a long, low, mellow-bricked house in a fashionable road overlooking the south-west edge of Hampstead Heath. While Elizabeth, John's mother, had been alive, and the children, Hugh and Jeanne, were growing up, it had often seemed too small for their various lives and activities. Now there were just the two of them, it was undoubtedly too large, and they often spoke of moving.

As John swung the Volvo through the gates and up the short drive to the garage, he saw his wife wave from a window. She was waiting at the open front door when he reached it. Colette was tall, almost as tall as her husband, and slender, her grey hair cut short to frame her face, her eyes an unusual green. She looked considerably younger than her sixty years, and, as was true of so many Frenchwomen, she managed to look elegant whatever she wore.

Before she spoke she kissed John firmly on the mouth. He held her for a moment, and then said, "You know." It was not a question.

"Yes. I just heard it on the radio a short time ago. I phoned your Chambers but Lander said you were already on your way home." In spite of the many years she had spent in England, Colette still spoke with a slight French accent. "I thought of trying Carmela but, being a coward, I decided to wait for you. It must be dreadful for her, John—that he should have taken his own life. Dreadful!"

"It may not be too pleasant for any of us, darling, once things start rolling. There's going to be a hell of a lot of publicity."

"I was afraid of that. No matter. I'll fix us both an early drink while— perhaps?" She smiled at him.

"Of course," John agreed. "I'll phone at once."

He went into his study and tapped out the number of Fauvel Hall. At first it was engaged, but when he tried again a few moments later a voice answered, "Yes?" When John had explained who he was, he was asked to hold the line. It seemed a lengthy wait. Then someone else spoke, though it wasn't Carmela.

"Mr. Mourne, sir, this is Simpson, the houseman, you remember. I regret it's not possible for you to speak to Lady Mourne at present. The doctor has given her a sedative, and she's resting, but she asked me to tell you she'll telephone you later this evening."

John barely had time to say thank you before the line went dead, though it rang again as soon as he had replaced the receiver. It was his sister, Helen.

"John, dear, I'm in Jersey, staying with friends for a few days. They've been driving me around their beautiful island, showing me some of the sights, and we heard the news on the car radio. Poor old Peter! He was a bit of a shit, but I wouldn't wish that sort of death on anyone."

"Nor would I," replied John. Helen had always been outspoken, he thought, and wondered whether she had heard the rumours about the Viscount. "Helen, when are you coming back?"

"I was planning on Wednesday, dear. When's the funeral? Towards the end of the week? I suppose all the Mournes will have to rally round."

"Yes," John said shortly, thinking that in the course of the next few weeks his sister might regret having reclaimed her maiden name after her disastrous marriage had ended in divorce so many years ago. "I hope to speak to Carmela later tonight," he added, "but at the moment she's incommunicado. Anyway, I doubt if anything's been decided yet—about arrangements, I mean. We'll keep in touch."

"Do that," said Helen. "I'll give you this number."

After a few more words they said goodbye. By now Colette had brought drinks into the study, and John threw himself gratefully into an armchair. Helen had reminded him that he must contact his son and daughter, both of them abroad.

"Wait till you've heard from Carmela," Colette advised. "It'll be easier for Jeanne and Hugh to make plans if we know what Carmela intends."

"I suppose so." John sighed. "It's difficult to know what to do."

"Yes." Colette smiled sadly. "If it were my French family, I'd know all right. By now, you and I and everyone else would be on our way to Fauvel Hall. But the Mournes—you're different."

"Yes, we're different," John admitted. "But in all fairness it was Peter who distanced himself from us. A psychiatrist would probably say it was because he resented our father marrying again, and extended his resentment to the new wife—and to Helen and me, her offspring. But these are deep waters. Anyway, we've no choice. We've got to stand by Carmela now, whether she likes it or not—especially in view of these damned rumours about Peter."

The death of Viscount Mourne was the lead item on the BBC news at nine, though, surprisingly, there was no mention of the manner of his dying. The newscaster merely said that the former Foreign Secretary had been found dead at his country residence, and that there was no question of foul play; an appreciation would follow after the news.

The appreciation took the usual form of a TV obituary. A senior Cabinet Minister said that with Mourne's death the nation had suffered a grievous loss, and that the Prime Minister was most upset. It was understood that Her Majesty was expressing her condolences to Viscountess Mourne.

"I'm glad to see the Establishment's rallying behind Peter," John remarked. "It may help to quash these bloody rumours, though of course the cat's out of the bag and the tabloids will make hay tomorrow, and even the

BBC can't be expected to ignore them for ever. Incidentally, I wonder when Carmela's going to phone."

He and Colette had had supper and were back in the study waiting for the phone to ring. The delay had been so lengthy that they had changed their minds, and had already phoned Hugh in Madrid and Jeanne in Paris. The responses had been similar; each of them would fly home for the funeral, as and when needed.

At this point the phone purred. John picked up the instrument immediately and, hearing Carmela's voice, nodded to his wife. "Hello, Carmela," he said. "My dear, we were so grieved to hear about Peter. What can we do to help? Would you like Colette to come down to Fauvel and stay with you? I could drive her down right away if you wished—or she could drive herself tomorrow morning. Personally, I've got to be in court—" He grimaced as he was cut short.

A minute later the call was over, and John's smile was regretful as he turned to Colette. "I get the impression that neither we nor our help are wanted. Carmela sounds composed, and completely in control of the situation. She says she's receiving excellent co-operation from the authorities. There has to be a post-mortem and an inquest, of course, but the funeral is scheduled for Friday. Family only. You and I and Helen are welcome to stay the weekend at Fauvel. There'll be a memorial service for Peter in a few weeks. End of message. All very businesslike. It must be the Spanish grandee influence."

"My dear, don't feel like that. She may be afraid of breaking down if she doesn't keep tight control of herself," Colette said charitably. "She didn't say anything about why Peter should have chosen to die like that?"

"No, and she didn't give me a chance to ask, either. She wasn't exactly unfriendly, just—just—impersonal." John sighed.

"What shall we do, then? Go down for the funeral and stay the night?"

"Yes, I'd like to, darling. And we'd better be prepared to stay for more than one night. At least it'll give us a chance to see what the form is. I'm afraid it may turn out to be a pretty ghastly weekend."

"It doesn't matter," Colette reassured him. "John, you've had a long day, *chéri*. Let's have a nightcap and go to bed."

It was easy to go to bed, easy to make gentle love, but not so easy to sleep. After a while Colette's breathing became regular, but John remained awake, lying on his back, hands behind his head, careful not to disturb her. His thoughts turned to Carmela, and his conversation with her. In retrospect, it had been less of a conversation than a statement she seemed to have rehearsed in advance to make to him—or to any other member of the family. He realized he was worried.

He told himself that Colette's explanation was probably correct, but he found it hard to credit. He wondered idly what Carmela would do now. It was most unlikely she would think of returning to Spain. Presumably she would stay at Fauvel; presumably she now owned the Mournes' family home.

He had no idea of the contents of Peter's will. Their father had died a few months after the "great row"—indeed, it was claimed that his stroke might well have been induced by it—and, even if he'd intended to do so, he had not disinherited his elder son. Fauvel Hall was to be the home of his wife, Elizabeth, for as long as she wished to live there and bring up her children there. Afterwards it would go to Peter and his heirs.

It had been supposed that by then Peter would be married, probably with a son of his own. Married he had been, but there had been no children. And now—John Mourne drifted into an uneasy sleep.

CHAPTER THREE

The morning after Viscount Mourne's death, Mark Ryle was in his office in the suite occupied by his unit in Cork Street. By nature he was an orderly man, and as a rule he liked to keep his room tidy and uncluttered, but today order and tidiness had been abandoned. His desk was deep in newspapers, and on the chair beside him was a pile of cuttings, with paragraphs sidelined in red.

He continued to read. He had started with the qualities and was now down to the gutter press. He found several suggestive comments, remarks that were liable to a variety of interpretations, innuendoes. There was no doubt that the rumours concerning Peter Mourne had spread, and were being voiced as a result of his suicide. He suspected that in the next few days the outright accusation that Viscount Mourne had been a Soviet agent would be made. The media would be quite safe from legal action; one cannot libel the dead.

Of course there would be a storm of protests and denials, both official and unofficial. Undoubtedly the matter would be raised in the House, with demands for a public inquiry. No matter what the Government's reaction was, suspicion would persist. It would be levelled at Peter Mourne's relations, his friends, his colleagues—innocent people. Hugh's career in the FCO might suffer a setback, at least temporarily. Thankful that this was not his business and that, apart from his affection for John and Colette and their family, he was not directly concerned, Ryle became aware of the buzz of his intercom.

It was the voice of Maggie Stewart, his resourceful and efficient personal assistant and secretary. Selfishly, Ryle was thankful that she was married to a man who had been crippled in a car accident and so was unlikely to leave her job, which was well-paid and occasionally intriguing, though it had certain drawbacks. "Mark," Maggie said, "the Director would like to see you—five minutes ago."

"Thanks, Maggie, I'm on my way."

Ryle looked at the piles of newspapers around him, and decided to leave them. He knew that "five minutes ago" was a warning he shouldn't ignore. He was wanted, urgently.

He found the Director, hands clasped behind his back, staring out of the window of his office. He turned slowly as Ryle came in, but for a moment said nothing. General Sir Walter Bannol was a tall, heavily-built man in his late fifties. A widower for some years, he was happy to work all hours at his job as Director of one of the smaller and lesser-known off-shoots of the SIS, and he expected his staff to follow suit. He liked to emphasize that theirs was not a nine-to-five occupation and, whatever other commitments individuals might have, the work came first. His group was in fact usually called on by the Cabinet Office Intelligence Co-ordinator for super-sensitive operations that bridged the apparently un-bridgeable gulf between the SIS and the Security Service—a fact that made him less than popular with both services. His staff invariably operated under a variety of covers at home and abroad, and made contact with their intelligence colleagues in embassies overseas only when secure communications were required.

In spite of his hours of work, and his demands on his staff, General Bannol had his virtues. He always gave his staff as much information as he deemed right and safe—a procedure not always followed in the intelligence and security services—and when operations went awry, as they did occasionally, he always supported his people. As a result they liked and trusted him.

"Good morning, Mark," he said at last.

"Good morning, sir."

"Sit down. I'll stand, if you don't mind. My rheumatism's bothering me today."

"I'm sorry about that, sir."

"You don't really give a damn, do you, Mark?" said the General absently.

Such a response was typical of his superior, and Ryle made no reply, but sat and waited. It was unlike the Director not to come to the point quickly, and this morning he seemed singularly indecisive. When he finally did speak, the question was surprising.

"Mark, would you object to making inquiries about people you considered to be friends of yours?"

Ryle hesitated. Then, "It would depend on the circumstances, sir, wouldn't it?"

"I'm afraid circumstances have made it necessary. I'm talking about the Mournes, as I expect you've guessed. They are friends of yours, aren't they?"

"I met the late Viscount Mourne and his wife a couple of times. I doubt if she'd remember me," Ryle said carefully. "I'm very fond of John and Colette Mourne. Hugh, their son, is an old schoolfriend, and I—I know their daughter."

He braced himself for some comment—probably scathing—but it didn't come, though he was sure Bannol knew of his former relationship with Jeanne. "What's the problem?" he asked. "What is it you would want me to do—sir?" He added the last word as an afterthought.

"Mark, don't play silly buggers!" Bannol was annoyed. "You know perfectly well what the problem is. There's a rumour—more than a rumour by now—that our ex-Foreign Secretary was in the pay of the Soviets, and had been for years. Think what the consequences would be if this could be shown to be true. For years Mourne was in a position of inside knowledge, of suggestion, of influence, of power."

"I know, sir. I've heard the gossip, and I've just been studying the papers—"

"So you are interested in the affair. Why?" The question was sharp.

"Because, as you say, the Mournes—or at least some of them—are close friends, dear to me."

"Which means you're in a better position than most to ferret out the truth."

"But—" Mark Ryle spoke uncertainly. "Are you putting any credence in the—the rumours, sir?"

"If I were a betting man, I'd say the chances were a hundred to one against there being any truth in them. Probably the odds are higher still, but then I'm a cynical character." Bannol lowered his bulk carefully into the chair behind his desk. "In any case, there's a good deal more to it than that. What I—and the Prime Minister—want to know is why the rumours were started, and who started them? It didn't just happen. And it wasn't a seed planted out of a moment's spite. If you'd been following developments as closely as I have, you'd know that seed's been carefully watered."

"You mean Mourne's been deliberately set up?"

"That appears to be a strong possibility," Bannol said. "And this raises other problems—vital problems. The Opposition will probably cry out for some kind of inquiry—or even a Royal Commission—but the PM's already decided that the rumours are a lot of nonsense and don't warrant an investigation. A statement to that effect will be made in the House this afternoon, and appear in the media immediately. The PM expects to get away with it, at least for the time being. But the PM's no fool and shares my view that the gossip may have been planted for a purpose. If so, as I say, it's essential to know why. You follow me?"

"Only too well, sir, I'm afraid," said Ryle grimly. "No official inquiry, but unofficially . . . I see where we come in. What exactly is my brief?"

Bannol nodded his satisfaction. All his staff were intelligent—they wouldn't have stayed long otherwise—but Mark Ryle was among the brightest. The General shifted in his chair; he hadn't been joking about his rheumatism.

"First, you report direct to me, Mark, and I report to the PM. No one else, except the Director-General—and Maggie, of course—is to suspect that any sort of investigation is taking place. Do I make myself clear?"

"Yes, sir, but if it's to be off the record, what authority do I have to ask questions?"

"None! That is, not unless you can persuade Lady Mourne, or failing her, John Mourne, to authorize you."

"I see." Mark Ryle kept his voice neutral, devoid of bitterness. "How do you expect me to do that, if no one's to know there's an inquiry?"

"I thought you might say you were interested in writing a biography of Viscount Mourne. Naturally, as an old friend of the family, you would hope for their co-operation. After all, you're supposed to be a writer with a biography to your credit."

"That was a life of my father."

"So? A lot of books are going to be published about Mourne, and I'm sure the family would be pleased to have someone known to them—and sympathetic—to write a definitive work."

Mark Ryle said nothing. There was nothing to say. The old bastard had thought it all out in advance. It was possible to refuse the assignment. General Bannol had never been known to force anyone to undertake a task against his will. But—In the circumstances there was really no choice.

When he returned to his paper-strewn office Ryle sat at his desk for some five minutes, considering. Then he made a phone call to the Mournes' Hampstead house. The receiver was picked up immediately, and he recognized Colette's voice.

"Yes. Who is that?" she snapped.

"Mark Ryle. I'm back in London, Colette."

"Oh, Mark! My dear, I am so sorry. I thought it was another damned reporter wanting to ask questions about Peter. You know about Peter?"

"Yes. I—I'm sorry. You have all my sympathy."

"It's not exactly a personal grief," Colette said honestly. "But I'm afraid it's brought trouble for John, and probably will for Hugh. They— We can't talk on the phone, Mark. When can you come to see us? Tomorrow? Could you come to supper tomorrow?"

"I should love to. Many thanks. About seven-thirty?"

"That would be fine. Earlier if you like."

The next day, when he arrived in Hampstead, Mark Ryle was unsure whether to be pleased or annoyed to find that Helen Mourne was already at her brother's house and would be joining them for supper. However bizarre John and Colette might think the idea of him as Peter Mourne's biographer, they would at least show a pleasant interest, and avoid asking unanswerable questions; indeed he sometimes suspected that John had made a good guess at the real nature of his work, that he would probably have put two and two together and arrived at something like the right answer.

Helen was different. She had no inhibitions, and was likely to roar with laughter, blast the whole project with some caustic comment, and then begin to probe. On the other hand, he reflected, because she had no inhibitions and didn't care a damn what she said, he might learn more about Peter from her than from any other member of the family.

He greeted John and Colette with affection, then dutifully kissed Helen on both cheeks. "You're looking very well," he said to her.

"Thank you for nothing," she replied lightly. "When men start saying you look well, as opposed to beautiful, radiant, desirable or some such word, you know you're over the hill. They no longer find you attractive and are merely being polite."

Mark laughed. "You're fishing for compliments," he said, "and you don't need to."

"Now, that's a considerable improvement. Keep trying on those lines, dear boy."

Helen grinned. She knew perfectly well that she had never been beautiful, but she didn't care, and hadn't done so for many years. When she was younger she had complained about her "Mourne nose." Now, just sixty, the same age as her sister-in-law Colette, she looked older, perhaps because she lacked the inner tranquillity that was so much a part of Colette's charm. Helen herself was very thin, and always seemed to be in motion, the bracelets she made a habit of wearing jangling on her wrists.

She was clever and artistic, but had made little use of her gifts. A large once-and-for-all payment from her rich husband on their divorce, plus a little money inherited from her parents, provided an income that enabled her to live modestly in a small flat in Kensington. Over the years she had had lovers, but had refused to marry again and, now old age was approaching, seemed content with her way of life and showed every sign of enjoying it.

One quality Helen did lack, however, was tact, and Mark had barely sipped his pre-dinner drink before she said, "You say you've been abroad for weeks, Mark. Did you miss the announcement of Jeanne's engagement?"

"No. I did see it. I've been meaning to write to her."

"She'll be here for Peter's funeral," John said. "Hugh, too."

"So maybe you can tell her in person how pleased you are—that is, if you *are* pleased," said Helen. "Personally, I think it's a great mistake."

"Helen!" Colette protested.

"What's the matter? Why shouldn't I say what I think?" Helen demanded. "This Simon fellow is never going to make her happy. He's a smug, self-centred creature. She'd have done better to marry you, Mark."

"Obviously she didn't think so." Mark's voice was taut.

"And as for you, Helen, you scarcely qualify as a marriage counsellor," Colette said tartly.

"No." Helen smiled. "Anyway, I'll do my best to love my new nephew-in-law."

Before Colette could respond, John suggested a second drink. Conversation became general, and turned first to the weekend Helen had just spent in Jersey. Mark was able to relax. The evening passed pleasantly, but he hesitated to mention the idea of a biography of the late Peter Mourne to the family so soon after the tragic death. Eventually, however, he broached the subject.

"Why you?" Helen reacted at once.

"Why not me?" said Mark mildly. "Writing's my job, especially about politics and politicians. I shall be one of many prospective biographers, of course. Viscount Mourne was an important man. But I know the Mourne family, and I hope you'll agree I would be—be sympathetic, shall I say?"

"Yes, I'm sure you would—will—be," John said quickly, glancing at

Colette, who was unresponsive, not happy with the idea. "But—Mark, you've heard this—this story that's suddenly surfaced—about Peter being a—a communist?"

Mark nodded. "Yes. I'm sorry to say that by now it's more or less in the public domain."

"And you'd like to cash in on it?" Helen said angrily. "I hold no brief for Peter. He was a shit, if you want my opinion, but I'm damned if I'll believe that any Mourne was a traitor."

There was a long and uncomfortable silence. Mark was silently cursing General Sir Walter Bannol. The idea of a biography had been stupid, mad even—a non-starter. So far it had done nothing, except come close to losing him friends whom he valued highly. He had better leave.

Helen forestalled him. As he made to get up, she said, "Mark, I apologize. That remark was quite uncalled for. If you want to write this damned book I'll help all I can, though that won't be much. I've no letters or photographs, and I hardly ever saw Peter."

"That goes for me too," John said. "You've got to realize what a difference the age gap made when we were children—and then there was the war. Mother thought Fauvel was too close to London to be safe, though in fact no bomb ever fell near it, and we spent our school holidays with cousins in Somerset. We didn't see Peter for literally several years after he came back from Spain. Fauvel was technically our home, I suppose, until 1950, but what with university and national service for me, and finishing school for Helen, we weren't there much. When we were, Peter was usually away, nursing his constituency or being an MP. You know that he and Carmela had a flat in Westminster in the Division bell area?"

Mark caught himself grinning in his relief that after all there seemed to be no serious quarrel between them. He nodded and said, "You mentioned 1950. Was that an important year for the family?"

Helen answered. "In some ways it was a watershed for John and me. In effect, we lost Fauvel, our home, the family's home. Peter and Carmela made it clear that they proposed to do a lot of entertaining, and neither we nor our friends would be welcome, unless we were given a specific invitation."

"But why did they wait till 1950?" Mark still failed to understand.

"I'd come down from Oxford," John said. "I'd taken my Bar exams and eaten my dinners, and I'd been admitted. In fact, I was a fully qualified barrister, and I had found some Chambers who would take me on. I didn't have many briefs, admittedly, but I needed to live in London. And Helen was about to get married. I'm sure Helen would agree that she and I were pretty well on our way out when Peter and Carmela issued their edict.

Still, it was a bit of a shock to hear it put so bluntly. And we had our mother to consider."

"They—Peter and Carmela—couldn't turn Elizabeth out of the place," Helen continued, "but it wasn't difficult to make her feel unwanted. Carmela's a forceful character, and Mother wasn't too well at the time." She shook her head in disgust. "I've never forgiven Peter for what he and Carmela did to her. As I said, in many ways he was a shit—but that doesn't make him a Soviet agent."

Choosing his words with care, Mark said, "As far as I'm aware, no one seriously believes that your half-brother was a traitor. This is merely an unpleasant rumour that's been started by either a personal or a political enemy. Would you know of anyone who might fill the bill? Did he have any enemies?"

Here they were no help, though they argued around the subject for a while, finally agreeing that most politicians had enemies of one kind or another. Also, as John pointed out, there was always the possibility that some madman, someone who had imagined a grudge, was trying to get even.

"Of course, Carmela would know better than anyone," Colette said. "And she'll have private letters and photographs, if she'll show them to you."

John nodded his agreement. "Yes. If you're going to write the authorized version, Mark, you'll need to get on the right side of Carmela, and get her to sponsor you—not financially, of course, but in the sense of getting her approval and co-operation."

"We have met, but she won't remember me," said Mark. "I suppose you couldn't help, John?" he added tentatively.

John hesitated, then he said, "Why not? The funeral's on Friday. It's meant to be private—family only—but there'll be plenty of others there, and I could introduce you as an old friend of Hugh's. I think he's Carmela's favourite among us, if she has one."

"That's a good idea," Helen said. "You can practise your well-known charm on her, Mark."

Mark looked at John. "I'd be most grateful," he said. "Thanks a lot."

And as he drove back to his flat in Marylebone, he thought with some bitterness that General Bannol would have called it a most satisfactory evening.

While Mark Ryle was returning from Hampstead, Carmela Mourne, who had been unable to sleep, was standing at her bedroom window, gazing out across the lawns of Fauvel Hall. The moon, three-quarters full, was shining brightly, shedding a fair light when not obscured by cloud. The night was still. Carmela heard the purr of a motor-cycle coming up the drive and turning towards the stables. The sound didn't worry her. She knew it would be the houseman, Simpson. Wednesday was his half-day, and he always went out in the evening.

Her thoughts returned to her husband. She had asked the police a direct question, and the Detective Superintendent had assured her that there had been no sign of foul play. The security guard who had found Peter Mourne, and Fauvel's resident staff, had all been questioned closely, and the grounds had been searched. The Superintendent had spoken with regret; he knew that relatives hated to accept the idea of suicide because, according to the psychiatrists, it made them feel guilty.

Carmela had given him a sad smile in acknowledgement of his kindness, revealing none of her feelings. As she stared out of the window now, she thought what fools men were. Then she reminded herself that the Superintendent didn't know what she knew. Suddenly shivering, she pulled her robe tightly around her body.

Peter hadn't killed himself. If he had decided to take his own life, because of some mistaken idea that his death would save her, that once he was dead she would be left alone, he wouldn't have done it that way. Peter hadn't liked pain. He would have been afraid of hanging there for long minutes, choking, scrabbling with his feet, gasping for breath. No, he would have chosen an easier death—probably taken an overdose of sleeping pills—and he would have left her a note; she had searched everywhere he might have secreted a message, but had found none.

It was time, she knew, that she accepted the fact. Peter had been killed. She didn't ask herself why. She thought she knew the answer to that question. But if it was murder, it had been carefully planned. At that hour Fauvel's big iron gates would have been closed and locked, and there was a guard with a dog patrolling the grounds.

Yet someone had got in, someone who knew or had been told of Peter's habit of taking Charlie for an early-morning walk. And surely more than one person would have been necessary. Suddenly she thought of Simpson. The houseman had only been with them for about a year, replacing old Tim Grant, who had been killed in a hit-and-run accident. She had never liked or trusted Simpson, as she had Grant, but she had no reason to believe—

And where did that leave her? she wondered despairingly. What should she do? There seemed to be no positive answer. Waiting was the only option, and she had never been very good at waiting. What was more, she was afraid.

CHAPTER FOUR

It was on the following morning—Thursday—that Mark Ryle first became aware of the possibility that Viscount Mourne's death might not be a simple suicide. He was in his office, reading back numbers of *Hansard,* the official verbatim record of debates in the House of Commons, when the Director thrust his head round the door.

"Just studying Mourne's parliamentary track record, sir," Ryle said, getting up.

Bannol nodded, motioning to him to be seated. "I'll be surprised if you don't find it true blue and to the right of centre. But have a look at this." He tossed a large manila envelope on to Mark's desk. "Courtesy of Special Branch," he added.

"Thank you, sir."

"The PM wants to see me this morning. I'll have a talk with you when I get back, Mark. There might be some developments. Anyway, read the SB's report. I'll be interested to know what you make of it."

The door had scarcely closed behind the Director when Ryle was extracting the report from its envelope. The initial investigations had been carried out by the local police, but the SB had been over the ground again. They concluded that there was no hard evidence to suggest that Viscount Mourne had not taken his own life. However, there were one or two anomalies. First, he hadn't left a note, which was unusual, though not unknown, in such cases. Secondly, it was arguable that the knot of the noose had been tied by a left-handed person, whereas Mourne was naturally right-handed. Finally, there was the question of motive, or lack of it. No one, not even Lady Mourne, had been able to suggest one.

Between them, the ordinary police and the Special Branch had been very thorough. Both Mourne's general practitioner and the cardiac specialist who had treated him had been interviewed. They agreed that for his age, his health had been good; with reasonable care to avoid over-exertion and stress, he might have lived for five or more years. Certainly if, after his coronary, he had been afraid of death, he had chosen a strange way to meet it.

Ryle returned the report to its envelope and sat thinking. There was one serious omission from the document. It made no mention of the rumours circulating about Peter Mourne, though it was inconceivable that Special

Branch was ignorant of them. And here, of course, was the perfect motive —not fear of death, but fear of possible disgrace. But surely this only became a viable idea if the late Viscount had known there was at least some truth in the rumours.

Or did Mourne really have an enemy, someone with such hatred or malice in him that he was prepared to kill the man—or have him killed— in order to give credence to a lie that he himself had fabricated? This scenario seemed highly improbable to Ryle. But the apparently left-handed knot intrigued him.

He thought of going in search of a piece of rope, but dismissed the idea. Someone might notice and make some crack about hanging; some character might even connect his activities with Viscount Mourne. He decided to settle for a bit of string. He was contemplating it and fiddling with it— almost as if he were playing cat's cradle—when his secretary brought in the morning coffee.

"Heavens, Mark, haven't you anything better to do? Or have you reverted to your childhood?"

"Hello, Maggie. Coffee? Good." Ryle straightened out the string. "Do me a favour, there's a dear. Tie a knot in this for me—the kind where one end of the string slides through a knot in the other. Turn the bit of string into a small lasso."

"You're crazy," she said.

Nevertheless, she did as he asked. Ryle watched attentively while she bent her neat blonde head over the task. She had small hands with plump fingers, and nails painted bright red, and the knot took her only a few moments.

"There you are, Mark."

"Thanks a lot."

Ryle picked up the string, but didn't glance at it until Maggie had gone. Then he took a second piece of string, and tied the same knot himself. He studied the two knots through a small magnifying glass. There was no doubt about it: the knots were dissimilar—mirror images of each other. He was right-handed, while Maggie was left-handed.

Troubled, Ryle turned to his coffee.

General Bannol was not impressed by Ryle's research with bits of string. He pointed out, unnecessarily Ryle thought, that string was not the same as stout rope. He also demonstrated that he could tie knots as easily one way as the other.

"But the PM would agree, Mark, that someone had it in for Mourne, hated him enough to start these rumours and, having started the fire, to stoke it up." Bannol spoke bitterly. "It's extremely worrying. The Opposition's getting in on the act, as we expected. A question's been put down in the House for this afternoon—on the lines of whether the PM is aware of recent comments in the media concerning the late Viscount Mourne, and what action the Government proposes to take. The answer is to repeat that the PM and the Cabinet have absolute faith in the Viscount's integrity, and no inquiry is being envisaged. But God knows how long they can hold that position. It depends on how much pressure is exerted."

Ryle, who knew his Director fairly well by now, noted the set mouth and the excessively clipped speech. Both indicated tension. It was becoming increasingly vital to discover the truth.

"Mourne?"

Jeanne Mourne raised her chin and regarded the Heathrow immigration officer down her long thin nose. Apart from this Mourne feature she had taken after her mother, Colette. She was tall and slim, with dark-brown hair and Colette's green eyes. And she wore her clothes with the same casual elegance. Today, in a black silk suit and white blouse, she looked particularly French.

"What's the trouble?" she demanded.

"No trouble, Miss Mourne." The officer shut her passport and handed it back to her, but he continued to eye her curiously.

Beyond the customs area she caught sight of her brother, Hugh, waiting at the barrier. As they had arranged, he had arrived from Madrid on an earlier flight. He gave her a hurried kiss.

Hugh Mourne took after his father rather than his mother. He was only an inch or two taller than Jeanne, a solid man, intelligent, efficient, assured, but lacking his sister's inspiration and artistic flair. He also lacked her volatile temperament. Yet no one seeing them together, the conservatively dressed young man and the elegant girl, would have failed to guess they were brother and sister. Perhaps more surprisingly, they were devoted to each other.

Colette, waiting in the car, watched them approach with affection. As she drove off, she said, "You've heard these preposterous stories about Peter, haven't you?"

"If you mean this tale about Uncle Peter being some kind of communist, maman, and working for the Soviet Union, I've seen some references to it, yes," said Hugh. "They've worried me, but I've no idea how widespread they are or how seriously the Government's taking them."

Jeanne interrupted. "The idea's crazy. How on earth did the story start? I knew nothing about it."

"Didn't your beloved mention it? Or has he stopped phoning you every day?" Hugh, who didn't particularly like Simon Maufant and would have preferred Jeanne to marry Mark Ryle, was apt to make snide remarks about his brother-in-law-to-be.

"If you mean Simon, as I assume you do," said Jeanne acidly, "he hasn't mentioned it." She didn't add that Simon had indeed not phoned her for a couple of days. Disregarding Hugh, she turned to her mother. "This isn't really serious, is it? I mean no one's paying any attention to it. Surely it's just a media scare."

"We shall have to hope so," Colette said, but she didn't sound very hopeful and the three of them lapsed into silence.

The Mournes were having drinks before dinner when the phone rang. "I'll answer it," said Hugh at once.

"If it's a reporter or anyone like that, just put the receiver down," Colette said quickly.

"Have you been bothered much today?" John wanted to know as Hugh went into the hall.

"A couple of calls, that's all. But I've not been home most of the time." Colette spoke casually. She didn't want to worry her husband, so she didn't mention a caller—a woman—who had made a speech about traitorous politicians, and spat out a string of obscenities; it had taken Colette a few moments to realize what was happening, and hang up.

"It's for you, Jeanne," said Hugh, returning. "Your Simon wishes to speak to you."

"Thanks."

Jeanne didn't hurry to the telephone, and her greeting was less than enthusiastic, but Simon Maufant didn't seem to notice. On the contrary, he sounded rather aggrieved because he had had trouble in locating Jeanne.

"I didn't realize you were in the UK," he said.

"I flew over this afternoon. The funeral's tomorrow at noon. I told you it probably would be. Will you drive me down?"

"No, I—I—Jeanne, you said the funeral would be family only, and I'm not family. I wouldn't want to intrude."

"You *will* be family in September, Simon."

"I know, darling, but until then— Anyway, I have to go to my constituency for the weekend. There's another ghastly debate on the death penalty coming up shortly and my agent wants me to sound out local opinion. Actually it'll be a free vote, as always, and I'll act according to my conscience. But the voters like me to listen to their views, as if—"

"So you won't be coming?" Jeanne cut him short. "Probably wise of you. Funerals are dreary occasions. I expect to go back to Paris directly afterwards, so phone me there, will you?"

"Yes, of course, darling. I'm terribly sorry to miss you this time, but it *is* a brief trip and, as you say, not a very happy one. I—I'll be in touch as soon as the weekend's over. Okay?"

"Yes, that's fine. Goodbye, Simon."

Jeanne put down the receiver, cutting her fiancé off in mid-sentence. She walked across to the dining-room window and stared out at the garden. Everything looked neat and tidy, but lacking in colour. She was angry, though she couldn't have explained why. She thought about the man she was to marry in September.

The Honourable Simon Maufant was in his early thirties, a Member of Parliament with every prospect of obtaining Government office in the next reshuffle, and eventually gaining a post in the Cabinet. His elder brother was already married, with two sons, so that he had no chance of inheriting the family title, and with it responsibility for the estate. But Simon had money in his own right. He was also good-looking and agreeable, and there was more than one girl who would have been pleased to marry him.

Jeanne had met him over a year ago at the wedding of a mutual friend. He had pursued her, and within weeks they had become lovers, but she had been surprised and a little gratified when he suggested marriage. Now she was suddenly unsure of herself and her feelings.

It was several minutes before she returned to the sitting-room and the family, to find them talking of Mark Ryle.

CHAPTER FIVE

It was a suitable day for a funeral—grey and with rain threatening. Mark Ryle drove to St. John's Church near Fauvel Hall, parked his car on the road outside, and walked up the gravel path to the big double doors, which lay open. For what was meant to be a private family affair, there seemed to be a great many people about. Some were clearly Press; others he assumed to be plainclothes police officers, or even Special Branch officers. Some policemen were in uniform, two of them controlling what appeared to be a group of spectators, presumably present out of curiosity.

Mark was stopped in the porch by a man in a black gown he took to be the verger, who said, "May I have your name, please, sir?"

Ryle answered, hoping that John had played his part.

The verger referred to the list he was holding, and put a tick against Ryle. "Thank you, sir. Please go in."

Another man, in a black suit and a black tie, opened the inner door for him. There was no need for Mark Ryle to wonder what would have happened if his name had not been on the list and he had nevertheless tried to enter the church. He recognized the second man as a Special Branch officer, who in turn recognized him and saluted. Ryle suspected he was armed, and would have had little trouble dealing with an unwanted intruder.

Viscount Mourne, when in residence at Fauvel, had quite often attended St. John's on a Sunday, accompanied by his wife. Once a year the vicar was invited to dinner at the Hall, and in return the Viscountess was invariably asked to open the summer fête, a function she sometimes performed. So it was not surprising that Peter Mourne had expressed a wish to be buried in the churchyard adjoining St. John's.

As the organ voluntary swelled, Mark Ryle stood at the back of the church and surveyed the scene. There were flowers aplenty in the sanctuary, but the coffin lying before the altar was bare, except for a single wreath of white roses. The congregation was very small and seemed to be split into groups. Lady Mourne sat in the front pew, alone at her own wish, as Ryle was to learn later. Behind her were John and Colette Mourne with Hugh and Jeanne. Helen Mourne sat across the aisle with a couple who eventually turned out to be cousins of the dead Viscount Mourne.

These were all the relations who were present; the Mournes were not a prolific family. Apart from them, there were two other small parties of mourners. Ryle identified one of these as probably composed of the late Viscount's medical and legal advisers, his constituency agent, perhaps his former Personal Private Secretary. There were scarcely more than half a dozen of these, and to balance them on the other side of the aisle was a group Ryle took to be the household staff of Fauvel. It wasn't easy to recognize people from their backs, especially when they were all dressed sombrely and similarly, but he was able to assure himself that Simon Maufant was not among those present. There would be vastly more people at the Memorial Service, Ryle reflected—presumably this would be held in some appropriately fashionable London church.

Thankful for the absence of Maufant—he hadn't been looking forward to seeing Jeanne and her fiancé together—Mark Ryle slid into a pew towards the rear as the parson came in from the vestry, said a brief prayer in front of the altar, and went to stand by the coffin. The organist ceased playing. There was no choir, and the service was brief—some prayers, an apparently sincere encomium from the parson with no reference to the manner of Mourne's dying, then more prayers, a blessing and, as the pallbearers lined up and lifted the coffin on to their shoulders, the music resumed.

The congregation rose. The service was over. To strains of a Bach fugue the procession moved down the aisle, the parson, the coffin, the widow, her face obscured by a black veil. Behind her walked John and Colette Mourne, who nodded at Mark as they passed him, followed by Jeanne with downcast eyes and Hugh, who smiled a greeting. Then came the Mourne cousins and Helen, who gestured for Mark to join her.

Had he not done so, he would have missed the extraordinary incident that took place outside the church. Those who left more slowly saw only its aftermath.

The parson, heading the procession, had just turned right towards the churchyard and the open grave that awaited the mortal remains of Peter Mourne, when there was a stir among the sightseers. Someone shouted, "Traitor!" The cry was repeated, and taken up by others: "Traitor!" "Spy!" "Red agent!"

Such a demonstration was totally unexpected, and the police were slow to react. Then a girl in a neat grey flannel suit and a cream-coloured blouse ran forward. She had short brown hair and a pale complexion. Seen walking in the street, she might have been taken for a secretary or a young housewife, pleasant, law-abiding, but not especially memorable in any way.

In her right hand, which she had been holding behind her back, she clutched a medium-sized can. Now she brought her arm forward, and lobbed the can and its contents at the coffin. "Traitor!" she screamed. "Betrayer of England!" Red paint spattered over the coffin and the pall-bearers, who were to be praised for not dropping their burden; a little even reached Carmela Mourne.

For a moment the scene was frozen. Then someone gave a shout, which seemed like a signal for action to recommence. The girl had fled. The group who had been shouting offensively opened to let her through, but closed again so as to hamper those who pursued her.

Ryle quickly stepped to one side, out of the way of John Mourne, who was urging Carmela and the rest of the relations back into the safety of the church. He found Hugh standing beside him.

"Bloody idiots!" Hugh said angrily, making no attempt to go with his family. "What the hell do they think they're doing? Who the hell do they think they are to judge a dead man?"

The parson approached, wringing his hands. "Dear God," he said, "what a dreadful occurrence. Dreadful. Sacrilege." As if unable to decide what to do he stared desperately at the coffin, which had by this time been laid down on the ground, while the pallbearers, without apparent success, tried to mop some of the red paint from it, and from their own clothes.

A woman who had deliberately obstructed a police officer was being taken into custody; a couple of her friends were arguing with the police about this arrest. A plainclothes man hurried into the church, presumably to inquire after Lady Mourne. Another was giving orders.

Suddenly a police whistle screeched, and three or four of the plain-clothes officers dashed towards the sound. From a distance came the roar of a motor-cycle, gradually diminishing.

By now the uniformed policemen were trying to clear the area of the church, to the annoyance of the reporters, but the television camera continued to roll. There would be plenty on the news later in the day, and in the evening and morning papers, about the "private" funeral of Viscount Mourne.

Gradually order was restored. The staff were the first to leave, escorted by Simpson, the houseman. Then Lady Mourne, somewhat against her will, was driven back to Fauvel under police escort. Colette accompanied her, and the female members of the family followed. The males, and those of the mourners who were returning to the Hall, including Mark Ryle, stayed for the committal.

John Mourne threw a handful of earth on to the coffin of his half-brother. It had proved impossible to remove the red paint in the available time, and a covering had been sought in the church. Ironically, the only available material that was remotely suitable was a flag, so the coffin had been draped in an old and tattered Union Jack.

"Thank God that's over," said John Mourne as the parson, showing more signs of strain than anyone else, insisted on shaking hands, first with Mark Ryle, whom he seemed to mistake for the chief mourner. "Come on. Let's go. I've had a word with the senior police chap," he added to Hugh and Mark, who were nearest to him as they walked to the car. "He believes the whole show was laid on."

Mark, who himself had spoken to the Special Branch man he knew, said, "That's pretty obvious, isn't it? Such an orchestrated fracas could hardly have been spontaneous."

"But why?" John shook his head. "I suppose I'm old-fashioned, but a funeral—"

"Nothing's sacrosanct these days, Dad," said Hugh with forced cheerfulness. "There's no point in worrying about it. Let's get back to Fauvel. I'm sure we could all do with a drink."

At Fauvel Hall the scene was comparatively normal, though the police guard in the grounds had become more conspicuous, and fewer people than expected had come on from the church. The houseman was serving drinks in the drawing-room, and a cold buffet had been laid out in the dining-room. Carmela Mourne, her small body upright and her eyes bright, either with anger or with unshed tears, was receiving her guests; she had refused all attempts to make her go and rest in her room.

John Mourne introduced Mark Ryle as an old friend of Hugh's, and Carmela gave Mark her hand for a moment. Then Mark saw John open his mouth again, and knew that he was going to raise the question of the proposed biography. Mark could think of no less suitable moment to mention the idea, and raised a hand in an attempt to stop him. But he was too late.

Surprisingly, although Carmela appeared to receive the idea coldly, she didn't immediately dismiss it as irrelevant or inappropriate. Instead, she turned again to Mark.

"You knew my late husband, Mr. Ryle?"

"Yes, Lady Mourne, though unfortunately not well. But I've known Mr. and Mrs. Mourne for a very long time. I was at school with Hugh, and they befriended me as a boy. I used to spend a lot of my holidays with them. I know this is hardly the moment to talk about a—"

"True. But you've written biographies before?"

"One. I am a professional author, Lady Mourne."

"I see." Lady Mourne's tone of voice made it clear that she was not overly impressed by Ryle's credentials or qualifications. "Well, I'm sure a biography by someone who can be trusted to understand and sympathize with my husband is necessary. Actually, before he was hounded to death by these disgusting rumours he was considering an autobiography. We shall have to ponder the matter." She gave Ryle a small, cool smile, and moved to speak to someone else.

Mark grinned ruefully at John, who said, "Perhaps this wasn't an auspicious moment to broach the subject. I'll have another go before Colette and I leave."

Mark could do no more than thank him, and add, "I'd be grateful," though he knew that the initial approach to Lady Mourne had been handled clumsily. Nor was this entirely John's fault. In the end Mark himself had been distracted by the sight of Jeanne across the room. She gave him a casual wave, and he went on, "Now I really must say hello to Jeanne. I haven't spoken to her yet."

Leaving John, Mark made his way towards her. She was speaking to her aunt, Helen, but broke off as he approached them. She kissed him casually on both cheeks, like the old friend he was, and he made suitable noises about her engagement.

"All best wishes, Jeanne. I hope you'll be very happy."

"Thank you, Mark."

"Lucky you're not getting married in that hideous church we've just left," said Helen. "John and I used to be taken there sometimes as children when Father was alive, and I hated it. I suppose Peter went there as a boy," she added, as if surprised at the thought, "but he can't have minded it as much as we did—or else he'd never have wanted to be buried there."

"So where *are* you getting married?" said Mark to Jeanne.

"In London."

Helen laughed. "St. Margaret's, Westminster. A posh society wedding. I shall have to buy a new hat for it."

"Don't be horrid, Aunt Helen." Jeanne had flushed. "It's not my first choice, I admit, but it's what Simon wants. You'll be getting an invitation, Mark."

"How nice! I shall look forward to it," Ryle lied. "When's the great day?"

"September the fifteenth."

"I'll make a note of it," he said lightly, thinking that nothing on earth would make him watch Jeanne Mourne marry another man. "Now I must be going. I've got work to do this afternoon. Goodbye to you both."

Abruptly he left them. He went to say goodbye to John and Colette, who made him promise to phone when he had a free evening, and to express his final condolences to Lady Mourne. She was gracious, but didn't refer to the mooted biography. Hugh asked him for a lift as far as Heathrow.

"I was going with Helen, but I'd sooner trust your driving. Anyway, it'll give us a chance for a chat. I'll get my bag."

"Okay."

Fond as he was of Hugh, Mark would have preferred to drive back to London alone. He had been shocked at the depth of his feeling on meeting Jeanne again. As far as he was concerned, he knew that nothing had changed; he was as much in love with her as he ever had been.

Fortunately Hugh had no immediate intention of talking about his sister. He was still understandably upset by the paint-throwing at the funeral, and first he wanted to talk of Peter Mourne. For Mark, this wasn't an easy subject either; Hugh was not someone to whom he could lie readily.

Hugh said, "That was a bloody awful thing to do, throwing that paint.

And those abominable cat-calls—traitor and so on." He shook his head in disgust. "I'd read about the rumours, of course, but I had no idea there was this sort of public feeling against Peter, although—"

"I'm not sure there really is—a great deal of public feeling, I mean," replied Mark. "But what there is does seem to be growing. However—you were going to add something, Hugh?"

"Yes—about Jeanne."

Mark's grip tightened on the wheel. It was true, Mark thought as he listened. Public outrage was indeed gaining momentum, becoming more intense, more virulent. As a result, it was beginning to affect all the Mournes. The fact that it was almost certainly being stimulated artificially made no difference. Suddenly he realized that Hugh was still speaking.

"—sorry for poor Carmela. I know she's never been particularly pleasant to our part of the family, but she was devoted to Peter. His death must have been a blow to her—especially as he killed himself—and to have this communist business on top is too much."

"Would it be tactless to ask if he was equally devoted to her?" said Mark, thinking of a photograph of the man and the girl in the shower.

"Mistresses tucked away somewhere?" Hugh laughed. "That's an odd question. But I don't think she gave him much chance. She was a possessive wife, I gather. She always travelled with him, and accompanied him to parties and receptions. I wonder what she'll do without him."

"Might she go back to Spain?"

"No, I shouldn't think so for a moment." Hugh paused, then he repeated, "No. Definitely not. She never has been back, you know. She always said it would cause her too much unhappiness because of the dreadful memories she has of the place. She lost everything in the Civil War. Both her parents and her two brothers and a sister were killed by the Reds, and their home was burnt to the ground. She only escaped by hiding in a ditch or somewhere. That's why she's always hated Russia and communism and all they stand for, and I suspect that's why she encouraged Peter to be so right wing. Not that he needed much encouragement. Which makes these extraordinary accusations so—so incredible. You've only to look at his record—"

"Yes," said Mark, and refrained from adding that he had already studied it in detail.

"Do you seriously intend to write a biography of him?" Hugh wanted to know.

Mark hooted at a car that had cut in too sharply in front of him. It relieved his feelings. The question was one he had been hoping Hugh wouldn't ask.

"Yes, indeed I do," he said firmly. "After all, my first book was a moderate success, and I've been thinking about another."

"Well, today's given you an interesting chapter, at any rate," Hugh said bitterly. "That and all these damned rumours should help make it a bloody bestseller."

CHAPTER SIX

"Would you care for a nightcap, sir?" the houseman asked.

John Mourne looked interrogatively at his wife and his sister. They both shook their heads. "Are you quite sure?" John said.

"I wouldn't mind a Perrier with some ice in it," Colette answered.

"Nothing for me." Helen was positive. "I'm off to bed in a minute or two, when I've summoned up sufficient energy. I've had enough of today. To be honest, though earlier I'd said I had to get back to London, I was thankful when Carmela repeated her invitation to spend the night here at Fauvel. I didn't fancy driving home after all the excitement at the funeral. It was lucky that Hugh and Jeanne were both able to get lifts, so there was no reason for me not to stay."

"Right." John turned to the houseman. "One Perrier with ice and one brandy, Simpson, please. Then I suggest you lock up and get to bed yourself—unless Lady Mourne has asked for anything."

"No, sir, thank you. I've already taken up the hot milk her ladyship has every night. There were no other requests."

"That's fine then," said John.

When Simpson had brought the drinks and, wishing them all a good night, had left the drawing-room, Colette asked, "Do you think one of us should check on Carmela before we go to bed?"

"No!" Helen was definite. "When she retired after dinner she bade us a firm good-night. I'm sure she wanted to discourage us from calling in on her later. After all, she's been under a considerable strain. Sleep is what she needs."

"Perhaps you're right." Colette still sounded doubtful.

"And that's what I want now, too. It's after eleven and I'm dead tired." And a few minutes later Helen was as good as her word. She kissed them both and left them to finish their drinks. But they were also tired, and less than half an hour afterwards they followed her upstairs.

Colette Mourne had fallen asleep immediately, but she woke about two and sat up in bed. She was both tired and restless, her mind hyperactive as she reviewed the events of the day. In the other bed, John slept peacefully, and she asked herself what she would have done, how she would have felt, if it had been John, not Peter, who lay buried in St. John's churchyard. She knew she would have been devastated. And Carmela?

Carmela had appeared calm and well in control of herself, though a close observer could see signs of her grief. She had wept; her eyes were red and bloodshot. There were lines of strain around her mouth, and she was almost too controlled. It would be better for her to break down, Colette thought, and allow herself to be comforted. But who was to comfort her? She seemed to have no close friends, and she had always kept the family at arm's length. She cared only for Peter—and now Peter was gone.

Shaking her head sadly, Colette slid out of bed, put on a robe, and went to the window. Gazing out over the lawns of Fauvel she told herself that it was not her business. She and Carmela had never got along particularly well, in spite of the fact that the De Chantals had been so kind to Peter Mourne and Carmela when they had come out of Spain at the end of the Civil War. They had nursed Peter back to some semblance of health and had made every effort to help both Peter and Carmela at a time when, with France on the verge of war, they had worries of their own. Yet in later years neither Peter nor Carmela had shown a great deal of gratitude.

Colette sighed. If anyone should go to Carmela to make sure she was all right, that she was not awake and in distress, it ought to be Helen, she supposed, but Helen had made it clear that she had no such intention. Telling herself that she was a fool, that Carmela was almost certainly asleep, Colette turned away from the window, and went quietly from the bedroom.

It was dark in the corridor and Colette switched on the light. Her gown was thin, and she shivered, partly from cold and partly from nervousness, which she knew was absurd. She paused at Carmela's door and listened, but the doors in the old house were thick and she could hear no sound. She knocked and went in.

By a trick of moonlight Colette's attention was immediately focused on the bedside table, where stood a milky glass and an empty pill bottle with its top lying beside it. A step inside the room and she saw Carmela's face, washed of all colour by the pale moon. She had hurried to the bedside before she saw that Carmela's face was indeed white, and heard her shallow breathing.

"Carmela! Carmela!"

The recumbent woman made no response. Mouth open, she began to make strangled noises deep in her throat. Colette took her by the shoulders and shook her, but without result. She wasted no more time. She ran back to her room as fast as she could, burst into it, switched on the light and called to wake John.

"Quick! John! It's Carmela. I think she's taken an overdose. Call her doctor! I'll wake Helen and organize black coffee. All we can do is try to walk her up and down until the doctor comes. Hurry, John!"

John Mourne, startled into wakefulness, practically fell out of bed. There was no telephone in their room, and the nearest instrument he could think of was in what was called the library. Not bothering about gown or slippers, he raced along the corridor and down the stairs. As he ran he cursed himself for not having foreseen that something like this might happen.

It took him a minute to find the doctor's number and tap it out on the keypad of the phone. While he waited for an answer, he heard Colette go through to the servants' quarters, calling to the houseman and the cook-housekeeper, banging on doors to wake them. Helen, he knew, would already be doing what she could for Carmela.

The doctor promised to be there in fifteen minutes. John dashed upstairs again. He was breathing hard, but he didn't notice. He went first to his own room and hastily pulled on some clothes in case it was necessary for him to go with Carmela to a hospital. Then he went along to her room. Colette and Helen had got Carmela out of bed and were trying to force her to walk. Actually they were dragging her, and although she was small this wasn't easy.

"I'll take her," he said. "Colette, you go downstairs, ready to let the doctor in."

"All right. Mrs. Compton's making coffee. It'll be here in a minute. I couldn't find Simpson. When he didn't answer I looked in his room, but he wasn't there."

John wasn't really listening. He gave Colette an encouraging smile and turned to his sister, who was supporting Carmela. "Come on," he said, and together they began to haul the pathetic figure of Viscountess Mourne to and fro, ten steps this way, then ten the other. They heard the sound of a motor-bike receding into the distance, but paid it no attention, too occupied even to comment. Later, however, they were to remember the sound.

It was after eight the next morning before it became apparent that Simpson was missing.

John and Colette Mourne were with Helen in the dining-room. By the
time the doctor had arrived, Carmela was already beginning to recover
consciousness. The doctor had approved all that her family had done for
her. With Colette's assistance he had washed out Carmela's stomach as a
precaution, and decided that in the circumstances she could be spared the
publicity that would attend transfer to a hospital. When he left, after the
appearance of the nurse whom he had summoned, Carmela was sleeping
naturally.

"Thank God she's going to live," said John.

"Yes." Colette nodded. "I only wish I'd gone to her earlier."

"Be glad you went when you did, darling. You were only just in time,
the doctor said. Half an hour later and she could have been dead."

"And she didn't want to die," Helen said.

"What do you mean?"

"Why do you say that?"

Colette and John were both surprised. Helen shrugged. She wished she
hadn't spoken. It was stupid to create unnecessary complications. Carmela
had been in a stupor; she hadn't known what she was saying.

"Oh, because she mumbled, 'I don't want to die' a couple of times as I
was trying to walk her up and down. If they're saved, intending suicides
often regret what they've done, I believe."

John might have questioned Helen further, but at that point the cook-
housekeeper brought in the coffee and toast they had requested. She was
obviously worried and on edge, and John got up to take the tray from her.

"Thank you, Mrs. Compton. That's very good of you."

"Sir, I—I can't find Simpson anywhere. He's not in his room. His bed
looks as if he spent the night in it, but he's not done any of his usual
duties."

"He must be somewhere," John protested.

"I dare say, but I don't know where, sir."

"Perhaps he's had an accident," Colette suggested.

"All right, Mrs. Compton," John said, taking control. "I'll get on to the
security men, and they'll find him."

But they never did find him, neither the security men nor the police.

The guard at the gates of Fauvel had seen him leave on his motor-cycle.
He had said that Lady Mourne had been taken ill, and he was going to
fetch the doctor because the phone was on the blink. And later in the day,
when it was discovered that a small but very desirable Corot and some
valuable Georgian silver were missing, there seemed an obvious explanation for the houseman's sudden disappearance.

"Young fool, that guard," said the senior security officer. "He should have remembered I was in direct radio contact with the police station, and thus there was no need to send a servant off for help on a motor-bike. And he should have noticed if the panniers on the bike were bulging." He shook his head in disgust.

"I heard the bike go, and so did my sister," said John Mourne sadly. "But at the time we never associated it with Simpson. We had other things on our minds."

"Of course, sir," the security officer agreed. "He must have been planning it for some time. Too bad that Viscountess Mourne was—er—taken ill this particular night. An unfortunate coincidence."

CHAPTER SEVEN

Any hope of preventing the news of Carmela Mourne's attempted suicide from becoming a matter of common knowledge was foiled by a series of anonymous telephone calls to the media late on Saturday morning. In spite of the family's determination not to comment, it took experienced journalists only an hour or two to check the facts to their satisfaction, and during the afternoon items appeared in television and radio programmes.

During the evening, a further story broke: while Lady Mourne was on the point of death, the Mournes' houseman had absconded with the family silver and a valuable French painting. The Sunday papers made the most of this, and the whole incident gave an added boost to the public's craving for sensation—an appetite already stimulated by the events at Viscount Mourne's funeral.

By Sunday morning Fauvel Hall was under siege. No interviews were given to the press, and the police, when appealed to, provided extra men to guard the grounds, and a Detective-Sergeant to answer the phone; he did so curtly and unhelpfully. But there was a plethora of photographs in newspapers and agency morgues of the late Viscount Mourne and his wife at various stages of the Viscount's career, and many which hadn't appeared during the past week since his death were published now. The few stills of the girl throwing red paint over the coffin were reproduced, and part of the TV tape taken at the funeral was repeated several times.

As for text, that was simple. Some pundit could always be found to comment, and imagination supplied what papers feared to print. Some of the papers had no hesitation in providing fictitious quotes. Colette

Mourne, for instance, was reported as saying that she had woken on the night in question from a dream that had warned her that Lady Mourne was dying. The family agreed that such fabrications were unworthy of denial.

Naturally, though care had to be taken not to libel the living in the person of Carmela Mourne, there were many hinted connections with the rumours alleging that Peter Mourne had been a long-time traitor and spy. Most of the media were reasonably sympathetic to Carmela, taking the line that it was not unnatural that, faced with her husband's death and the horror of the scandal suddenly associated with it, she had been tempted to take her own life. Some, however, were less kind and implied that if Peter Mourne had indeed been a traitor, his wife must surely have suspected it.

There were some interesting sidelights, too. A Labour MP, by name Tom Chariber, was quoted as saying that he had received telephone calls threatening physical violence if he persisted in asking questions in the House about the late Foreign Secretary. A journalist, who claimed to be writing an in-depth report on the late Viscount Mourne's political career, chimed in: he, too, had received similar threats. Such stories, of course, led to accusations of an attempted cover-up, more demands for an official inquiry, and the expression of more fears for national security. By now it was clear from the media that the rumours concerning Peter Mourne's treachery were not going to die a natural death.

By eleven o'clock on Sunday morning Mark Ryle had read and digested the material concerned with the Mournes in all the newspapers he had hastened to buy on the Marylebone High Street. The carpet in the sitting-room of his flat was now littered with them. Kicking his way through the newsprint, he reached for the telephone.

He had tried to contact John Mourne the previous day at Fauvel Hall, and had left messages for him, but John had not returned his calls, and he wasn't eager to phone there again. He checked the Hampstead house, but there was no reply. Then he tapped out Helen's number.

A sleepy voice answered him. "Hello."

"Good morning. This is Mark Ryle."

"It was a good morning till you woke me."

"I'm awfully sorry. I wanted to talk to John and find out how Lady Mourne is, but I can't get hold of him."

"He's still at Fauvel. He's coming back to London tonight. Colette's staying on for another couple of days, though she's scarcely needed with day and night nurses attending to Carmela."

"So how is Lady Mourne?"

"She'll live. For some reason Colette took it into her head to check on her in the wee small hours. But she's pretty weak. It's no fun having your stomach pumped out, and she's not young any more."

"No, I suppose not."

There was a silence, which seemed longer than it was because they couldn't see each other. Mark started to speak. Helen laughed; it was a surprisingly nervous laugh, almost as if for once in her life she wasn't sure what to do. In fact, she wanted someone in whom to confide. She didn't want to worry John, and Hugh was back in Madrid. Mark was an old friend of the family. Mark knew everyone involved. Mark was here in London and accessible. She made up her mind.

"Listen," she said. "Why don't we have lunch together one day this week, so that we can talk properly? What about tomorrow, if you're free?"

"Tomorrow would be fine," Mark said at once, cloaking his surprise. Helen hadn't indicated what she wanted to talk about "properly," but obviously it was a subject of importance to her. "Where? When?"

She named an Italian restaurant in Knightsbridge. "It'll be full of yuppies on expense accounts," she said, "but Orlando doesn't cram in too many tables, so there's a reasonable amount of privacy. And the food's wonderful. Twelve-thirty? My treat."

Mark thanked her, and promised to arrive on time. He put the receiver down thoughtfully. Another mystery, but one to which tomorrow would presumably bring a solution. Meanwhile he had work to do.

The next day was Monday, and it began badly for Mark Ryle. When he reached his Cork Street office, Maggie greeted him with the news that a Miss Mourne had telephoned and wanted to speak to him urgently. At once he thought of Jeanne. But why—

"From Paris?" he asked stupidly.

Maggie regarded him with some amusement. "Not unless you were planning to pop over to France for lunch," she said, and then added in her most businesslike manner, "I gathered you had a luncheon date with Miss Mourne which she cannot now keep. I put her London phone number on your pad."

"Thanks."

Ryle went through to his office, cursing himself for his instant reaction. He should have thought of Helen, not Jeanne. After all, he was meant to be meeting the former in a few hours. He tapped out Helen's number and waited.

"Hello. Mark Ryle here."

"Mark, about our lunch. My apologies, but I have to break our date. I had a silly accident. I slipped on the kitchen floor last night when I was getting supper, and I've twisted my ankle. It's not serious, but I need to rest it."

"What a shame! I *am* sorry, but it doesn't matter about the lunch. We'll have that some other time."

"Yes, of course. But what about today? Can you come to my flat? For coffee? Or a drink at noon?"

"It's very kind of you, but—"

"Mark, I need to talk to you."

Ryle swallowed his irritation. There had to be some very good reason for Helen to insist on seeing him so urgently. He would have to go.

"Fair enough," he said. "I'd like that. I've a few things I must attend to here in the office, but I'll be along during the morning."

Among the things he had to do was make two appointments. First he tried one Cecil Dornford, who for many years had been Peter Mourne's political agent in the constituency he had held before his elevation to the House of Lords. Dornford, now retired, lived with his daughter in Richmond, and Ryle hoped to arrange a meeting.

But, brought to the telephone, Cecil Dornford flatly refused to have anything to do with Ryle. "I've got nothing to say," was his immediate response. "I'm honoured to have been able to call Viscount Mourne my friend, and I've no intention of helping anyone to write a lot of scurrilous rubbish about him."

Ryle protested, but Dornford put down his receiver, cutting him off in mid-sentence. Mark Ryle swore. Someone who had promised to be a good source of information about Mourne's early political career had proved completely useless. He wondered if it would be worth while writing a formal letter to Dornford, explaining that he was a family friend and so on, but finally he decided against any such move. It was clear that for the present at least Cecil Dornford was in no mood to be co-operative.

Ryle fared better with his next call, though only marginally. The Labour Member of Parliament, Tom Chariber, agreed to be interviewed on the subject of Viscount Mourne and the threats he himself had received, but he did so with some reluctance, and he refused to set a specific day or time. He also asked a great many questions, to which Ryle did his best to provide palliative answers.

"No," said Mark Ryle, "I'm not a newspaperman. I'm a serious writer concerned with domestic and international politics. I've got a First Class degree in politics and economics from Oxford, and the Mourne family whom I have known since childhood believe that I am a suitable person to write a biography of the late Viscount."

"You mean a cover-up?" said Chariber quickly.

"No, I do not, I assure you. I hope to produce a good, readable, unbiased picture of Viscount Mourne."

"Warts and all, as people say? But you can't do that until there's been an official inquiry. I'm determined to push for one at whatever cost, as you probably know." Chariber paused. His breathing was heavy, and he seemed to expect some reply to this last remark. When none was forthcoming, he added, "Very well, but I'm a busy man. I can't make an appointment now. I'll have to contact you. How do I do that?"

Ryle gave the MP the phone number that the office used for calls from outside—and outsiders—and asked Maggie to warn the switchboard that one Tom Chariber would be phoning. To his surprise Maggie remarked that she knew Chariber; her parents lived in his constituency.

"A nice man," she said. "He really cares about people. I suppose that's one of the reasons why he keeps getting re-elected time after time, even though it could scarcely be called a safe Labour seat."

"He's a moderate, isn't he? Not too far left, not hard left, as they call it?" Ryle asked idly.

"He's certainly not extreme in any way, but he's staunch Labour. And he lives up to his principles. No sending his kids to public schools, as some of them do, and he and his wife live in a very modest little house. She's something of an invalid."

"You sound as if you like him, Maggie."

"I do. And so do most people. He's popular inside and outside the House."

"You won't greet him as an old friend when he phones, will you?"

It was an order; Maggie realized this and raised her eyebrows. "That was not necessary," she said. "I know my job, and anyway the man's no more than an acquaintance. There's no chance he'll recognize my voice."

"Sorry." Ryle gave her a rueful smile.

He spent the next couple of hours with a colleague. On security grounds General Bannol considered it good practice to keep his staff strictly compartmentalized, so that only he and his immediate deputy were at the centre, holding all the threads. Nevertheless, sometimes it was necessary for the staff to share information among themselves. This was such an occasion, and Ryle had to brief a man who was going to the Middle East.

It was noon before they had finished, and he had time to remember Helen Mourne. Apart from satisfying his curiosity, he hoped the visit would be productive; it could hardly be less helpful than the earlier part of the morning. To add to his frustration, as he was about to leave, Maggie reminded him to take an umbrella, pointing out of the window; it had begun to rain heavily.

But he was lucky, and caught a taxi in Burlington Gardens which deposited him at Helen's ground-floor flat within twenty minutes, in spite of the lunchtime traffic. When she let him in, he was appalled at how unwell she looked. Her hair was untidy and she had no make-up on her face. The green housecoat she was wearing, made of some shiny material, did little for her either. It gave her complexion a sickly hue, and emphasized the dark circles under her eyes.

"Sorry I look such a hag," she said, limping into the living-room ahead of Mark. "This damned ankle kept me awake and I started thinking, which made everything worse."

"Have you seen a doctor?"

"Yes. Luckily he lives upstairs, so there was no problem. Cold compresses, keep the weight off the ankle and take painkillers. If it fails to improve he'll order an X-ray, but he doesn't think anything's broken."

Helen sat on the sofa and carefully put her legs up on it. "Pour me a large pink gin will you, Mark, and help yourself to whatever you want." She gestured, her bracelets jangling, to a side-table on which stood an array of bottles and glasses and an ice bucket.

Ryle poured the pink gin, and a whisky for himself. He gave the gin to Helen and then, holding his own glass, went to the windows at the end of the room and gazed out. Helen had taken great care with the design of the garden, to which, as the ground-floor tenant, only she had access. It consisted of a small paved courtyard, surrounded by flowering shrubs and trees. In the centre of the paving stood a replica of the *Manneken Pis* in Brussels, the small boy who peed eternally into a shallow marble bowl. Altogether, it was a delightful town garden, peaceful and secluded.

"Admiring my garden?" Helen said. "I should miss it terribly if I had to give it up."

Ryle gave her a sharp glance. "There's no reason why you should have to give it up, is there?"

"The lease of this place won't last for ever. When I bought it, that's what it seemed like, of course, but time passes and now I'm afraid it may not see me out."

"How long has the lease to run?"

"Oh, fifteen—twenty years."

"I see," Ryle said untruthfully.

In twenty years' time Helen would be about eighty. He studied her surreptitiously, but he couldn't believe that she was really worried about the lease on her flat. If she had been, she would have known to the day when it would expire. Nevertheless, it was evident that she was concerned about something. She had finished her pink gin very quickly, and was nervously twisting one of her bracelets round and round on her thin wrist.

"Pour me the other half before you sit down, there's a dear, Mark," she said, "and help yourself."

Ryle poured her second gin, but left his own drink, which he had barely tasted, alone. He came and sat in an armchair opposite Helen, and glanced round the room. Blending with the modern furniture, there were one or two good old pieces—an escritoire and a butler's tray, for example —which he guessed had originally come from Fauvel.

He said, "Have you heard how Lady Mourne is today?"

"Yes. I telephoned earlier and managed to speak to Colette. Carmela's condition's quite satisfactory, though she's still weak and exhausted. But she refuses to talk about why—why she did it. Mark, I—I don't know what to think."

"There's a problem?" he asked quietly.

"Yes! By God there is!" Helen was suddenly her normal forceful self. "I'm sorry to bother you with it, Mark, but John's got enough on his plate. He's worried about the effect these ghastly rumours will have on Hugh and Jeanne—all the Mournes, in fact. It's not a name one's glad to have just at present. I would have told Hugh, but he's not here, and I thought you would understand and not dismiss me as an old fool."

"I'll never do that, I promise you, Helen. And if I can help, I will."

"Thank you, Mark. The problem—my problem—put baldly—is that I've doubts about Carmela's suicide. I'm not sure she did try to take her own life—and there's no possibility of an accident. She'd taken many too many capsules for that. The only alternative is that someone tried to kill her. But who? Simpson seems an obvious answer. But why on earth should he? Perhaps he didn't mean her to die, and was just using her to act as a diversion while he got away with the loot. But it doesn't make much sense, does it?"

"Not much," Ryle admitted. "I hate to say it, but isn't attempted suicide the simplest explanation?"

"The simplest, yes, Mark, I agree—and I wish I could accept it."

"You said you had doubts. You haven't told me what they are yet."

"I'm going to, but remember they're only doubts—ill-founded suspicions, if you like." Helen sounded impatient. "First, when Carmela was beginning to wake up, and I was trying to make her walk, she muttered, 'I don't want to die' several times. Okay, perhaps she was regretting what she'd done, but it seems to me, looking back, that as an immediate reaction it was odd. I'd have expected, 'Oh God, I feel sick,' or even, 'Let me alone, for God's sake.' And, unless I'm imagining it now, after the event, I'm sure she was frightened."

"There's something else?" Ryle queried as Helen stopped speaking. "You said 'first' earlier."

"Careful man!" Helen managed to smile sardonically. "You're not prepared to commit yourself till you've heard all the facts."

"I'm not sure I'm prepared to commit myself at all," said Ryle, "that is, if you want me to pronounce a clear-cut verdict."

"I'll settle for not proven, Mark, providing you consider the evidence seriously and advise me what, if anything, I should do."

"Of course. I'm here to help," replied Mark simply.

"Right. Well, have you ever heard of anyone setting their alarm clock when they had no intention of ever waking up again? Carmela had set her alarm for eight in the morning. It's a small clock, and I had to pick it up to see the time—I'm a bit short-sighted—and by chance I noticed."

Mark Ryle sipped his whisky. It gave him a moment to disguise his quickened interest. Helen was right; it was a strange act on the part of Carmela Mourne if she expected to be dead when the alarm sounded. And suddenly Mark remembered the left-handed knot in the rope that had hanged her husband. He distrusted coincidences.

He said, "The business of the alarm is peculiar, I admit, but I can think of at least two explanations. Lady Mourne might have set it from force of habit, scarcely knowing what she was doing, or she might have set it and afterwards decided on the spur of the moment that without her husband life was no longer worth living."

"Yes," Helen sighed. "I suppose you're right."

"Not proven, in fact." Mark Ryle smiled. "But surely, when her health improves, Lady Mourne will at least have to offer her family some explanation. How can she avoid it?"

Lying in bed in the room in which she had so nearly died, Carmela Mourne knew that she couldn't continue indefinitely to refuse to discuss the tragedy—if indeed it would have been a tragedy—that had been avoided by so narrow a margin. But what was she to say? What line was she to take? She had *not* tried to kill herself, but if she said so, would she be believed? And, more to the point, did she want to be believed?

She thought of the houseman, Simpson. She had no doubt that it was he who had doctored her milk, and set the suicide scene. She hated him, not because he had planned her own death, but because she was now sure that he had been responsible for Peter's. True, he might well not have put the noose around Peter's neck himself, but it was a certainty that he had arranged it. The police, of course, were trying to find Simpson. She didn't believe they would ever trace him. If they did he would admit to the thefts, but deny everything else, and an old woman's accusations would be a waste of breath.

Better to say she couldn't remember, she decided finally. She had gone to bed, taken her sleeping pills as usual, drunk her milk. Perhaps she had dozed, thought she hadn't taken any capsules, and taken two more. Perhaps she had been confused or light-headed, and then taken still more. She couldn't remember. It was a thin story, she knew, but it was the best she had, and she must stick to it; no one could force her to remember, and the world could think what it liked.

She wished that Colette Mourne would leave Fauvel. She had no need of the Frenchwoman. She preferred the nurses who simply treated her as a patient, were kind and efficient and made no attempt to probe. The Mournes were too curious; they would probably have called it "concerned," but she knew it was curiosity. She suspected that before he left Fauvel, John, having failed to get any answers to his own questions, had urged Colette to find out what she could about the supposed suicide.

Helen had been the best of them, Carmela thought. Helen hadn't tried to make any inquiries. Helen had gone back to London almost immediately. It was ironic that her cry for help—"I don't want to die"—had been to Helen, who was the most disinterested member of the family.

Perhaps, Carmela mused, it was a pity she hadn't died. Her death would have been painless, she would have known nothing about it, and it would have solved all her problems. But she had always been combative —a fighter. In the beginning she had been Peter's strength. If it had not been for her, he would have died of his wound, and never even reached Paris.

Of course, it was different now. She was alone, most terribly alone. She had never been so isolated before. Her situation was cruel, unfair; surely she had deserved better.

Viscountess Mourne groaned softly, and the nurse, who had been busy at the other end of the bedroom, hurried to her side.

CHAPTER EIGHT

Traffic was heavy for a Tuesday morning, Mark Ryle thought, even though he was driving against the rush hour, out of Central London on his way to Putney. On his return from Helen Mourne's the day before, he had found on his desk a note saying that Mr. Chariber had telephoned and would see Mr. Ryle at ten o'clock the next day; he hoped this would be convenient. Attached to the note was a file, including a full *curriculum vitae* of Thomas Edward Chariber. Ryle had been amused; as usual, Maggie had been ultra-efficient.

Moving in fits and starts amid the traffic, Ryle had plenty of time to consider Tom Chariber. He had been born sixty-seven years ago in South Wales to Edward and Mary Chariber, and was the youngest of their eight children. His father and three brothers had been coal miners, but his mother had been determined that Tom, who had promised to be a clever boy, should not go down the pit. Accordingly, though the decision had cost her considerable anguish, she had sent him away to her childless sister, who was married to a small shopkeeper in Hereford.

Mary Chariber lived long enough to know that Tom had won a scholarship to the local grammar school, but not long enough to see him go up to Oxford and later become a Member of Parliament. Subsequently Tom had married a girl who was, like himself, a devout Methodist, and had had three children of his own, all now adults and doing well for themselves. In the course of time his wife had unfortunately become an invalid, suffering from asthma and multiple allergies. But certainly on the surface it seemed that they had always been a happy, devoted couple; if they had any regrets, it was that Tom had remained a mere back-bencher throughout his political life.

Ryle sat in his car on Putney Bridge. There had been a minor accident, and part of the roadway was blocked. The police were on duty directing traffic, but even when Ryle could move it was only at a snail's pace. By the time he reached the block of flats where the Charibers lived while the House was sitting, he was twenty minutes late for his appointment.

He parked his car in one of the spaces marked "Visitors" and went into the hall of Paradise Court, as the place was called. It was unattractive, though clean, and some effort had been made to dress it up; in one corner a large vase of dusty dried flowers stood on a table. Ryle's first thought was that it was far from his idea of paradise. He rang the bell beside the name Chariber.

"Mr. Ryle? Come up. Flat thirty-four."

The voice was firm and gravelly, and well suited to the man who opened the door to Mark Ryle. Chariber was big, over six feet, with a head of shaggy grey hair and intelligent brown eyes. But his shoulders were bowed, and he moved heavily. He didn't offer to shake hands.

Ryle apologized for being late as Chariber led the way into a room which, judging from its furniture, was used as an office. Chariber ignored the apology. Instead, he waved Ryle to an uncomfortable-looking chair and sat himself behind his desk. He spoke at once.

"I'm a busy man, Mr. Ryle, so let's get down to business and not waste more time than we have to. You want to talk to me about the late Viscount Mourne, I gather."

"Yes, Mr. Chariber. I'm doing research for a book, as I mentioned."

"Why come to me?"

"I thought you might have some interesting insights. You've been asking questions in Parliament and demanding an official inquiry—"

"And I'm buggered if anyone's going to stop me now!"

Chariber suddenly banged his fist down on his desk, as if to emphasize his determination. He frowned fiercely, and glared at Ryle as if it were Ryle who was trying to dissuade him. The overall impression he gave, however, was that beneath his façade he was tense and nervous.

"Is anyone seriously trying to stop you?" Ryle inquired.

"I'll say. The wife won't answer the phone these days in case it's someone threatening to beat me up—there was one chap said he'd kill me if I didn't lay off. And you ask if they're serious?" Chariber laughed scornfully. "You can take it from me, they sound bloody serious."

"You say 'they,' so you think there's a group, or certainly more than one person involved. What do the voices sound like? Have you told the police about these threats?"

"The voices? They're foreign, most of the ones that utter threats. Russian, I suppose, or from one of their satellites. They're the lot that are most likely to want to avoid any inquiry into the doings of Viscount Mourne, aren't they? As for the police, no, I haven't brought them into it. What could they do? Put a tap on my phone? Try and trace calls? I've no time for all that nonsense."

"You sound as if you're assuming Viscount Mourne was a traitor, Mr. Chariber."

Chariber shrugged. "I'm not prepared to voice an opinion on that. All I want is a full and fair inquiry that'll get at the truth. No cover-up. No whitewash. Mind you, there have been some other phone calls, too," he added suddenly. He leant forward over his desk and almost leered at Ryle. "You'd be surprised!"

"I'm sorry. I don't understand," Ryle said, though he had a fair idea of what Chariber had in mind.

"Calls from fools trying persuasion instead of threats, saying how bad it would be for Britain if her ex-Foreign Secretary were to be shown up as a spy, and how none of our allies would ever trust us again. Well, maybe that's so, but nevertheless the people have the right to know the truth."

The last sentence emerged in a burst of sincerity that seemed to surprise even Chariber himself. He breathed heavily, and there was an appreciable silence as if he had forgotten what he intended to say next.

"Anyway, I'm not to be bought," he continued. "I never have been and I never will be. I'm a man of integrity. You ask anyone in the House, whatever their politics, and they'll tell you that Tom Chariber's a man of integrity."

"I'm sure you are, Mr. Chariber," Ryle said quietly.

"You know, you won't believe this, but I've been offered a substantial sum of money paid into a Swiss bank account, no questions asked, and a directorship in a reputable company, if I'll lay off Mourne. Not that I've the least intention of doing so, threats or bribes notwithstanding, but it goes to show, doesn't it?"

"Do you think the source of the bribes was the same as the source of the threats?"

"You mean the communists, trying a different approach?" Chariber appeared to consider the question carefully. "Could be. Alternatively, the bribery crowd might have been close pals of Peter Mourne, and now afraid for their own reputations. I'm trying to be fair, you see," he added ingenuously. "But it's Mourne you're interested in, not me. What do you want to know about him?"

"Whatever you can tell me."

"Not much that isn't public knowledge already. We were on opposite sides of the House. He was a Cabinet Minister, and I remained the lowliest back-bencher. We came from different backgrounds, and didn't move in the same circles. We were acquaintances, no more. I disagreed with his politics and almost everything he stood for, but I can't honestly say that I disliked him as a man."

Tom Chariber talked for the next ten minutes with few promptings from Ryle. What he had to say was of only moderate interest, and Ryle learnt more about Chariber himself than about Viscount Mourne. Chariber was beginning to intrigue him. The MP came across as a genuine, committed socialist, a forthright man, honest and to be trusted. Maggie, Ryle thought, had drawn an accurate picture of him. And yet—

Mark Ryle was a trained observer; it was an essential part of his job to note those small details that others might miss, and to question the reason for them. On this occasion, he asked himself why the tension and nervousness he had noted in Chariber seemed to be on the increase as the near-monologue proceeded, when the reverse might have been expected.

For instance, as he talked, Chariber had begun to fidget in his chair. He picked up a pen and put it down again. He took surreptitious glances at his watch and at the telephone standing on his desk; it was obvious he was expecting a call. And when the phone did bleep, Chariber sighed audibly. Whatever else the MP was, Ryle thought, he was a poor actor.

The telephone call was brief. On Chariber's side it consisted of "Yes," "Yes," and "Right. Five minutes." Now he openly consulted his watch, but made no immediate move to end the interview. He seemed to be having difficulty in concentrating his thoughts.

At last he said, "Perhaps there is one point I should add, Mr. Ryle. It was something that happened in the Fifties. Some members of the Labour Party were in Moscow for a conference and a friend of mine—I won't tell you who he is—swears he saw Peter Mourne go by in an official car in the centre lane of those wide streets—you know, the lanes reserved for VIPs. When he got back to London, my friend tackled Mourne about it, but Mourne swore he'd been in France at the time. Of course, my friend could have been mistaken, but he was damned sure and, in retrospect, it makes one wonder, doesn't it?"

The interview ended on this somewhat anti-climactic note, as Chariber didn't wait for Ryle's reply. Instead, he stood up and said, "I'm afraid that's it, Mr. Ryle. I have to go out now. I've a committee meeting at the House in an hour, and I don't have to tell you what the traffic's like. I hope I've been of some help. Give me a mention when your book's written."

"I will indeed," Ryle lied, "and I'm most grateful to you for giving up your valuable time. It's been fascinating to talk to you."

Chariber gave Ryle a doubtful glance, obviously distrusting the seeming compliment. He was sweating, and he rubbed his upper lip with the back of his hand. "If you'll excuse me for a moment while I say goodbye to the wife," he said, "I'll come down to the car park with you."

Ryle would have much preferred to go ahead alone, but Chariber had left him little choice. He waited inside the front door of the flat and heard a murmur of voices, a short silence, and the flush of a toilet. Chariber reappeared.

"I've just remembered someone else who might help you, Mr. Ryle," he said, opening the door and ushering Ryle towards the lift. "He's a French politician, a *Député* in the *Assemblée Nationale,* a socialist who believes that President Mitterrand has been too accommodating. But then, when you get into power it's almost impossible to stick firmly to principles, isn't it? You have to compromise."

"I'm not a politician," Ryle said, privately adding, Thank God. "I wouldn't know. This Frenchman's a friend of yours?"

"No. An acquaintance merely. We've met at various meetings." Chariber pressed the button for the lift. "But he knew Peter Mourne and on one occasion, when he was in London, he got rather drunk and made some odd remarks about the late Viscount."

"Such as?" Ryle prompted.

At this point the lift arrived. There was a couple already in it—an elderly man and his wife—and further conversation was impossible until they reached the ground floor. Chariber let the couple leave the lift first, and in the hall put out a hand to detain Ryle.

"I suggest you talk to him yourself," he said. "His name is Marcel Le Rougetel and he lives in Paris, in Neuilly, not far from the house the French Government gave to the Duke and Duchess of Windsor for life. I can't tell you the exact address, but you should be able to find it out easily enough."

"Yes, I'm sure I can," said Ryle. "Thank you once again. I'm most grateful to you."

Chariber opened the front door of Paradise Court, and let Ryle precede him into the open air. He waved his hand towards the right. "You'll be parked in one of the visitors' bays over there, I imagine," he said. "I'm on the other side of the building, so I'll say goodbye here."

"Goodbye, Mr. Chariber."

As at their meeting Chariber made no attempt to shake hands with Ryle, but contented himself with a nod before he turned and started to walk away. Ryle set off for his car.

He had scarcely gone ten yards when he heard the screech of tyres behind him. He swung round, tensed to leap out of the way of any oncoming vehicle. He was in time to see Tom Chariber standing in the path of a large black car. Chariber appeared to be rooted to the spot, and made no attempt to save himself. The car hit him squarely, throwing his body into the air, to fall to the ground with a dreadful dull thump. Then the car was almost on top of Ryle but, as he jumped and rolled sideways, it swerved away from him and roared out of the car-park.

Ryle caught a glimpse of the driver's profile under a chauffeur's cap pulled well down, and knew that he would never be able to identify the man. The car was a black Volvo, but that was little help; he had been unable to read the number plate, which was coated with mud, and anyway in all probability the car had been stolen or the plates changed.

Ryle got to his feet, bruised but unhurt. Tom Chariber, however, was lying quite still. Ryle was not the first to reach him. Two people had dashed out of Paradise Court, alerted by the horrific sounds. One was the caretaker, the other a young woman, a neighbour of Chariber's, who happened to be going out to shop. They both looked up in anguish as Ryle reached them; neither of them had ever before seen a dead man—certainly not a corpse as mutilated as Chariber's. The woman suddenly gagged, turned away and vomited. The caretaker, who was middle-aged, swallowed hard but managed to contain himself.

Tom Chariber was indeed an unpleasant sight. The big, heavy man lay on the ground like a sack, inanimate and covered in blood. His head was twisted at an odd angle, and no longer seemed to belong to his body. His mouth hung half-open, blood dribbling from the side of it. His eyes, staring, were filled with fear. As his bowels relaxed, the smell grew revolting.

Other people appeared, seemingly out of nowhere. A small group gathered round the corpse, though keeping at a respectful distance. Someone went to phone the police. A neighbour said something about Chariber's wife, and there was a general murmur of distress; she would have to be told, but no one was prepared to volunteer, not yet, not at this moment. More people came, but there was still no one to take charge, no one in authority.

Mark Ryle edged to the rear of the spectators, then walked quietly away, his departure unnoticed. Better than most, he knew what his citizen's duty was, but he had good reasons to avoid involvement. Tom Chariber was dead and there was nothing he could do to help him. Nor could he be of much use to the police, who would seek the hit-and-run driver. He couldn't identify the man, and others had seen the black Volvo. Besides, he couldn't afford to waste time here; he had more important work to do.

As he drove away from Paradise Court he passed the first of the approaching police cars, its siren screaming.

CHAPTER NINE

The same evening Mark Ryle was on the last British Airways flight to Paris. The aircraft was full, and an irate businessman had been given the excuse of over-booking and bumped so that Ryle could have a seat. It was by a window and, as they took off, Ryle stared out, first at the receding earth below, then at the cloud formations around, and concentrated on his thoughts.

Inevitably these centred on Thomas Chariber, MP—the late Tom Chariber. As Ryle had told General Bannol on his return to Cork Street, there was no question of an accident. Chariber had been deliberately run down and killed. He, and only he, had been the intended victim. The driver of the car couldn't have mistaken Chariber for anyone else; the MP had been walking towards the oncoming vehicle, and after hitting him, it had taken care to swerve to avoid Ryle. But why should anyone want to kill Chariber?

Chariber had claimed that he had received warnings threatening him with violence if he continued to demand an inquiry into the alleged communist sympathies of Viscount Mourne. There was no proof of these claims, but certainly Chariber had been tense and nervous as if he believed in them, though he had maintained they would make no difference to his future actions. Indeed, Chariber had given the impression that he personally had little faith in Mourne's integrity, and felt it his duty to persevere.

Nevertheless, duty or not, it was unlikely that Chariber had faced up to the real possibility that he might lose his life. At worst he might have feared a beating-up, and perhaps he would have taken precautions to avoid being caught by himself in a lonely spot. But it seemed that someone or some group had decided that the danger he posed was too great, that in order to prevent whatever appalling results might follow a finding that the accusations against the late Foreign Secretary were true, Tom Chariber had to be killed.

Of course, there was an alternative explanation, Ryle thought—the purpose might have been not to protect Mourne, but to help to condemn him. If someone wanted to give credibility to the rumours that Mourne had been a traitor, the death of Chariber, which could be linked to an attempt to prevent him playing his part in exposing Mourne as a long-term communist agent, was an excellent ploy.

Ryle's ruminations were suddenly disturbed by a juddering of the aircraft. He hadn't noticed that the "Fasten Seat-Belts" sign had flashed on. A reassuring voice came over the public address system. "This is the Captain. We are encountering a little local turbulence, as a result of nearby thunderstorms. They will not delay us. We shall be landing in Paris in sixteen minutes."

Ryle passed through immigration and customs with no difficulty; he always travelled light and had only hand luggage. In a taxi on the *autoroute,* taking him past Le Bourget towards the Porte de la Chapelle and the centre of the city, he made himself relax. It would be late when he reached the small hotel close to the Madeleine where he always stayed, too late to commence operations tonight. But tomorrow . . .

The next morning, after a good night's sleep, two large cups of coffee, and a couple of croissants, Mark Ryle reached for the telephone in his room with a sense of anticipation. He hoped for a successful few days in Paris, combining business with pleasure.

First, business—and a great deal would depend on Marcel Le Rougetel's response to his approach. He tapped out the unlisted number Maggie had somehow found for him. A woman answered, a *femme de ménage* he guessed, who took his name and said that she would see if Monsieur Le Rougetel was available to speak to an English friend of Monsieur Chariber.

Ryle had to wait for so long that he wondered if the call had been cut off, but at last a man's voice said, in English, "Le Rougetel here, Monsieur Ryle. What do you want of me?"

"Half an hour of your time, *Monsieur le Député.* I'd prefer to tell you what it's about when we meet."

"You say you're a friend of Tom Chariber's?"

"A casual friend. He gave me your name. You—you know he's dead, monsieur?"

"Dead? *Mon Dieu!* Tom! When? I didn't know. How did he die?"

"A traffic accident. It happened yesterday."

"I—I see," Le Rougetel said slowly. It was clear that the news had been a shock to him, but he recovered quickly. "All right, Monsieur Ryle. You have my phone number, so I assume you know my address. Could you come along this morning? I shall be here until noon."

"I'll be there, monsieur. Thank you very much."

Ryle's next call was to Louis De Chantal, Colette Mourne's brother, and was a mixture of business and pleasure. It immediately produced an invitation to dinner that night; this suited Mark perfectly as it left the day free, and yet would enable him to question the De Chantals tactfully about their early memories of Peter Mourne. Louis, who was a year older than his sister, would have been only a small boy when Mourne had come out of Spain with Carmela Drelano, as Lady Mourne then was. But Louis's mother, Ghislaine De Chantal, who lived with Louis and his wife, Annette, had nursed Peter when he was sick and cared for Carmela over some months. Ryle wondered how good Madame De Chantal's memory would be at eighty.

But his mind was now on the last call he must make, and firmly he told himself that it *was* essential. The De Chantals would be sure to tell Jeanne that he had been in Paris, and the family would think it strange if he didn't contact her. When there was no answer from her apartment, he tried the *galerie* where she worked as an interior decorator. Jeanne answered the phone herself.

"Mark, how nice to hear from you—and so soon." She sounded slightly amused.

"I'm dining with the De Chantals tonight, but if you're free tomorrow—"

"You're in Paris?" She was surprised. "I—I assumed you were in London."

"No, I came over last night." Mark resisted the temptation to ask why she should think he would phone her from London. She wasn't making much sense. "Jeanne, what about dinner tomorrow night? I'm not sure how long I'll be here or I'd offer you a choice."

"Tomorrow would be fine. Come to my apartment around eight, and we'll have a drink there first."

He had half-expected Jeanne to say that she was too busy, or that she already had a date, and he felt absurdly pleased at her ready acceptance. "That's great," he said. "I'll be there."

Mark Ryle arrived punctually at the junction of the Avenue Richard Wallace and the Rue de Longchamp in Neuilly, where Marcel Le Rougetel lived in an apartment overlooking the Bois de Boulogne. He was admitted by a *femme de ménage* in a starched white apron. Immediately she showed him into the salon, a long room full of heavy, dark furniture, that stretched from the front to the back of the building.

The Frenchman came forward to greet him, and offered his hand. "Good-morning, Monsieur Ryle. Please to sit down. My wife is out so we will not be disturbed." He led the way to two chairs by the long windows facing the formal gardens at the rear of the apartment block. "That was sad news you brought me. I didn't know Tom Chariber well, but I respected him as a colleague and an honest socialist. How did the accident occur? I assume it was an accident."

"It seems so, *Monsieur le Député,*" replied Ryle, wondering at Le Rougetel's implied suggestion that Chariber's death might have been other than accidental. Ryle was sure that he had mentioned a traffic accident in their conversation earlier that morning.

By now he was watching Le Rougetel closely, but the Frenchman's face gave little away. It was a pale round face, characterized by a small neat moustache. But almost everything about Monsieur Le Rougetel was small and neat. From his well-shined shoes to his sleek head, the only word to describe him was "dapper." Mark Ryle had taken an instant dislike to him.

"As far as I know," Ryle said carefully, "Monsieur Chariber was knocked down by a car and killed instantly. The only odd point is that the driver failed to stop. So it could have been a hit-and-run accident—or I suppose it could have been deliberate."

"Ah, mon Dieu! Surely not? Why should anyone—?"

"You may know that Chariber had received threats because of his insistence that there should be an inquiry into the activities of the late Viscount Mourne—the former British Foreign Secretary—about whom certain allegations have been made. You're aware of these, monsieur?"

"Of course, of course. One cannot help knowing. It is all over the media. But I knew nothing of any threats to Tom." Le Rougetel paused, then asked sharply, "But you, monsieur, who are you? I agreed to see you as a friend of Monsieur Chariber, but—are you from the police?"

"Most certainly not!" Ryle laughed. "I'm a writer." He explained his plan to publish a biography of Viscount Mourne, and Le Rougetel listened politely.

"I doubt if I shall be able to help you, monsieur," Le Rougetel said, "though I shall do my best. I knew Peter Mourne, but not intimately. Far from it. Socially I found him—and his wife—delightful. Politically, of course, we disagreed, as was only to be expected. Our—what shall I say in English?—our philosophies of life were so different . . ."

Le Rougetel talked for some time, and all that was expected of Ryle was a nod of the head or a murmur of interest, but the Frenchman had spoken the truth when he said that he couldn't—or wouldn't? Ryle wondered—offer much help. His knowledge of Viscount Mourne, he stressed again and again, was superficial, and he really failed to understand why Tom Chariber should have thought otherwise.

"But you must have formed some opinion of Mourne," Ryle persisted.

"You say you were shocked when you first heard these rumours about him. I think everyone was. But now that you've had time to consider the matter, perhaps discuss it with your colleagues, are you still so shocked, monsieur, or do you feel that possibly—just possibly—they could have some basis in fact?"

Monsieur Le Rougetel gave a Gallic shrug. "One could perhaps argue that Peter Mourne was too good to be true, too anti-red to be blue." He waited a moment, and then laughed at his own aphorism. "He took every opportunity to denounce *détente* as a Soviet trick, for example, even when his own party was in favour of it. And mutual reduction of nuclear weapons—another trick, according to Mourne. It is always possible to twist facts; one can argue any case if one is sufficiently clever."

"Then you yourself wouldn't accept the idea that Mourne was too good to be true, as you say?"

"Monsieur Ryle, it is difficult to believe, is it not? As for me, I do not know, but I will tell you of someone who might. I have heard him claim to be a close friend of the late Viscount. His name is Vladimir Brolov, and he is a White Russian, but born in France, in Paris. He is, perversely perhaps, an avowed communist. He makes no secret of it. In this country we respect another man's religion—and his politics. We do not believe in McCarthyism here in France."

"Where would I find this Vladimir Brolov, monsieur? What does he do?"

"He runs a small but excellent restaurant on the Île de la Cité. I recommend it. For the food it is worth a visit, even if Brolov cannot help you with your inquiries—your book. If you will excuse me one minute I will get the exact address and phone number for you."

Le Rougetel was gone several minutes, and it occurred to Ryle that he might be telephoning Monsieur Brolov. He did not trust the Frenchman. It was more than a merely instinctive dislike. Le Rougetel had struck him as evasive and unreliable—someone whom his uncle, Brigadier Ryle, would have called "a tricky customer." Tom Chariber had been tense, uncertain, fearful even, but he had come across as basically honest. Le Rougetel did not. He had suggested, subtly, while at the same time denying it, that he would not be all that surprised if Peter Mourne had indeed been a communist. But, even if Le Rougetel himself were a phoney, it didn't necessarily follow that his beliefs or suspicions were false.

When the Frenchman returned with a card on which he had written the address and phone number of the restaurant, he did not sit down again. Ryle accepted the hint; Le Rougetel had had enough of him. He stood up.

"Thank you very much, *Monsieur le Député*. I'm most grateful."

"I can guarantee you'll have a good meal, but that is all I can guarantee, Monsieur Ryle. Brolov takes his politics seriously, and he may not wish to talk to you about Viscount Mourne. It is one thing to be an acknowledged Communist Party member, but quite another to be a traitor—or even a suspected traitor."

Mark Ryle left the apartment building with a sense of frustration. He was certain that Le Rougetel had told him exactly what he wanted to tell him, and no more. In spite of hints and innuendoes, he had learnt nothing that he hadn't known before.

Immersed in thought, he strode up the Rue de Longchamp in the direction of the Avenue Charles de Gaulle—the main street of Neuilly, where he knew he would find a taxi to take him to the Île de la Cité. Subconsciously he noted the white Renault. He had seen it, or its twin, as he came out of his hotel that morning. There had been two men in it then; there were still two men in it now.

He had walked only a few yards when he spotted a taxi disgorging a passenger in the Place de Bagatelle, and he sprinted to catch it. He gave his destination, and the cab moved off, only to be halted almost immediately by a line of toddlers crossing the road, each one clinging hard to a long piece of cord. It was at this point that Ryle, glancing back in amusement as the children reached the safety of the pavement and his taxi shot ahead once more, became aware again of the white Renault behind him.

It was still there when the taxi turned into the Avenue and joined the traffic roaring towards the Arc de Triomphe. Wedging himself in a corner, Ryle watched it through the rear window. The driver was clearly an expert, because the distance between the Renault and the taxi scarcely varied, though twice the Renault could have drawn out into a different lane and overtaken the cab. Ryle knew that this might mean nothing; the occupants of the Renault might not be in a great hurry. But he needed to be certain.

The small convoy had passed Porte Maillot and was heading down the Avenue de la Grande Armée when Ryle leant forward and spoke to his own driver. "When you get to the Arc," he said, "make two complete circles before you go on down the Champs-Élysées."

"As you wish, monsieur. You're paying."

Ryle grinned, but made no attempt to explain. He sat back and watched the Renault, whose driver didn't hesitate. First the taxi, then the Renault, went twice around the Arc de Triomphe. It was a mildly exciting progress through the mass of traffic, but at least there was no longer any doubt, Ryle thought; he was being shadowed, and whoever was following him didn't seem to mind if he realized it.

But who? And why? He had only been in France twelve hours or so, most of them spent in sleep, and his decision to come across the Channel had been sudden. Yet someone was already intensely interested in his movements. There was no immediate answer to the "who?" or the "why?" but at least one point was pretty certain—his tail had some connection with the late Viscount Mourne.

CHAPTER TEN

Mark Ryle's taxi reached the end of the Champs-Élysées and turned right around the Place de la Concorde. The white Renault had closed up in the increasing traffic, and was now directly behind the taxi, as if pulled along by a tow-rope. Together, starting and stopping as the other vehicles moved in erratic bursts of speed, they drove along the *quais* beside the Seine, past the Tuileries gardens and the Louvre, until at last they reached the Place du Châtelet. Here they turned right over the Pont au Change on to the Île de la Cité. Ryle's spirits rose. This was a part of Paris he loved and knew well; he had spent several holidays staying on the neighbouring Île St-Louis with French friends of Dick and Penny Ryle.

And in the narrow, cobbled, mainly one-way streets of the old city he would have one great advantage over his pursuers in the Renault. He himself had no car to park and, he reflected, if he couldn't lose a follower in these conditions, among the housewives busy shopping, the tourists with their clicking cameras, children playing, dogs, pushcarts, delivery vans, then he should offer the Director his resignation.

By this time they had reached the Place du Parvis outside the west front of the great cathedral of Notre-Dame. Ryle leant forward and tossed some notes on to the seat beside the driver. "Go along beside the cathedral," he said, "then turn into the Rue Massillon. Drop me just after you get round the corner, and wait as long as you reasonably can. The street's narrow and you'll block it, but that won't matter for a few moments."

The man collected the money with one hand, and noted the very generous tip. "I understand, monsieur. Whatever you wish," he replied.

"Merci!" Ryle said as the taxi slowed to a stop. He jumped out hurriedly, and slammed the door behind him. He was twenty yards down the street when, glancing over his shoulder, he saw his driver engaged in a fierce altercation with one of the occupants of the white Renault. He grinned to

himself as he hurried towards the corner of the Rue Chinoinesse, where Abélard and Héloïse once walked, and where Vladimir Brolov now kept L'Oiseau d'Or. The air was redolent with the smell of freshly-baked bread and good French cooking, only slightly overlaid with petrol fumes.

Ryle consulted his watch. It was a minute or two after noon, and waiters in black trousers and gold shirts were taking down the shutters from L'Oiseau d'Or. The restaurant was presumably open for business, though this was not immediately obvious as its windows were so heavily curtained that only a glow of light could be seen from the street. The legal requirement that a menu should be displayed was met in the least obtrusive manner by a small frame in a corner of the glass by the entrance.

Glancing behind him to make sure he was free of any tail, Ryle quickly pushed open the door and went inside. Here, the decorative theme was also black and gold and behind the bar hung a tapestry of a large golden goose.

At once a waiter—obviously the maître d'—came forward to greet him. "Good-day, monsieur. You have come for lunch? You have reserved a table?" he said in English.

Ryle replied in French. "What makes you think I speak English?" he asked.

"Er—your clothes, monsieur. Or am I mistaken?"

"No, you're not mistaken, and you're certainly very observant." Ryle smiled; his shoes were English, made to his own last, but his suit, shirt and tie had all been bought in Hong Kong. "As for your questions, I've not come to lunch, but to see Monsieur Brolov, if that's possible."

The maître d' reverted to French. "If you will tell me your name and your business, I will ask if Monsieur Brolov is available. He may not yet have arrived."

"Please give him this." Ryle found a pen, took a card from his wallet, and scribbled a sentence on it.

"Very good, monsieur. Perhaps while you wait you would like a drink at the bar."

Ryle went to the bar and slid on to one of the tall stools. A barman appeared immediately, and Ryle ordered a double whisky. The drink arrived, and moments later the maître d' returned, full of apologies. Monsieur Brolov had not yet arrived, as he suspected, but he was expected in half to three-quarters of an hour. If Monsieur Ryle would care to wait, a table would be put at his disposal and the chef would be happy to prepare whatever he would like to order for lunch.

"You will be Monsieur Brolov's guest, of course, monsieur," added the maître d'. "This is understood."

"That's extremely kind. Please express my thanks to Monsieur Brolov."

"Mais, monsieur, je ne comprends—" The maître d' was unable to hide his bewilderment. He had just explained that the *patron* was not present, and the stupid Englishman was asking that a message of thanks be conveyed to him. Hadn't the Englishman understood him—or had he failed to believe him? The maître d' abandoned his problem, and said, "If you would come this way, monsieur."

Ryle followed the man to what would have been a choice table for two in a secluded corner of the main dining-room. Another waiter was already removing the second *couvert*. Ryle sat, allowed a gold napkin with a black goose in one corner to be spread across his lap, and took the elaborate menu that was handed to him. The nearly-empty whisky glass that he had left on the bar was immediately brought across to his table.

Ryle finished his drink, refused a second, and studied the menu. It was quite obvious that the maître d' had been in touch with Brolov on the phone, or that the man was already on the premises in spite of the waiter's disclaimer. Ryle couldn't believe that everyone who turned up unexpectedly at the restaurant and asked for the owner would be treated with such extraordinary courtesy. Why was he different?

He could imagine only one answer: on the back of the card he had given to the maître d' he had written in French, "To talk of Peter Mourne at M. Le Rougetel's suggestion." He assumed that it was one or other or both of these names that had occasioned the display of hospitality, quite apart from the strong likelihood that Brolov had been warned of the probability of his visit by Le Rougetel—which would also account for the maître d's expectation of the arrival of an Englishman.

He ordered. Mindful that he was dining with the De Chantals that evening, he chose onion soup, an omelette with a green salad, and cheese to follow. The waiter allowed his disappointment to show, but suggested that, if monsieur insisted on such a sparse meal, a bottle of Chablis would greatly improve it. Ryle agreed without demur; it saved argument, and he need not drink more than a glass or two of the wine.

He nibbled a breadstick and looked around the restaurant, which was beginning to fill. The clientele seemed to consist mainly of youngish men, presumably on expense accounts, though there was a party of four chic women who exuded business efficiency, and one family group of mother, father, and three children; as so often in France the children's table manners and general behaviour were exemplary. In the evening, Ryle surmised, the customers would be quite different. There would be a larger number of couples, and the average age would be greater. But one thing, being French, they would all have in common—their intense interest in what they ate.

The wine arrived. Ryle tasted it, and noted the label on the bottle with approval; Brolov had done him proud. He took another breadstick, and yawned. He wondered if Jeanne knew L'Oiseau d'Or and whether it would be advisable to book a table and bring her here the next evening. A great deal, he supposed, would depend upon his meeting with Brolov— that was, if he ever got as far as seeing the White Russian. He yawned again.

The onion soup was set before him, and he began to eat. It was delicious. He was enjoying it, or he would have been enjoying it were it not for feeling so tired and almost inert. He forced himself to sip at the soup, but his head was nodding, his neck seemingly too weak to sustain it.

The maître d' was standing in front of him. "Monsieur is not well?" he asked solicitously.

"Yes, I'm—I'm fine," Ryle said.

But it wasn't true. Even as he spoke, he knew it wasn't true. He knew that he'd been drugged. His eyes wouldn't focus and their lids were heavy. The somnolence grew stronger, until what he wanted above all else was to sleep. He fought against the sensation but it was useless. There was no doubt that the drug was beginning to overwhelm him.

A second waiter had appeared. With his help the maître d' assisted Ryle to stand and, half carrying him, half forcing him to walk, propelled him through a nearby doorway, previously concealed behind a wall tapestry. The incident caused little or no excitement. Two or three people glanced up from their meal, but their interest was short-lived. A man who inquired if anything was wrong was reassured: the gentleman was a trifle indisposed—perhaps, one waiter suggested, a little too much to drink—but there was no need for concern. A moment later, and everyone was again concentrating on the food before them, or on their conversations. The man who had been sitting by himself at the corner table was forgotten.

Mark Ryle opened his eyes to find himself lying on a couch in a room that was furnished mainly as an office, with a desk and a couple of filing cabinets. Nevertheless, the atmosphere was one of the utmost comfort. There was a good Wilton carpet on the floor, and the curtains were made of some heavy brocade material. On one wall was a large modern painting that might or might not have been a David Hockney.

Ryle took in all this without appearing to do so. He made no effort to move. He needed to give himself time, time to recover from the effects of the drug they had given him. It must have been in the whisky, he reflected, and it was not a strong dose; he had no feeling of hangover, but merely an immense thirst. In a few moments his wits would be adequate to confront the man who sat astride a chair, regarding him with interest.

The man was huge, well over six feet tall and proportionately broad, his features correspondingly large. His hair was grey, worn fairly long, and he had a superb Che Guevara moustache. Ryle guessed his age to be about seventy. His expression seemed to combine in equal parts charm, benevolence, and amusement.

"Good, Mr. Ryle," he said in English with a strong French accent. "You are recovering, I'm glad to see. I was afraid I might have to send for a doctor. Incidentally, I am Vladimir Brolov, as you may have already guessed. My friends call me Vlado."

Unsure of the meaning of this remark, Ryle chose to remain silent. He could only assume that he had been searched while he was unconscious, but he was carrying nothing of interest—nothing which might suggest the nature of his real occupation. He wondered what on earth they—presumably, Brolov's minions—could have hoped to find: a weapon of some kind, perhaps. In any case, he thought, the result of drugging him had merely been to put him on his guard.

Suddenly Brolov gave a great belly laugh. "You know, Mr. Ryle, you aren't a very good advertisement for my restaurant, collapsing like that after a mouthful of onion soup. L'Oiseau d'Or prides itself on its onion soup."

Oh well, if that was the kind of charade they wanted, he'd play along, Ryle decided. Aloud he murmured, "I'm sorry. I'm sure it wasn't the soup. I just felt faint."

"But you're improved now?" Brolov didn't wait for an answer. "Excellent. Would you like a drink? Coffee? Tea? You have only to ask."

"Thank you," said Ryle. "You're very kind, but what I'd really like would be a glass of water." He paused. "Plain water." He couldn't resist the addition.

While Brolov went to fetch the water Ryle swung his legs carefully off the couch and sat up. His mouth was still dry—he would certainly be glad of a drink—and he felt very slightly giddy, but otherwise he was back to normal. They had done him no real damage. Once again he asked himself, why had they bothered with all this nonsense? Surely not merely to search him? They must be sophisticated enough to assume that, even if he were an agent of some kind—official or unofficial—he wouldn't carry obvious identification. For that matter, what was the connection between the Communist Party, as represented by Brolov, and the late Viscount Mourne? Ryle could only hope that he was about to find out.

"Monsieur Brolov, I do apologize," Ryle said, as Brolov returned with the water. "It's too bad of me, when you were so hospitable to a stranger." His voice was devoid of sarcasm.

"A stranger in person, perhaps, Monsieur Ryle, but any friend of Viscount Mourne is a friend of mine."

"But you are mistaken, monsieur. I cannot claim such a friendship."

Once again Ryle explained about his intention to publish a biography of the late Viscount. As far as he himself was concerned, the story had begun to sound less and less convincing, but Brolov listened with great concentration, as if he were extremely interested. As Ryle progressed, however, Brolov's formerly mild expression became clouded. He frowned. He pulled at his moustache. Finally and surprisingly he exploded.

"Non! Non! Non! Merde! Monsieur, vous—vous faîtes des bêtises. Vous êtes venu pour des prunes . . ."

Ryle's French was excellent—he was almost bilingual—but he was more accustomed to cocktail party chatter or political or philosophical discussions across a dinner table than to rebutting the flood of vituperation that poured forth from Vladimir Brolov. But, if he failed to understand all the colloquialisms and imagery, their meaning was abundantly clear.

According to Brolov it was outrageous to suggest that the late Viscount Mourne had been a communist, a crypto-communist, an undercover communist. Peter Mourne had been an honourable man. If he had been a communist he would have declared himself as such, and not lived a life of lies. It was only the scum of the media that had made those vile accusations. The plan to give these lies status and permanency in a printed volume was—he, Vladimir Brolov, could find no words to describe his abhorrence. But he did, at length. He was especially shocked that an Englishman should contemplate such a publication, he said, staring at Ryle. Everyone these days was obsessed with communism—and in particular undercover, secret communists—but that the English, whom Peter Mourne had served so well, should suspect him was disgusting. Yet here was Monsieur Ryle . . .

Ryle was beginning to lose patience. He had been drugged, searched somewhat amateurishly—there was no doubt about that since his handkerchief had been replaced in the wrong pocket—and now he was being abused. He had had enough.

"Monsieur Brolov," Ryle interrupted his host. "Among a lot of other epithets, you've called me a fool and told me I'm on a fool's errand. But you have totally misunderstood my purpose. I have no wish to prove that Viscount Mourne was a communist or had communist leanings—which in his case would mean he was a spy and a traitor. On the contrary, I am very fond of his family. I had hoped that you, who are indeed a known member of the Party, might help me to deny the rumours and gossip and accusations."

Brolov listened to Ryle attentively, and became calmer. "And I do deny it, monsieur, absolutely. I have known Peter Mourne for many years and I would deny that he was at any time a communist or even a fellow-traveller. Vehemently I would deny it. I hope that satisfies you."

Too damned vehemently, Ryle thought, and in any case, how would Brolov know? If Mourne had in fact been a KGB agent-in-place, an acknowledged Party member, especially a Party member in another country, would be the last to know—unless, that is, some double deception, some ultra-complex ploy had been in progress, or was now being played with Brolov a part of it.

With these thoughts in mind, Ryle bowed his head in apparent acceptance of Brolov's words. Then, deliberately clumsy, he got to his feet. He apologized once again, thanked Brolov, and said it was time for him to go. Brolov protested that he should perhaps rest a little longer, but it was a merely formal protestation, and when Ryle paid no heed to it Brolov escorted him through the restaurant and shook hands with him at the entrance. If anyone had been interested, all he would have noted was that Mark Ryle was leaving L'Oiseau d'Or in apparent perfect health and on the best of terms with its proprietor.

Once outside in the Rue Chinoinesse, Ryle strode off briskly. By now the street was less busy. There were still a few tourists about, and some locals hurrying home to lunch with long loaves of bread under their arms, but the shopkeepers were putting up their shutters for the afternoon *méridienne.* The man lounging in the doorway opposite L'Oiseau d'Or was thus considerably more conspicuous than he might have been earlier.

Ryle noticed him, but only from training and habit. He hadn't forgotten the men in the white Renault who had been following him since he had left his hotel that morning, and the thought flashed across his mind that perhaps he had been over-confident that his trick with the taxi would lose him his tails, and had been less than careful.

He shrugged. In any case, now he was intent on getting away from Vladimir Brolov's haunts, intent on breathing fresh air to clear his head of the residue of whatever drug he had been given. He made for the blunt eastern end of the Île de la Cité, where the French have built their Memorial to the Deported, one of the most affecting memorials in the world to a country's dead.

It was a cool day with a wind coming off the river, but Ryle paid no attention. Taking gulps of air, he walked at a steady pace through the rough grass of the treeless Square de l'Île de France, which is washed by the Seine on two sides. Soon he came to the Memorial, a low stone and concrete structure, not unlike a gun emplacement, on whose wall are incised the words: *"Aux deux cents mille martyrs français morts dans les camps de la déportation."* He remembered that Jeanne Mourne's grandfather, Colette Mourne's father—the man who, before the other, all-encompassing war had begun, had welcomed into his house the young Peter Mourne and his Spanish girlfriend—had been one of these two hundred thousand martyrs.

Iron gates closed the twin entrances to the Memorial during the midday period, but Ryle had no wish to descend the steep stone steps to the courtyard below with its barred narrow space on a level with the waters of the Seine, and the underground chambers leading from it. For several seconds he stood, gazing across the muddy green waters of the river towards the Île St-Louis, his thoughts on the past. Then abruptly he turned and retraced his steps.

It was not until he was half-way across the adjoining Square Jean XXIII that he sensed he was again being followed. This Square is not rough and open like the Square de l'Île de France but is, in reality, a neat small park with trees and flowers, normally frequented by people walking their dogs, mothers with children, and visitors taking photographs of the fine flying buttresses along the east front of Notre-Dame. At this time of day it was almost deserted. Glancing briefly over his shoulder, Ryle saw a man some twenty yards behind him, who seemingly had appeared from nowhere.

His first thought was that the man might have been relieving himself behind a tree, and that he hadn't noticed him as he passed. But there was something familiar about the shape of the squat, broad-shouldered figure that immediately reminded him of emerging from Brolov's restaurant and seeing a man—the same man?—in a doorway across the street.

Ryle stopped suddenly, crouched, and pretended to tie up a non-existent loose shoelace. It was an old trick. By turning his body fractionally sideways he could see the legs of the man behind him. An innocent stroller would come straight on without pause, since he would have no particular interest in anyone ahead of him, but it was difficult for a tail, however experienced, not to show a momentary hesitation. On this occasion the legs came to a complete standstill, leaving Ryle in no doubt.

Ryle stood up, swung on his heels, and walked back towards the man. Planting himself firmly in front of him he said in French, "What the hell do you think you're doing following me around? I don't like it, do you understand me?"

The man, in spite of his aggressive build, had a pale and frightened face. He stared up at Ryle, as if unexpectedly overwhelmed, and made no immediate reply. Ryle repeated his question, though less fiercely. The man's attitude surprised him. He had anticipated heated denials and angry protestations of innocence. None came.

Instead, when it seemed that the man was finally able to speak, he said, "Monsieur Ryle, I'm very sorry to have annoyed you."

In spite of his surprise, Ryle managed to snap, "Don't apologize! Tell me who you are! How do you know my name? *Et pourquoi vous filez le train à moi?*"

"*Monsieur, je m'appelle Jean-Paul Pinel.* But my name is of no importance. I am following you because those are my instructions. I am a member of DST, and my *patron* said we were to watch you in case there was any trouble."

The DST, thought Ryle—*La Direction de la Surveillance du Territoire,* the French internal security service, an approximate equivalent of MI5. If they had some idea of his mission—which, if his entry into France had been noted, they might well have suspected—it was perhaps not unreasonable that they should take an interest in him. He said, "What sort of trouble?"

"My *patron* gave me no hint, monsieur, but I think perhaps he is concerned for your safety here in France."

"You said 'we.' Do you have a companion? Or is there a whole team tailing me?"

"Just two of us, monsieur. *Mon copain*—my partner—is driving the car. A white Renault, which monsieur may have noticed."

Ryle nodded. The man was a fool, he thought, or at least incompetent, but the problem of the Renault was solved, unless—he had better make sure that Pinel was not lying.

"Show me your papers," he said. "Take them out, very slowly and very carefully. Don't make any sudden moves that I might misinterpret."

Pinel made no objection, but did precisely as he was told; he took no chances, but clearly he was confident that his papers were in order and would convince the Englishman. Ryle glanced at them and returned them to him; the mere fact that he was carrying such identification showed that his mission was not under cover in any sense.

"Okay," he said. "So where did you leave the Renault?"

"On the Rue du Cloître, monsieur."

"Then that's where we'll go. You can give me a lift back to my hotel," said Ryle. "I know I don't have to tell you where it is, and it'll save me a taxi fare."

Ryle's hotel did boast a restaurant, which is unusual for a small hotel in Paris, but by the time he reached the place the last stragglers had finished their meal and were lingering over coffee. To speed them on their way, the waiters were clearing the empty tables and re-laying them for dinner. Ryle's arrival was greeted with some dismay, gestures expressive of inability to serve him, and voluble regrets.

Luckily for Ryle, however, the manager arrived in the dining-room at this point, and an accommodation was soon reached. The hotel did not normally provide room service, but as a favour to Monsieur Ryle, who was always a welcome guest, the manager would arrange for a tray to be sent up to his room. So, with profuse thanks, Ryle, who was by now extremely hungry, hastened towards the lift.

Once in his room, he washed his hands and face and, feeling refreshed, found the telephone number of an old acquaintance in the DST, one Pierre Avaine, who sounded amused to hear from him. Ryle made no response to his bantering.

"Why are you having me followed all around Paris?" he demanded bluntly. "Do you think I'm some kind of threat to the security of the French Republic?"

"It is for your own protection, *mon cher.*" Avaine didn't bother to deny the accusation. "We both know why you're here and if—I emphasize *if*— our friend who shall be nameless was indeed what is rumoured there may be powerful interests who will wish to conceal this fact. They might well be prepared to do you harm in order to achieve their purpose."

"If you think your current minions are going to protect me, you can think again," Ryle said angrily. "They're totally incompetent and merely a nuisance as far as I'm concerned. I want them called off. Do you understand, Avaine? I mean it." He paused, thinking he had better sweeten the pill. "I promise you, if I come across anything of importance I'll keep in touch." That was vague enough, he added to himself.

"Very well, my dear colleague, it shall be as you wish. But please, please, for my sake, if not for your own, try to avoid any trouble."

"I'll do my best," Ryle assured him, and as there was a knock on the door and a waiter brought in a tray with chicken sandwiches, salad, and a pot of coffee, he quickly and firmly added, "Goodbye" before replacing his receiver.

CHAPTER ELEVEN

Mark Ryle woke slowly, drifting up from a deep sleep. After his belated lunch he had kicked off his shoes and lain down on the bed. Hands clasped behind his head he had stared at the light fitting in the middle of the ceiling and tried to organize his thoughts. The thread led from Tom Chariber, who had drawn attention to himself by his demands for an official inquiry into the activities of Viscount Mourne, via the French *Député,* Le Rougetel, to Vladimir Brolov, the restaurateur of Russian descent. Each in his own way, whatever he had said or affirmed or denied, had tended to undermine belief in Mourne's integrity.

But had this been calculated? It was a question that Ryle not unnaturally found impossible to answer with any degree of confidence. And if it had all been deliberate, why precisely? Taken together, Chariber, Le Rougetel, and Brolov were a most unlikely trio to have been engaged in some kind of conspiracy directed towards throwing suspicion on Mourne. Chariber had been no irrational anti-government firebrand, like some of his colleagues on his side of the House. On the surface at least, Le Rougetel would seem to have little to gain whether or not Mourne had been a spy and whether or not he were to be exposed as such, though as a politician he might have a professional interest in the truth.

Brolov was more difficult to judge since he was an avowed communist. The Party—presumably in the shape of the KGB or the GRU—would scarcely welcome an exposure which, although Mourne was dead, could lead to inquiries, damage assessments, and even perhaps the unmasking of additional assets. The Soviet authorities were more likely to take every possible measure to ensure that their agents preserved their anonymity beyond the grave. Whatever the real motivation, Brolov seemed an odd vehicle. Unless of course, Ryle repeated to himself, he was taking a vastly simplistic view of a complex plot, the ramifications of which had yet to appear.

At this point Ryle's thoughts became personal. Here we are again, he reflected. It's always my impulse to refuse to take obvious facts at their face value. He remembered bitterly that this, in essence, was one of the accusations that Jeanne had flung at him before she had finally walked out. At the time he had denied it with some vehemence. By now he was sure that it was at least partially justified. His occupation necessitated considerable scepticism, but even at such work a man could become too mistrustful.

The phone rang. Ryle put out a long arm and pulled the instrument on to the bed beside him. He said hello. Maggie's voice answered him.

"Hello, dear. How are you? As I'd not heard I thought I'd better ring and make sure all was well."

"I only got here last night."

"I know, but time passes slowly without you. You're enjoying Paris?"

"Er—moderately. The city's wonderful, but from a personal angle my contacts are both provocative and frustrating. My first call produced nothing of great interest, but suggested a second. I lunched at a place called L'Oiseau d'Or on the Île de la Cité, run by a White Russian called Vladimir Brolov. Unfortunately I ate—or drank—something that disagreed with me and I passed out briefly. But no damage was done."

"Oh Lord!" said Maggie. "Are you okay now? Are you sure?" She was no longer bantering.

"Positive. Incidentally, my French friends appear to be interested in what I'm doing. I complained to Pierre, told him I didn't like to be too closely monitored."

"Pierre?"

Ryle ignored the query. Maggie might not understand the reference to Pierre Avaine and the DST, but the Director certainly would when she relayed the conversation to him. "So much for my news," he said. "What about the home front?" He guessed that Maggie wouldn't have phoned unless she had some news to impart. "Any gossip?"

"Lots! I suppose it's not very surprising. One might have guessed. But I've only just heard that Tom's been having it off with his secretary, and a few months ago she took some sick leave. She went into a private clinic to have a cyst removed from her womb—or that was the official story."

"I see. Does his wife know?"

"Certainly not. He'd have done anything to keep it from her. In spite of his jolly on the side he was devoted to his wife. There's also the point that he was a pillar of his church, and it wouldn't have gone down well in those circles either."

When Mark Ryle arrived at the De Chantals' apartment for dinner that evening, Louis, Colette's brother and thus John Mourne's brother-in-law, and his wife, Annette, welcomed him as a dear friend. Annette kissed him three times, French fashion, on alternate cheeks, and Louis shook his hand firmly, at the same time drawing him into the salon, a long and elegant, typically Parisian room.

"Maman, you remember Mark Ryle? I'm sure I don't need to ask."

"You don't, especially as I've been expecting him—and looking forward to it. So I won't bother with your stupid question, Louis. Welcome, as always, *mon cher* Mark."

From her wheelchair, Ghislaine De Chantal held out both her hands, sadly deformed by arthritis, to Ryle, who bowed and brushed each of them lightly with his lips. She smiled, pleased with the old-fashioned courtesy. She was in her eighties, frail and confined to her wheelchair, but she was still mentally alert, a fact that Ryle, who had not seen her for some time, registered with relief.

"We are *all* pleased to see you," said Annette, a small, vivacious woman, ten years younger than her husband. "We're anxious for all your news. Letters and telephone calls are useful, but it is a great relief to talk to someone else—someone involved as a friend of the family, but not too closely."

"You mean to someone who, you hope, will tell us the truth." Louis smiled wryly at Mark. "We're worried about Colette and—and all the Mournes. We know you understand. It's inevitable."

"Yes, of course," said Ryle quietly.

Naturally he understood their interest, but he had not expected the subject of Peter Mourne to be broached so candidly or so straightforwardly. The speed with which they had raised it was, he realized, a measure of their concern. Nevertheless, he found it disconcerting, a feeling which he had obviously revealed. For the sensitive Annette immediately interrupted to say that Louis must get him a drink. She asked what he would have.

"Scotch with a spot of soda, please," Ryle said.

"Ah, *le Scotch,*" said Annette. "It's become the smart thing to drink in Paris nowadays."

But Louis wasn't to be deterred for long. Ignoring his wife's efforts to deflect the conversation, he served drinks and then at once returned to what he had been saying. Mark had decided, within limits, to make no attempt to parry questions.

"It's not pleasant for any of the Mourne family," he said. "There are always people ready to make scandalous phone calls and send hate mail, and of course there was that dreadful incident at Lord Mourne's funeral."

"You were there? You saw what happened?" Madame De Chantal said anxiously.

"Yes." Ryle hesitated, but realized that there was no reason not to tell the truth. He described the shouting and the hurling of the red paint, and gave his opinion that the whole thing had been an organized demonstration. "It was worst for Lady Mourne," he added. "She was right behind the coffin."

"We don't mind that much about Carmela," Ghislaine De Chantal said with an unexpected and brutal frankness. "It's Colette we're concerned about, and John, and the effect this whole affair will have on the children."

Surprised by the old lady's abrupt dismissal of Carmela, it was a moment before Mark realized that the "children" she was referring to were Hugh and Jeanne. He now began to choose his words carefully, wanting to reassure the De Chantals, but remembering that he was meant to know no more than might a close friend of the family.

"I'm afraid that in the short term it's being extremely unpleasant for Colette and John, and for John's sister, Helen. They all live in London, which is naturally the centre of the controversy. But fortunately the most difficult period shouldn't last too long. The media will get bored and blow up another scandal." Or let's hope so, Ryle thought, because that's how it should be, unless whoever is engineering this decides otherwise. Out loud he added, "Of course a lot depends on how the British Government decides to play it, but I don't believe that in the long run it'll make much difference to the Mournes."

"But what about Hugh—in the Foreign Office?" Annette asked.

"In Madrid he's well away from it all, and I feel sure there'll be no lasting effect on his career, if that's what you mean. The powers-that-be do have some sense, you know, and to take any action against Hugh would be the equivalent of admitting that the absurd rumours about Peter Mourne had some validity, wouldn't it?"

Louis was quick to respond. "Don't ask us. Our business is wine—an honest enterprise compared with politics."

Ryle laughed. "Anyway, Hugh should be okay. It really ought not to have any more effect on him than on Jeanne. It's a good thing they're both out of the country, but—"

He stopped, conscious that there was a sudden tension among his three listeners. They were staring at him as if he had made a comment so stupid that he couldn't expect it to be taken seriously. He glanced questioningly from one to the other.

"You mean you don't know?" Annette said at last.

"Know what? About Jeanne?" He felt a tremor of apprehension. "No. I was speaking to her on the phone this morning. She was all right then. What's happened?" His voice was tight.

"She didn't tell you, say anything?"

"No!" The single word sounded like an expletive.

"Well, that wretched man she was going to marry has broken off the engagement," Louis said. "Officially the marriage will not take place by mutual consent, but in fact he told Jeanne that he couldn't risk his political future by marrying into the Mourne family while a cloud of suspicion hung over it. He suggested postponing the wedding in the hope that the accusations against Peter would be proved false, but Jeanne told him to go to hell."

"Quite right too!" interjected Ghislaine De Chantal. "I'm extremely glad. In her place I'd have done the same. It's self-evident that this man's not worth marrying."

"Certainly not, maman," Annette agreed.

Mark Ryle said nothing. He was content to let the two women voice their opinions. His own feelings were in turmoil. He had steeled himself to accept the fact that Jeanne was about to marry Simon Maufant in September, but it seemed that, after all, this was not to be. He felt relief and joy, anger against Maufant, grief for Jeanne, and irritation that he hadn't known before. He recalled his conversation with Jeanne that morning, and the amused tone in which she had remarked that he had telephoned "so soon." He knew now what she had meant, he thought, with a spurt of resentment at her failure to explain.

"I—I'm very sorry," he heard himself say at last. "I had no idea. I must have missed the announcement, unless it hasn't appeared yet. I hope she's not too upset."

"I suspect it was her pride that was hurt more than anything," said Annette.

There was no need to reply to this. The subject was changed and shortly afterwards the *femme de ménage* came in to announce that dinner was served. Ryle was glad of the respite. He decided not to mention the biography of Peter Mourne he was supposed to be researching until after the meal, though he knew he shouldn't leave it too long. Old Madame De Chantal would retire early, and he mustn't miss the chance to question her.

His chance was provided by the old lady herself, and came as they were all having coffee. Jeanne and the Mournes had been uppermost in Mark Ryle's mind throughout dinner, but he had studiously avoided mentioning them, and instead had done his best to be an entertaining guest by recalling episodes from his recent visit to the Middle East. He was grateful when Madame De Chantal reintroduced the important topic.

"I have such happy memories of Fauvel Hall," she said suddenly. "Before the war we—my late husband and I—had two splendid holidays staying with dear Elizabeth and David. It was on the second occasion that I first met Peter Mourne. He must have been about sixteen at the time. John and Helen were still very small."

She appeared to lapse into a brief reverie, and Ryle said, "I wish you'd tell me about it." He briefly explained the planned biography.

Louis and Annette exchanged glances, but old Madame De Chantal would have considered it ill-mannered to show surprise. She smiled sweetly at Ryle. "There isn't much to tell," she said. "Little worth putting in a book."

"Nevertheless, I should be interested, madame." Ryle returned her smile.

She gave the faintest of shrugs. "Very well. Elizabeth and I were close friends, of course. It was one of those friendships formed when one is young and which lasts a lifetime. Unfortunately they are rare, but because of that especially precious."

She paused. Again, she seemed to be lost in a dream of the past. Mark waited, trying to picture the young girl Ghislaine De Chantal had once been, when her hair was long and beautiful, her face unlined, her body not confined to a wheelchair. Even now she sat upright and retained great elegance.

"Our mothers had known one another," she continued, "and we were sent several times to stay with each other, Elizabeth to improve her French and I my English. Neither of us had a sister, and we became close, as I said." She paused. "But it's Peter you're interested in. I remember him first as a quiet boy who wandered about the house—rather unhappily, I thought. It was a grief to Elizabeth that, although she had done her best as a stepmother, he had always resented her. She couldn't help feeling that it was because of her that he decided to go to Spain, instead of to university. And of course, afterwards—"

She stopped, shook her head, and sighed. Finally she added, "Peter was only a boy when I met him then, but after his experiences in the Spanish Civil War he was a man—and a sick one."

"That was early in 1939?" Ryle asked, knowing the answer.

"Yes. In January of that year. He must have been almost twenty-one. He arrived on our doorstep—before the war we had a house in St-Germain-des-Prés—without warning, and with Carmela—Carmela Drelano as she still was then. They knew no one in Paris except us and it was natural he should come here. Poor dear, he was in a sorry state."

"He smelt," Louis said suddenly. "He and Carmela both smelt."

"What?" Annette laughed.

"It's true! I was nine, pushing ten, at the time, and I remember going into the hall and the two of them were standing there with maman. They looked tired, exhausted, and as if they hadn't had a bath for a month—which probably they hadn't. Maman called to me to come and help because Peter was on the verge of collapse, but I'm ashamed to say I ran away. Carmela terrified me. I thought she was some kind of gypsy."

"Peter had a nasty wound which hadn't healed properly," Madame De Chantal continued, "and I have to admit that Carmela looked after him well. She insisted on sleeping in his room, and to begin with she scarcely left him."

"They were with you a long time?" Ryle said.

"Oh no," Madame De Chantal corrected him. "You must understand that this was a very difficult period for all of us. We were certain that war was coming. We knew that your Mr. Chamberlain with his piece of paper from Hitler had made no difference. It had bought us a breathing space, that's all. And we weren't sure what to do with it—any more than our politicians and generals. My husband wanted Peter and Carmela to go to England. It seemed the sensible thing to do, but there were many difficulties."

"Why?" Annette, who had previously heard only an outline of this complex story, had become curious. "What sort of difficulties? Money?"

"No. That was no problem. Elizabeth sent Peter money, and anyhow we could have helped them. The main complication was Carmela herself. She was Spanish. She had no papers. She had entered France as a refugee, I suspect illegally, but Peter claimed he'd have died in Spain if she hadn't looked after him. We didn't ask too many questions." Ghislaine De Chantal threw out her hands in a gesture of resignation.

"Of course, there was an obvious solution," she went on, "Peter could marry her. He wanted to, but yet another difficulty arose: they were of different religions. Oh, they had so many obstacles to overcome! Some of them, I'm sorry to say, of their own making. We did what we could, but naturally we had our own problems. It was not a happy time."

"You said they weren't with you for long," Ryle prompted.

Louis answered, after an anxious glance at his mother, who was clearly beginning to tire. "Not in Paris," he said. "We had a country house in the Bordeaux area where our vineyards were. Maman sent them there—luckily it was in the Zone that was at first unoccupied by the Germans—and from there they made their way to England. They got back some time after the war started, I gather." He stopped and added rather acidly, "And that was that."

Ryle looked at him sharply. "Surely they were grateful," he protested.

"Elizabeth was very grateful for what we'd done. She embarrassed us with her thanks as long as communication was possible," Ghislaine De Chantal said. "But by the time he reached home Peter was ill again, and perhaps Carmela found it difficult to write English. Then the war changed everything, and by the end of it they had forgotten, apparently, or they were too busy to think of us."

Louis made an almost imperceptible gesture to Annette, who rose to her feet. She went around to the back of the wheelchair.

"Maman, you have been up for long enough. Mark must say goodbye now, and I shall take you to your room."

"Yes, you are right. I must go. I'm tired." Ghislaine De Chantal held out her hands for Mark to kiss. "Come and see us again when you are next in Paris," she said, smiling at him. "And if you want to know more about Peter, ask old Brecquou. He's still alive."

"Your mother is wonderful," Ryle said, when Annette had wheeled her from the salon.

"Yes, she's splendid," Louis agreed. "Like so many of her generation, including old Jean-Paul Brecquou, whom she mentioned. Their bodies get feeble, but not their minds."

"Who is this Monsieur Brecquou?"

"He was my father's manager at the vineyards—and his close friend. He and his wife took care of Peter Mourne and Carmela after they left us. He's a widower now, and he lives with his daughter in Chantilly, where her husband is a doctor at *Le Centre Medico-Chirurgical des Jockeys.* He might well be worth a visit if you're so interested in the late Viscount."

Ryle took the opportunity to ask a question that had been nagging at his mind for some time. "Do I gather from your tone that you didn't like Peter Mourne much?" he said.

Louis hesitated, then decided to be frank. "Not much," he replied. "He was an ingrate, if ever I knew one. He might have shown a little appreciation for all my parents did for him—and for Carmela. What's more, from what I heard, he didn't treat his stepmother too well either, though she was very good to him and Carmela. But I agree that this doesn't make him a communist or a traitor."

"Let's hope he wasn't, for everyone's sake," said Ryle. "Do you by any chance remember if you ever heard either of your parents comment that he or Carmela had shown any sympathy for the Republican cause in Spain?"

"On the contrary." Louis De Chantal was quite definite. "They were both so violently pro-Franco that they annoyed my father. He believed, erroneously as it turned out, that when our war came, Franco would throw in his lot with Hitler, and against us."

"And of course Carmela had reason to hate the Republicans," Ryle admitted. "She lost her home and her family, thanks to them."

"I know. Which makes it incredible that anyone should think that Peter Mourne could have— If he had, Carmela must have known." De Chantal shook his head. "Ah well, what about some brandy, Mark? I'll drive you back to your hotel later. It's no bother. My car's outside."

"Thanks," said Ryle. "I'll gladly accept both offers."

CHAPTER TWELVE

Chantilly, with its famous *hippodrome, château*, and *forêt,* is only about twenty kilometres to the north of Paris—half an hour's drive once Ryle had reached the *Périphérique* and negotiated the suburbs immediately beyond. He left his hotel in a rented car the next morning in time to reach his destination at about half-past ten.

The weather had turned warm and thundery overnight, so he drove with all the windows down. This was why he smelt the smoke so soon after reaching the outskirts of Chantilly. By the time he had passed the racecourse on his right and come to the junction of the Avenue du Maréchal Joffre and the Rue du Connétable, the smell was unpleasantly strong. It was also all-pervasive, though it seemed to emanate from the populated area to the north, rather than from the *château* or the forest to the east. Somewhat nonplussed, Ryle raised his car windows. Better be hot, he thought, than breathe in that heavy, smoke-laden, acrid air, which might well do him as much harm as inhaling a couple of hundred cigarettes.

The man who was his reason for coming to Chantilly, Jean-Paul Brecquou, one-time manager of the De Chantals' vineyards, lived on the Rue du Haut, a street of tall, narrow houses not far from the Canal St-Jean. The area was off the tourist routes, and Ryle had only a faint recollection of it from earlier visits to Chantilly, mainly to attend the well-known *Prix de Diane* at the racecourse, but Louis De Chantal had given him detailed directions while driving him back to his hotel the previous evening. It was Louis who had suggested that Ryle should arrive without any advance notice.

"That way you'll be likely to find old Brecquou sitting in his garden studying a racing form, though I don't think he gambles a great deal," Louis had said. "Not that he gets much chance, poor man. As you know, there's no off-course betting in France, and there aren't many racing days at Chantilly during the year. In any case, if you warn her of your arrival, his daughter, who's a Madame Fourget, will want to know what you want, and she may suggest that he's not well and can't see you. She's a good woman, but sometimes she can be over-protective."

Ryle had taken Louis's advice and had not telephoned, but, as he turned off the Rue du Connétable, he wondered if this had been a sensible move. In fact, there turned out to be a police barricade across the street he wanted to enter, with a group of onlookers around it and a couple of gendarmes to keep them in order. One of the gendarmes stepped forward, holding up a forbidding hand, though it was quite clear that Ryle, who had slowed his car to a crawl, had no intention of attempting to crash past the barrier. Beyond the gendarme Ryle could now see that the street was crowded with police vehicles and fire service trucks, while men—some in uniform and some in plain clothes—appeared and disappeared among a row of shattered buildings.

"Défense d'entrer, monsieur," the gendarme said as Ryle wound down a window. The acrid smell was particularly pungent.

"I wanted to get into the Rue du Haut," Ryle said.

"Quel numéro? Who do you wish to see, monsieur?"

"Numéro sept," said Ryle, thinking it was none of the gendarme's business. "I intend to visit Monsieur Jean-Paul Brecquou."

The gendarme gave Ryle a long, almost suspicious stare, then slowly shook his head. "That will not be possible, monsieur."

"Pourquoi non?" Ryle demanded abruptly.

He was becoming irritated. The gendarme was far from young. His hair was grizzled and his skin weather-beaten, but his eyes were bright. He certainly was not unintelligent, yet he seemed to be purposely obstructive.

"Because, monsieur, and I regret to tell you this, neither the house nor Monsieur Brecquou is with us any more. Admittedly Monsieur Brecquou's body is at the morgue, what remains of it, but his soul is in Heaven." The gendarme, who by now had relaxed, crossed himself. "He was a good, kind man. Always ready to share a tip on the horses or stand a *copain* a drink at the café—when he managed to escape from his daughter, that is."

The gendarme paused reflectively, then continued, "Not that I'm suggesting Madame Fourget didn't look after him well, but—" He gave an expressive shrug. "You know women. Madame Fourget did what she thought best, but she didn't really understand Jean-Paul, and her husband never interfered. Jean-Paul hated to be cosseted. But I mustn't speak ill of the poor woman."

Once started, the gendarme seemed unable to stop talking. Words flowed from him in a steady stream, the people around him nodding in sympathy like a Greek chorus. It was a bizarre scene, and Ryle gathered a great deal of useless information about Monsieur Brecquou, his daughter, and his son-in-law. He waited patiently for the flow to ease, coughing from time to time in the smoky air.

"Monsieur, when did Monsieur Brecquou die?" he asked at last. "And what happened to the house? I don't understand. It must have been more than a simple fire to give rise to all this smoke and this commotion."

The questions set the gendarme off once more, but this time Ryle had no need to feign interest. *"Alors, vous avez raison, monsieur,"* he began. *"Vraiment,* it was much more than a simple fire."

At length the facts began to emerge. Jean-Paul Brecquou had died in the early hours of the morning. There had been an explosion which had wrecked the house in which he lived, and had caused considerable damage to the houses on either side. The explosion had been followed by a fire, which had spread along the street. The Chantilly fire service had been unable to cope, and by the time assistance arrived from Senlis and Compiègne it was too late to save most of the buildings.

"It was like a scene from Hell, monsieur," the gendarme went on. The man had a streak of poetry buried under his uniform, Ryle thought fleetingly. "The smoke, the dark, the leaping flames, the screams, the confusion, the chaos, the terror that another explosion might follow the first, husbands seeking wives, wives seeking children. It was horrific. I never want to see anything like it again," he concluded rather lamely. The people around nodded their heads in agreement.

"Was Monsieur Brecquou the only casualty? Surely not," said Ryle.

"Fortunately, Chantilly was lucky." The gendarme had reverted to his epic style. "So far, Monsieur Brecquou is the only inhabitant to have given his life. But many were hurt and are now in hospital. We await news of their fate. But mostly they appear to be suffering from burns, smoke inhalation, and shock. Madame Fourget has a broken leg and a crushed pelvis, though her husband escaped unharmed. The couple next door to the Brecquous are in an especially serious condition. Oh, it could have been much worse, monsieur, I agree. The good God was merciful to our people, monsieur. Nevertheless—" The gendarme spread out his hands helplessly. "You are about to ask who could have brought about such a wicked act, and why? As I said, the Fourgets are fine citizens, helpful neighbours who have never harmed an individual, and as for old Jean-Paul—it is beyond my comprehension!"

Mark Ryle had an idea that the disaster was not beyond his own comprehension, but he had to ask while this representative of the authorities, presumably overwhelmed by what had taken place, was in such an unexpectedly expansive mood. "You are suggesting that the event was not an accident, monsieur?" he said.

"Most certainly it was no accident. Perhaps it was not intended that the fire should spread, but the attack on the Fourgets was deliberate, and the perpetrators should have realized that with old houses, dry timbers, attics full of—"

Ryle interrupted him. "How do you know it was a deliberate attack?"

He cursed himself for having spoken so abruptly. The gendarme was reminded that he was on duty, and giving out information to a stranger—a stranger who might be a journalist, or— He was not pleased with himself, and he rounded on Ryle.

"And just who are you, monsieur, that you're so interested? Are you from a newspaper?"

Ryle coughed, partly to give himself a moment to think, partly because the smoky air was getting into his throat. The gendarme and the people around appeared immune from its effects; presumably they had become accustomed to it during the night.

"No, monsieur," replied Ryle more gently. "No, I'm not here as a reporter. I'm a historian. A friend told me that Monsieur Brecquou had some fascinating recollections of the war, and as I was in Paris I thought I would visit him. Unfortunately I am too late, but naturally I'm interested in this strange affair, especially as you said it was no accident."

The gendarme nodded, apparently satisfied with this explanation. "No accident, monsieur," he repeated. "There is no secret about how it happened, and I will tell you what is known. Monsieur Brecquou could walk all right, but stairs were too much for him, so he slept in a room on the ground floor, and he never closed his shutters at night. Some fiend threw a home-made petrol bomb through his window, and followed it with a cylinder of liquefied gas. The result? I have explained."

"Dreadful," Ryle murmured. "Dreadful."

For a moment the two men and the people surrounding them were silent, as if in respect for the dead and the injured. Then Ryle thanked the gendarme, and said he must be on his way. He turned the car, went back to the Rue du Connétable, and drove on, over the canals, past the *Jardin anglais* in the shadow of the great *château*, towards Senlis.

His object was to get out of Chantilly, and away from the smoke-filled air which now conjured up for him horrific images of the scene that had taken place on the Rue du Haut a few hours ago. He drove fast, forcing the car to eat up the ten kilometres to Senlis. Traffic was light, and it was not until he was nearing the town that he noticed the white Renault in his rear-view mirror.

Ryle swore softly. So much for demanding that Pierre Avaine call off his dogs, he thought; the DST hadn't even bothered to use another car that he might not recognize. He had intended to by-pass Senlis and take the *autoroute* straight back to Paris, but now, on impulse, he drove into the old town to the Place du Parvis in the shadow of the fine cathedral, parts of which date from the twelfth century.

It was almost midday. The Place du Parvis is the main parking area near the centre of Senlis; Ryle had trouble in finding a space, but finally managed to squeeze his car between a large truck and a badly-parked private vehicle. He had some difficulty opening his door to get out.

Ignoring the Renault that had followed him, he set off on foot up the steep hill to the cathedral itself. Inside he found a priest saying Mass in a side chapel, seemingly for a congregation of half a dozen elderly women. A mother was helping her child to light candles in front of a statue of a saint unknown to Ryle. There were a few sightseers, but the Cathédral Notre-Dame in Senlis is less famous than its namesake in Paris, though its original construction was commenced some ten years earlier. Ryle sat down in a rear pew and thought about Jean-Paul Brecquou.

First he admitted to himself that he was badly shaken. He had no faith in coincidence, but to his mind there could be no explanation but that Brecquou had been eliminated because of his one-time connection with Peter Mourne and Carmela, and probably as a direct result of his own— Ryle's—inquiries. The gendarme had insisted that the attack had been deliberate, even though Brecquou and the Fourgets were well-liked in their neighbourhood. What was more momentous was that, unlike the killing of Tom Chariber, this had been an act of blatant terrorism which could easily have resulted in wholesale disaster, and showed an almost impudent disregard for the lives of the uninvolved.

Why? Ryle asked himself. With an old man like Brecquou a clean kill would surely have been possible, even if time had been pressing. Was it then intended as a warning that, when necessary, counter-action would be taken regardless of any consequences? Was the enemy—enemy?—becoming bolder, or had he panicked?

As Ryle asked himself this last question, he realized that he was beginning to form a mental image of the so-called enemy. And instinctively he rejected the idea of panic. The killing of Brecquou had been bold, he decided, but not rash, and not without purpose. Whoever he might be, or whatever organization might be represented by the word, the "enemy" was a professional—a tactician who would play the game at its limits; at present it seemed impossible to out-think him.

The priest at the side altar had said his Mass, and was leaving the main cathedral on his way to disrobe. A small party of eight tourists had entered with a guide. Mark Ryle left the pew in which he had been sitting, and made his way outside and down to the Place du Parvis, in search of a café. He ordered a *demi* and a *croque-monsieur;* with the promise of dinner with Jeanne that evening, he had no wish for a large meal. He ate quickly, finished his beer and crossed the square towards his car.

To his annoyance he found that the truck was still beside him, making use of that near-side door impossible, while the white Renault that had followed him from Chantilly had parked even more closely to the left of his own car than the previous occupant of the space. In fact, it was so close that he would find it almost equally impossible to open the driver's door and get into his car at all. Nevertheless, he must try. He squeezed his way along the narrow space, and he had his key in the door lock when the two men converged on him, one from the front end of his car, one from the rear.

The Place du Parvis, especially at this time of day, was a well-frequented square. Some passers-by, like Ryle, had already eaten early, and were going about their business. Others were still enjoying their meals. But still others were making for a café or were on their way home to lunch.

Nevertheless, in spite of the fact that the Place was not deserted, there was little that Ryle could do. He had been taken unawares, intentionally cut off in a small, narrow, isolated space. The two men were on him before he could attempt to shout for help. They were big, strong bruisers, equipped with knuckle-dusters and steel-tipped boots. In the first few seconds it was clear to Ryle that they were professionals, probably hired for the job and likely to do a good one.

If there had been room to manoeuvre, Ryle might have been able to defend himself by dealing first with one man, then with the other. As it was, he had no chance. He heard the taller of the two grunt with pain as, in spite of the lack of space, he managed to kick him in the groin, but he couldn't turn quickly enough and the other attacker's knuckle-duster caught him on the temple and threw him back against the bonnet of his car. As he stumbled he felt a punch in the stomach which knocked the breath out of him, and he crumpled to the ground.

After that he was conscious of very little, as his assailants kicked and punched him. Fortunately it was all over in a couple of minutes. Then liquid was being splashed on his face, causing his split lip to sting. There was a strong smell of aniseed, the sound of glass breaking, and he was aware of the two men leaving him and getting into the Renault. Instinctively he rolled as close as possible to his own car, sure that they wouldn't care if a wheel ran over one of his legs, though he knew that if they had been ordered to kill him they would have done so already. Nevertheless, it was with great relief that he heard the Renault drive off.

For a moment he allowed himself the luxury of lying, half under his own car, eyes closed, breathing gently. He could taste blood in his mouth, and felt around carefully with his tongue to make sure that his teeth were intact; the blood was clearly coming from his lips. He moved slowly, knowing that he must make an effort to rise, though his body responded only feebly.

And near him a woman said, in a high-pitched English voice of the kind that was used to chairing committees, "Come away, dear. The man's drunk."

"Drunk? At this time of day? Disgusting!" said her companion. "But of course the French are famous for it, aren't they?"

Ryle squinted through half-shut eyes and saw two pairs of elegantly clad legs retreating. He would have grinned, but it hurt too much. Besides, the little incident had been a reminder. Others, who might be more charitable than his two compatriots, would see him if he remained where he was, and he had no desire for any kind of commotion—especially a commotion that might involve the police.

He finally managed to get to his knees and from there, pulling himself up by the handle of the car door, to stand. At least he had one piece of luck: the car key was still in the lock. He didn't have to search for it among the fragments of the bottle of *anis* that had been poured over him. He opened the car door and eased himself into the driving seat.

He assessed the damage. He was in one piece. There seemed to be no serious injuries and no bones were broken, he thought, though his ribs hurt when he took a deep breath; one or two of them might have suffered a crack. He had a split lip and an eye that wouldn't open properly. Apart from that and the fact that generally he felt as if an elephant had trampled across him, he was apparently unharmed. This was a good deal more than could be said for his suit: apart from being drenched in liquor, it was dirty and stained and had been deliberately torn. He looked—and smelt—like a drunk who had had an accident.

But he might easily have been dead. This was merely a warning. The bastards had accomplished their instructions precisely. To show their superiority they hadn't even bothered to steal his wallet. They had wanted him to be aware that this was no casual mugging.

So now Ryle had a personal score to settle with his shadowy enemy or enemies, and he had learnt his lesson. From now on he would be on his guard. He cursed himself for having been so careless in the last few days. After what had happened to Chariber he should have known better—and Jean-Paul Brecquou should have been the last straw.

He did what running repairs he could to his face and general appearance, and drove out of the Place du Parvis with more than his usual care. The last thing he wanted at this point was to be stopped by the police and forced to explain how he might be completely sober when he stank of *anis*. In spite of the French national reputation for consumption of alcohol, their drink and driving laws were strict. Or was an encounter with the police really the main thing to escape? Ryle didn't relish the idea of providing General Bannol with an explanation, either. Maybe this could be avoided.

But what could not be avoided was an explanation for Jeanne as to why he must cancel their date tonight. This more immediate problem occupied him for the time it took him to reach his hotel.

CHAPTER THIRTEEN

"Are you telling me the truth?"

"Absolutely. Cross my heart and—"

Mark Ryle hated lying to Jeanne, but there was no way he could explain to her the relationship between his present condition and his quest for the truth about Peter Mourne. Some time in the future, he supposed, though not over the telephone, it might be possible to tell her the whole story, but at the moment it was unthinkable. Ryle hoped in vain that she would accept his excuses, and cease arguing.

"I don't believe you!" Jeanne said bluntly.

Ryle had no alternative. "It's true, all the same," he replied. "I had a minor accident with the car in a parking lot in Senlis. Nothing to worry about, but a bit of—of bruising. Much as I regret it, Jeanne, I'll have to cancel our date tonight."

Jeanne was still not deterred. "What were you doing in Senlis, of all places? And what kind of accident?"

"I'd gone to have a look at the cathedral."

"You'd what? I had no idea you were a great fan of ancient monuments. And why Senlis?" She didn't wait for an answer, but went on less uncompromisingly. "Mark, you do sound odd. Are you really all right?"

"Yes, but I've a split lip, which is why my voice isn't normal. If you must know, the owner of the car I hit got nasty and hit me in the face before I expected it."

There was an appreciable pause before Jeanne Mourne answered. Then, "It sounds a bit much for a bump in a parking lot. Still, you say you're fine. Okay, then you are, Mark. But not fine enough to take me out to dinner tonight?"

"Jeanne, I've said I'm sorry. If there were any way I could manage—"

"Sure. Goodbye for now, Mark."

"Jeanne, listen!" Ryle protested, but he was too late; the line was dead.

He drew a deep breath, and winced as his ribs hurt. Damn Jeanne, he thought. Why couldn't she have been more understanding? He wondered how she would have reacted to the story he had told the *concierge* when he returned to the hotel—that he had been the victim of a friend's practical joke that had gone wrong. But at that time he had to explain away not only his appearance, but also the fact that he reeked of *anis*. At least a shower and a complete change of clothing had managed to get rid of that complication.

Lying in pyjamas and robe on top of his bed in the hotel room, he could see his face in the dressing-table mirror. It was not a reassuring sight. The left side was badly swollen, the eye almost closed, the mouth torn at the corner, and the cold compresses with which he had attempted to make himself look more presentable had merely had the effect of making his skin blotchy and mottled. In fact, he was a mess, and Jeanne—

Ryle cursed fluently but silently. Perhaps the answer was to forget Jeanne, he thought, and go back to London at the weekend; by that time his appearance shouldn't occasion too many interested stares at the airport and on the aircraft. All his Paris leads had apparently petered out, and, at least for the moment, he had no ideas for any fresh angles to explore. To be honest, he didn't feel like any form of mental activity, and he wondered if he might be suffering from a very mild concussion. But first, before he took any action or even tried to sleep, he must phone the office.

Maggie sounded bright, intelligent, and efficient—every virtue that he himself at present lacked. Ryle forced himself to concentrate. After a minute's casual chat, he gave her in elliptic terms the story of the incident in Senlis, and asked her to warn Macfarlane in the Paris Embassy to expect him to deliver a more complete account of his activities for ciphering on the London link the next day.

To his pointless dismay, but perhaps understandably as she was in a position to read a great deal between his carefully selected words, Maggie showed far more concern for his physical condition than had Jeanne. But, once she had assured herself that he was not badly hurt, she returned to business and began to ask leading questions.

"Was it your fault, dear?"

Why the hell can't she wait for the cable? Ryle thought, but he responded readily enough. "I have to admit I was careless," he said. "I should have noticed that the next car—the white Renault; incidentally, it clearly wasn't Pierre's—was parked unnecessarily close to mine. As I said, the trouble was that the two men in it were most—unpleasant; again, I'm sure they were nothing to do with Pierre.

"I see," said Maggie slowly. "Poor you! You didn't report it or anything?"

"No, of course not. I didn't want a fuss. Actually—" Ryle hesitated, wondering whether he should say any more over an open line, but the tap, if it existed, was probably one of Pierre's and he'd learn little from the conversation which he didn't know or couldn't guess. He decided to continue. "Actually, I'm not making excuses, but the whole thing might have been avoided if I hadn't already been a bit shaken. The old man I'd been hoping to meet in Chantilly—a friend of Colette's family—was killed in the night. A devastating fire at his house."

"My God! So you missed your chance?"

"Yes."

"Heavens, you are having a bad time! Any other excitements?"

"No, thank God. I'm thinking of coming back to London over the weekend, but I'll fix a flight myself. Any news from home?"

"Nothing important. More gossip. You remember I told you about Tom's sex life. Well, I managed to meet his girlfriend, the one who had a cyst removed a while ago. She told me the whole sad story. She really seems to have loved Tom, and their relationship continued even after the —the operation—right up till his death. But she swears she didn't know he was in any special trouble immediately before he died—and I believe her."

"You mean she hadn't noticed he was worried lately?" Ryle was sceptical.

"She said he did seem a bit *distrait,*" Maggie admitted, "but he said it was because of his wife and lack of money. Incidentally, there's no news of that driver, and I doubt if there will be. But they've found the car, abandoned in a multi-storey car-park. Stolen, needless to say."

"Needless to say." Ryle sighed.

Two possible leads had disappeared in the course of a single telephone call. True, he had had few expectations that the driver of the car that had killed Tom Chariber would be traced, but he had hoped that Chariber's girlfriend might provide some useful information.

Nothing was any bloody help!

Ryle dozed, then drifted into sleep. The next thing he heard was an insistent knocking on the door of his room. Blearily awake, he slid off the bed, and went to stand by the wall next to the door.

"Qui est-ce?" he demanded. *"Pourquoi vous trouvez-vous là?"*

"Mark, it's me—Jeanne! Aren't you going to let me in?"

Ryle unlocked the door and opened it. "Sorry," he said. "I must have fallen asleep."

Jeanne marched into the room, and turned to look him up and down. She took in the pyjamas, the robe, and the swollen, battered face. It was clear from the state of the bed that he must have fallen asleep lying on top of it. Without immediate comment, she put down a large and evidently heavy briefcase on the stool in front of the dressing-table, and glanced around her.

"You took a long time answering my knock," she said. "I thought you'd got an attractive little *poule de luxe* in here."

"That's because of your suspicious mind," said Ryle. "At the moment Helen of Troy couldn't bring a response from me—and that goes for you, too, *ma chère Jeanne.*"

"I don't call that much of a welcome."

Ryle shrugged, and winced as his ribs hurt. "I didn't ask you to come. Incidentally, why *have* you come?"

"To satisfy myself. When you said you couldn't make dinner this evening, I thought it was just like old times—one of your inexplicable changes of plan—due to some political crisis somewhere! Then I realized that this time you'd produced a really novel excuse, and it occurred to me to come and make sure it was genuine."

"Kind of you! And now you're satisfied, perhaps—"

"You look to me as if you'd been in a good deal more than a minor rumpus in a car park, Mark, but I suppose you know your own business best." Suddenly Jeanne's voice changed. "Mark, please don't let's quarrel.

Are you sure you really are all right? Is there anything I can get you from a *pharmacie?* Or do you need a doctor?''

"No, no. The concierge got me all I needed, and I've done the running repairs myself," Mark said. He made no comment on her remark about the extent of his injuries.

Then Jeanne said, "Mark, I'm sorry. I know I was bitchy on the phone, and I've been a bit bitchy since I got here, but I've not had a very agreeable time lately. You know that Simon's called it off, don't you?"

"I do now," Mark said more gently, "but I didn't when we spoke yesterday. The De Chantals told me last night that your engagement was off—and why. I'm sorry, Jeanne. The man's a fool."

"To put his career before me?"

This was a question Mark Ryle was not prepared to answer. In a way it was what he had done himself, he thought wryly, though the circumstances had been quite different. He certainly hadn't been driven by ambition to reach the top of his particular tree. He had just wanted to be free to get on with his job, a job he considered worth while, but which unfortunately necessitated an unpredictable and unreliable lifestyle almost totally incompatible with marriage. And it had been Jeanne—tired of broken dates, unexplained absences, vague and ambiguous excuses—who had walked out on him, not vice versa.

"I'm afraid I've nothing to offer you, Jeanne," he said, immediately aware of his unintended *double entendre.* "This place doesn't run to room service, except in emergencies," he added hastily.

"I thought of that. I came prepared."

"What!"

"Not what you think." Jeanne gestured towards the bed. "Go and lie down, and I'll show you. I hope you're hungry."

Ryle watched with amusement as she began systematically to unpack her briefcase, and arrange its contents on the dressing-table. There was a bottle of wine, complete with a corkscrew, two glasses, paper plates and napkins, knives, forks, spoons, and all the makings of a delicious picnic. Suddenly Ryle realized that, in spite of his ailments, he was hungry. It was a long time since that *croque-monsieur* in Senlis, and so much had happened in the interval that it seemed even longer than it was.

"I collected some of this from my apartment," Jeanne said, "and I called in at a *charcuterie* on the way here. We start with stuffed vine leaves."

"Wonderful!" said Ryle, hoping that his torn mouth could cope with the food. "But first let's open that bottle."

The evening passed rapidly, and it was good. By common consent they avoided the subject of Peter Mourne. They chatted about the relative merits of London and Paris as places to live, and what each city could offer by way of theatre, music, sport, and other amenities. Jeanne told a couple of amusing stories about her work as an interior decorator and the vagaries of her clients. Ryle talked about the Middle East.

Once Jeanne said, "You do go to a lot of intriguing places, Mark. Aren't some of them dangerous?"

"One can get knocked down by a bus in Oxford Street."

"Or assaulted in Senlis?"

"So it seems."

"Have you ever been attacked like that before?"

Mark temporized. "When I was at school. There were these two brothers—"

He recounted the anecdote. It had actually happened, and he made it sound entertaining. To his relief it also served to distract Jeanne from asking further and possibly awkward questions.

At ten o'clock she stood up purposefully. She said that she must go and it was time he went to bed. Ryle made no attempt to argue. The wine and Jeanne combined had helped him to forget his numerous aches, but he felt absurdly tired. Perhaps tomorrow—

As if reading his thoughts, Jeanne, who was busy packing the remains of their supper into her briefcase, said over her shoulder, "I'm going away tomorrow for the weekend, to my country house." She laughed. "Doesn't that sound grand? Actually it's a cottage in Brittany, in Dinan, small but very attractive. A friend of maman died unexpectedly a couple of years ago, and left it to me."

"How nice." Ryle hid his disappointment.

Then Jeanne said, "I was wondering if you'd like to come with me, Mark. I shan't be able to leave work before six, which means we'd get there pretty late, but I'll drive. I expect you'll still be fairly frail."

"Jeanne, it's a wonderful idea—"

"But—" she prompted.

Mark Ryle hesitated. His immediate impulse was to accept the offer; at that moment he wanted to do so more than anything he could imagine. Nevertheless, there was a reason why he should refuse. A weekend alone with Jeanne would almost certainly renew the old relationship, with all its joys, but also with its doubts and deceits, its rows and their aftermath, its rancour and discord; he wasn't sure he was prepared to face all that again. Besides, it was quite the wrong time, when Jeanne was on the rebound from Simon Maufant.

"You'd rather not come?" Jeanne said as Mark remained silent. "It would be comfortable, you know, and there'd be excellent food. Marie is a splendid cook."

"Who's Marie?"

"Marie-Antoinette. But I assure you we shan't be living on cake. She was ineptly named. Our Marie was just a simple country girl, though pretty. And, as was to be expected, she got herself into trouble. It's an old story, isn't it? Anyway, grand-mère took her in and looked after her when her baby died, so she became devoted to the family. She worked for the De Chantals on and off for years. Now she's my *femme de ménage* in Dinan." Jeanne, who had been speaking fast, stopped abruptly, then added, "Do come, Mark. I have to be in Paris early Monday morning, so it would only be two days, but it would give you a good rest and—and I could do with your company."

Ryle knew that this was the nearest Jeanne would come to an appeal. It must have hurt her to make it at all. It meant that Simon Maufant had damaged more than her pride. So, whatever the outcome, he couldn't refuse her.

"Jeanne, if we can be back by Sunday evening that'll be great," he said. "I should love to come with you. Very many thanks."

CHAPTER FOURTEEN

It was six-thirty on the Friday evening. Mark Ryle's weekend bag was already packed and he was ready to leave. Then his telephone rang and naturally he thought at once of Jeanne. Something had come up, and she was about to put him off. He felt a bitter disappointment.

"Yes," he said in English, keeping the monosyllable neutral.

"Ah, mon cher. C'est Pierre qui parle."

Avaine. The DST. "Hello. What do you want?" Ryle answered.

"Don't be ungracious," the Frenchman chided. "I merely wanted to make sure you were recovering from your spot of bother yesterday."

"You learnt about that, of course."

"Of course. But not because you were under observation, Mark, believe me. It was quite accidental. Two English ladies reported a drunk lying in the Place du Parvis in the centre of Senlis in the middle of the day. Disgusting, they considered it, and so do I."

Pierre Avaine laughed before he continued. "The drunk had gone by the time a gendarme arrived on the scene, but these clever ladies had taken the number of the car they thought might be his, and it has been duly traced. The news has just reached me. *C'est tout.*"

"I suppose they didn't also take the number of the white Renault parked right close to it, did they?"

"It wasn't ours," repeated Avaine quickly.

"I never thought it was. And incidentally I was not drunk, Pierre. I was beaten up by two thugs who broke a bottle of *anis* over me."

"I suspected something of the kind. I'll make inquiries about the Renault, but there was no mention of it in the report, so I have little hope. You didn't get its number yourself, I suppose?" The DST man paused.

Ryle cursed himself. "No," he replied shortly, "I didn't. I was much too busy."

"I see," said Avaine. Then: "Mark, it was a warning—and I suggest you heed it."

"Do you now? Okay. I'll take your suggestion under advisement."

"Do more than that, *mon cher.* Act on it! Go home. You're not popular here with anyone at present, either with your enemies or with your friends, and I wouldn't wish you to view your visit to Paris with any regrets. Do you understand?"

Sure I understand, Ryle thought, putting down the receiver. Peter Mourne was off limits; inquiries into his past were to be prevented by fair means (mild threats from Pierre Avaine, obviously acting under orders), or foul, like the attack in Senlis. The enemy's reasons might differ from those of his so-called friends, but on both sides the basic motive was presumably fear. If Mourne could be shown to have been a spy, then everyone associated with him would be tainted. Better to let sleeping dogs lie, perhaps?

Yet, on the other hand, this was too simple. What must be kept in mind was that someone—some group or authority—had initiated the original gossip, and was prepared to refuel it, whether it were true or false. And, what was more, they had no hesitation in taking violent action to sustain the accusations.

Ryle looked at his watch. It was time he went downstairs. He couldn't depend on Jeanne's arriving on time, and he didn't want to keep her waiting in the evening traffic. He picked up his bag and, with an automatic last glance round the room, closed the door and went along the corridor. In the foyer he handed in his key, reminded the *concierge* that he had arranged for his room to be kept for him until his return on Sunday evening, and stationed himself by the big glass doors of the outer lobby to wait for Jeanne's appearance.

Jeanne arrived within minutes. She nodded her approval when, almost as soon as she drew up, Ryle opened the door of her BMW, tossed his bag on to the back seat, and got in beside her. Someone hooted behind them, impatient to park at the hotel entrance.

"The traffic's awful tonight," Jeanne said. "It's always bad on a Friday evening, but usually the worst is over by now, the commuters well on their way home."

"It should thin out when we get on the *autoroute*," said Ryle. "Which way are you going—Caen, or Le Mans and Rennes?"

"Oh—Rennes, I think. I usually do. On the whole it's faster. There may be more traffic as far as Orly and Chartres, but after that it should thin out, as you say. And it's a simpler approach to Dinan."

"I'll do some of the driving if you want a rest," volunteered Ryle.

"We'll see. How are you, Mark?" Jeanne gave him a quick glance as they crossed the Seine and drove southwards to get on to the *Périphérique* at the Porte d'Orléans. From there it would be only a few minutes to the exit to the southbound and westbound *autoroute* system.

"You're looking better," Jeanne added, "though still not your usual handsome self."

"I'm fine," Ryle lied. In fact, his ribs still hurt and the irregular progress of the car, caused by the traffic, reminded him—even in the comfortable BMW—of bruises he had half forgotten. "Fighting fit," he repeated, and hoped it was not an unfortunate choice of words.

Jeanne grunted in disbelief and for a while was silent, forced to concentrate on her driving. But once off the *Périphérique* and on their way to Orly, she was able to relax a little. She asked how Mark had spent his day.

"Mostly lazing," he said, "but I did do some shopping. The suit I had on yesterday isn't wearable till it gets some attention." Actually Mark had decided that it would never be wearable again, and that he'd put the cost of a replacement on his expense account, though he doubted if the claim would be approved by the financial dragons. "I also bought some casual clothes for the weekend."

Jeanne laughed. "You *have* been splashing out."

"And I got you a small present."

"Mark, there was no need."

"I was taught that one should always take a present to one's hostess."

"I hadn't thought of myself in quite that formal a light," she said, suddenly thoughtful and withdrawn. "What else did you do?"

"Wandered around. Looked in at the Embassy, where an old chum gave me coffee. Had a long siesta." Ryle shrugged. "As I said, I had a lazy day."

It was more or less the truth, he thought, except that the "old chum" at the Embassy, where he had spent the morning, had been Fyfe Macfarlane, the local MI6 Head of Station, who, warned by Maggie to expect him, had provided coffee, and, after Ryle had parried some curious inquiries, an office and a typewriter for him to prepare a long private report for General Bannol's eyes only. Ryle had personally taken it to the cipher room and given the necessary transmission instructions. He had waited for a reply, but there had been no more than a routine acknowledgement.

While he waited, he was entertained by the thought of the necessarily uninformative signal no doubt already on its way from the disgruntled Head of Paris Station to his bosses in MI6 in Century House. After the fruitless wait, he had gone shopping.

"What about you, Jeanne?"

"Very busy, tidying up before I leave."

"You're still leaving?" Ryle couldn't hide his surprise. He had assumed that as Jeanne was no longer to marry Simon Maufant she would be staying on in Paris.

"Oh yes," said Jeanne. "It's all arranged. There's an American girl—excellent at the work—who's taking my place. It wouldn't be fair to change my mind at the last minute, and say I wanted to stay. Besides, I feel I need a change."

"Have you any plans?"

"Not definite. I thought I'd take a holiday, perhaps go and stay with Hugh in Madrid for a week or two."

"Sounds a wonderful idea," said Ryle, and wondered what Jeanne's reaction would be if he told her that it was quite likely he would be going to Madrid himself in the near future.

By now they were half-way between Le Mans and Rennes. Soon, progress would be slower after they left the *autoroute* and turned north to Dinan. In fact, it was about three hours after leaving the outskirts of Paris that they crossed the high viaduct over the River Rance and entered the charming Brittany town. It was a bustling place by day, especially when there was a market in the Place du Guesclin, but by eleven o'clock at night it was quiet and peaceful, most of its inhabitants already in bed.

Jeanne drew up in front of a small house near the Basilica of St-Sauveur, on the outskirts of the *Vieille Ville*—the famous Old Town of Dinan. "Here we are," she said. "Heavens, I'm tired."

"I'm not surprised." Ryle grinned at her. "You've done all the work."

Jeanne had insisted on driving the whole way, and they had stopped only once for fuel and to have coffee and quiche at one of the *Aires de Service* on the *autoroute*. But Ryle had been less somnolent than he had pretended. He badly wanted to know if they had been followed. While on the *autoroute* this was almost impossible to judge, without taking Jeanne into his confidence and asking her to vary her speed. However, no vehicle had turned off at the *Aire de Service* and none, apparently, had followed them over the viaduct and into Dinan. By now Ryle felt reasonably safe.

"Ah, here's Marie. She must have seen the car's lights," said Jeanne, as the metal-panelled gates began to open. She waved briskly as she drove through them into a small paved courtyard. The house was narrow and tall, with no garage, but, like all French town houses, it was well protected from prying eyes.

"I'll start to get our bags out," said Ryle, but Marie was forestalling him. He followed the two women into a small hall. Jeanne introduced him.

"Marie, this is my friend, Monsieur Ryle."

"Bonsoir, monsieur. Bienvenu à Dinan."

"Merci, madame. Bonsoir."

Marie-Antoinette Corbet made no attempt to disguise her interest in Mark Ryle. Slowly she let her eyes travel up until they came to his face. Then, after a moment, she nodded as if in approval.

Ryle restrained an impulse to grin at her. Jeanne had failed to warn her what a comical little figure Marie now made. She was under one and a half metres tall, and her figure had become broad. She wore a long black dress with a white apron, pulled in tightly at the waist so that her figure resembled nothing so much as an hour-glass. Her face still showed signs that she had once been pretty, and it was surprisingly unwrinkled for her seventy years, but altogether there was no denying that she looked like a fat child in fancy dress. Nevertheless, Ryle was sure that she was far from unintelligent.

"I'll show you to your room, Mark," Jeanne said. "Then what would you like? Sandwiches and a nightcap?"

"That would be wonderful."

Jeanne led the way up the steep stairs, and opened a door on the right. "I hope you'll be comfortable, Mark. Ask Marie if there's anything you need. You have a washbasin, and the bathroom's there." She pointed. "Luckily the place has been modernized. Come down when you're ready."

"Thanks," said Ryle sounding as off-hand as Jeanne had done.

He smiled as he went into the small bedroom. Jeanne was obviously a little embarrassed, but wanted to make it clear that there was no question of their spending the night together. In any case, he doubted if his ribs and bruises could have stood the effort. Possibly she appreciated this. Perhaps tomorrow—

He unpacked rapidly, went to the bathroom, washed his hands and face. Then he spent a moment wondering what to do about the present he had brought Jeanne. It was an ounce of her favourite perfume—Guerlain's "Chamade"—and he now felt that it was perhaps too extravagant a gift at such a moment. Finally he left it on the chest of drawers, deciding that he would give it to her in the morning.

Downstairs, Jeanne was already in what he supposed must be called the salon—a combined sitting- and dining-room which, apart from the kitchen, obviously occupied the whole ground floor of the house. He was surprised by the room's quiet elegance, until he remembered that Jeanne had a profession, and was good at it. Then Marie was bringing in a tray with bowls of soup and sandwiches.

"Monsieur, Mademoiselle Jeanne has told me that you are writing a book about her relation, Viscount Mourne," she said. "So it is very fortunate that you are here!"

"Here?" Ryle frowned; he didn't understand. "You mean here in France?"

Marie handed him a table-napkin and a bowl of soup. "I meant in Dinan, monsieur, where you can speak to me."

"Did you ever meet him, Marie?" Jeanne gave a small laugh of disbelief. "When was that?"

"When he came out of Spain, m'selle, with his—his lady-friend." She gave the words no expression, but her disapproval was obvious. "I was only a slip of a girl at the time, but I remember it as if it was yesterday. I was working for your dear grandmother when they arrived without warning at the De Chantals' Paris house. If monsieur is interested—"

"Indeed I am, madame." Ryle hid his surprise. He doubted if he would learn anything new from Marie, but it was intriguing that she had known the Mournes.

"Then I shall tell you about it tomorrow, monsieur."

"Thank you, madame," said Ryle, and when she had gone he turned to Jeanne. "You didn't know Marie knew Peter and Carmela?"

"No, I did not, Mark. It never occurred to me, though I suppose it might have done if I'd thought about it."

"I can't imagine Marie as a slip of a girl, but she'd have been young in 1939, wouldn't she?"

"Nineteen or twenty—and, I gather, quite pretty, as I said. She's changed a lot. At that time it would have been a couple of years after she'd lost her baby." Jeanne shook her head. "Mark, I'm afraid you'll be lucky if you get anything worth while from dear Marie, but—"

"Who cares?" said Ryle, reluctantly chalking up yet another lie. "It's great to be here."

Perhaps it was because the bed was hard, perhaps it was because he couldn't stop thinking of Jeanne—or Marie-Antoinette Corbet—but Mark Ryle slept badly. He woke finally at six. He put on a robe and went down to the kitchen. The old Frenchwoman was already up and dressed. She regarded him with mild benevolence.

"Petit déjeuner, monsieur? Qu'est-ce que vous voulez? Du café et des croissants? Freshly baked. I have fetched them from the bakers this morning."

"Je vous en prie, madame."

"I will take M'selle Jeanne's tray up later. It is good for her to sleep."

"Yes," Ryle agreed. "But you'll have a cup of coffee with me, madame?"

"If monsieur wishes."

Ryle was beginning to tire of pleasantries. "And maybe, as you promised, you'll tell me what you remember about Peter Mourne," he said, sitting down at the kitchen table.

Marie Corbet was not averse. Once she had got Ryle's breakfast and her own coffee she seated herself opposite him, fully prepared to reminisce. But, as Jeanne had warned, what she had to say was of peripheral interest, even if he had intended to prepare a biography of Mourne for publication; for his real purpose, it at first seemed useless.

Marie had not liked either Peter or Carmela, as she readily admitted. Initially they had been reasonably pleasant to her, but it was not her business to answer questions about the family, and when she couldn't or wouldn't satisfy Carmela's curiosity, the Spaniard had become irascible and deliberately discourteous. It was obvious, Marie said, that neither of them was used to servants, or knew how to treat them.

"Surely Peter Mourne—" Ryle objected.

Marie shrugged. "Perhaps, monsieur. But he was ill, though not nearly as ill as he pretended to be. Once I caught them making love, and I could tell from the bed linen that this was not the first time they had been together—in spite of him supposedly being so weak and in need of rest."

There was more gossip, and Ryle asked if Marie had ever heard them talking of the Spanish Civil War, and their experiences in it. Yes, indeed, she said, they spoke of it at length, of how dreadfully the Republicans had behaved and of how thankful they were that Barcelona had finally fallen to the Generalissimo.

"I had gathered they were both great supporters of Franco," Ryle volunteered.

Marie sniffed. "From the way they talked, they seemed to regard him as some kind of saint," she said. "It was too much, monsieur."

"Too much, Marie? What do you mean?"

"I'm not sure, monsieur." Marie paused. "Perhaps it didn't strike me as genuine. The fact is I didn't like them, monsieur, and I didn't trust them."

Marie was pushing back her chair and preparing to get Jeanne's breakfast.

"I regret that is all I can tell you about them, monsieur. Not much use for your book—though if you could manage to discover their secret—"

"Secret? What secret?"

"I've no idea what it was, monsieur, else it wouldn't be a secret. But I know they had one. There was a little balcony outside their bedroom and one day I was cleaning it. They didn't know I was there and I overheard them talking. I don't remember the exact words but Monsieur Mourne said something about there still being time to stop. She was angry and said that was nonsense, and he replied God help them if— Then they heard me. They were furious at first, but I pretended to be stupid."

Marie-Antoinette Corbet gave Ryle a broad smile and left the room with Jeanne's breakfast tray, leaving Ryle to reflect that the simple country girl, as Jeanne had described her, must have grown up fast in Paris.

CHAPTER FIFTEEN

It had been quite a weekend, thought Mark Ryle—everything he had hoped for. He glanced sideways at Jeanne, but the traffic into Paris was heavy on a Sunday evening and she was fully occupied with driving. Clearly she had no wish for conversation. Mark let himself relax and mentally reviewed the last two days.

In fact, they had done very little, except become reacquainted. She had shown him the picturesque *Vieille Ville,* with its cobbled streets and ancient buildings. They had walked around the ramparts overlooking the River Rance. They had eaten Marie's excellent food and drunk a lot of wine. Without effort, they had once more become companionable and sympathetically gentle with each other. And last night Jeanne, smelling fragrantly of the "Chamade" he had bought her, had come—expected but unasked—to his bed, and their lovemaking was as sweet as it had ever been.

"What are you grinning at?" Jeanne asked suddenly.

"I was thinking of your Marie-Antoinette," Ryle said with partial truth. "Oh, Jeanne, it's been a terrific weekend."

"Because of Marie or because of me?" Jeanne laughed.

"Both!" replied Ryle firmly. "My only complaint is that it was too short."

Jeanne made no comment on this remark. Instead she said, "When do you go back to London, Mark?"

"I don't know. I'll have to get in touch with my office tomorrow, and it'll depend on what more, if anything, they've found for me to do here. But I guess I'll be leaving by mid-week at the latest. I'll phone you anyway. Perhaps we could manage the dinner I failed to provide last Thursday."

"That would be pleasant," Jeanne agreed.

Five minutes later they had reached Ryle's hotel. There was a large limousine in front of the entrance and Jeanne had to double-park, so there was no time for a long goodbye. Ryle kissed her quickly, said thank you again, seized his bag from the back seat, and got out. He stood on the pavement and watched her drive off, her car soon lost in the traffic.

Ryle asked the *concierge* for his key, and inquired whether there had been any telephone calls or messages for him. He was given the key and an envelope addressed to M. Ryle in a handwriting he failed to recognize. There had been one phone call, but the caller—a man—had left no name. That was all.

Ryle opened the envelope as he went up in the lift. It contained an advertisement for a forthcoming sale at a well-known store in the Rue de Rivoli. His immediate reaction was that of anyone faced with unsolicited mail, but this was no ordinary junk mail. It had been sent to him personally by someone who knew that he was in Paris and staying at this particular hotel. Why? The oldest trick in the book? To discover the number of the hotel room occupied by an individual guest, one merely delivered a letter to the *concierge*. A moment's wait, and with any luck the *concierge* would slip the envelope into a numbered pigeon-hole behind him. Later it might be possible to obtain the key by requesting it when the desk was busy, or gain entrance to the room by forcing the lock. So, had someone been in his room? Was someone there now?

Silently Ryle took up a position to the side of his door. Silently he inserted the key and turned it. Then he flung the door open. It was almost an anti-climax when there was no response. He put his hand around the door-post and gingerly switched on the light. Still no reaction. A quick glance showed him that the room looked normal. He went in and shut the door behind him. Clearly a maid had been in to clean at some time, for the bedspread was smooth, the wastepaper basket empty, the towels in the bathroom neatly arranged. The clothes and oddments he hadn't needed in Dinan were still where he had left them. His laundry had been returned, and placed on top of the dressing-table. He lifted the telephone receiver and heard only the dialling tone.

Ryle decided that his judgement must have been at fault. No unauthorized persons had been in the room or, if they had, they had taken nothing and disturbed nothing. The room was as it should be. Yet as he unpacked his bag and prepared for bed he was unable to shake off a feeling of unease. There had to be some explanation for the stupid advertisement that had been sent to him.

For half an hour after he had lain down his mind worried at the problem. He had almost decided he would have to pay a visit to the Rue de Rivoli next day when suddenly he sat up and put his light on again. Nothing was missing, but had something been planted on him? He got out of bed and began a thorough search.

He worked systematically, beginning with the bathroom, and it took time, for he had no idea what he might be looking for. He was also hampered by the fact that he couldn't make much noise, though it was difficult to move furniture quietly. When the people in the adjoining room banged on the wall angrily for the second time he nearly abandoned his efforts. He could foresee the manager appearing at the door to say that other guests were complaining about the row he was making.

Fortunately the bedroom was not large, and by now his task was almost complete. He eased the dressing-table back into place, wincing as his hand slipped and it made a loud thud. Next was the bed. It was a double bed, and heavy, but he stripped off the bedclothes, and tilted the mattress on to its side. He found nothing.

The box-spring remained. His luck was in. Within seconds he found the packet taped to the canvas underside of the box-spring. It was about ten centimetres square, about five centimetres thick and wrapped in brown paper sealed with self-adhesive tape. He wrenched it off and placed it on the bedside table. Then he continued his uncomfortable exploration in case there was anything else to be discovered.

Satisfied at last, Ryle took the packet into the bathroom, and removed the brown paper with the utmost care. Inside was a white plastic bag containing what looked like a white powder.

Though he had half-expected what he would find, for a moment Ryle was appalled. There was little doubt about the nature of the powder, but he took a razor blade and, holding the packet carefully over the lavatory, made a very small slit in one side. A touch with a moistened finger and a touch to his tongue was enough. Cocaine—almost certainly the strengthened compound called "crack"—and worth God knew what on the streets of Paris.

He knew he must have no part of this. He must get rid of it—and all traces of it—before any tipped-off officers of the *Sûreté nationale* banged on the door. Slowly he let the white powder sift through the slit he had made into the lavatory pan, pausing several times to work the flush. He was left with the plastic bag in which grains of the substance inevitably remained, and the brown paper in which it had been wrapped. After forensic tests either, he knew, could condemn him, and he couldn't rely on the plumbing system to get rid of them, at least not in their present form. So both the paper and the bag would have to be burnt.

Ryle blessed the hotel, which, as a matter of course and as an advertisement, provided its guests with quantities of book-matches. He set to work on his laborious task, which was reasonably successful, though it took a great many matches, and he was finally able to flush the ashes away and swill the can out thoroughly. Then he cleaned everything in sight, taking particular care with the lavatory pan itself, scrubbed his hands, made up the bed and finally put out the light.

He had little hope of getting much sleep.

In the event, it was not until six in the morning that they came, with their demanding knocks on the door. Considerate of them, Ryle thought. He had been dozing and had no need to feign sleepiness.

"Who is it?" he called.

"Monsieur, it is the manager and—I am sorry, but it is necessary that you permit us to enter."

"All right. I'm coming. One minute." Ryle got out of bed and slipped on a robe. He stomped over to the door and flung it open. "What the hell is this? Do you realize what time it is?" he asked, now sounding indignant.

"Monsieur, I am desolated, but these—these gentlemen insisted." The manager lowered his voice. "They are from the police—the *Sûreté nationale*. I have seen their identification. There was nothing I could do."

"Perhaps we might continue this conversation inside the room, monsieur."

It was the oldest and clearly the most senior of the three plainclothes officers who had spoken. He was a tall, thin man with black hair and a walrus moustache which accentuated his pale—almost sallow—complexion. His eyes were brown, the colour of mud, and expressionless. He pushed past the manager and Ryle and strode into the bedroom. His two companions, who were both fair-haired and of medium height, but equally menacing, waved Ryle and the manager ahead of them.

"You are Monsieur Mark Ryle." The senior officer spoke good English.

"I am. Who are you?" Ryle saw no reason to be polite, as none of the men was in uniform.

"*Sûreté nationale.* Narcotics division." The man smiled as if at a private joke. "Your papers, please."

"When I've seen your credentials. You burst into my hotel room in the small hours of the morning, and—"

"Here!"

Ryle took the document that was offered to him and glanced at it. He had no doubt that the three men were what they purported to be. But he noted the senior man's name—Bernard Lemieux. He fetched his passport and handed it over. Lemieux leafed through it, then put it in his pocket.

"You travel a lot, monsieur. You have been in the Middle East recently, I see."

"Yes, I have," Ryle said coldly.

"A great place to acquire drugs—the Middle East."

"So?"

"Ah well, we propose to search your room, monsieur. Do you object?"

"It's not my room. It belongs to the hotel. You should ask the manager. He might."

Lemieux made no attempt to ask the manager. He nodded to his two men to go ahead, and gestured to Ryle to sit down. He perched himself on the side of the bed. The manager stood uneasily near the door.

"If—if I am no longer needed, perhaps—" he began nervously.

"But you are needed, monsieur. You are what we might call a neutral witness."

"Witness to what?" Ryle demanded. "If you expect to find any drugs secreted in this room, you're going to be disappointed. That is unless one of your goons planted them here while I was away for the weekend—or is busy planting them now."

"The authorities do not do such things in France, monsieur. Perhaps it is common practice in your country, but it is certainly not so in ours. So, please be patient, and we shall see."

Lemieux got up from the bed and walked over to the window. The movement seemed to be some kind of signal, for the two men who had been searching the bathroom and bedroom with a fair show of efficiency at once turned their attention to the bed. Ryle watched grimly as first the mattress was upended, then with a loud thump the box-spring. There was an appreciable pause.

"Nothing here," one of them said.

"So, go on! Look elsewhere. There are plenty of other places," Lemieux ordered quickly, glancing at Ryle. "And you, monsieur," he added to the manager as the irate guest in the next room banged on the wall. "Go and apologize for the noise. Say it will be finished soon."

The manager left, and the search continued, though now it was half-hearted. Ryle wondered what would happen if the occupant of the next room put in an appearance to complain about the earlier and similar disturbance, but he was saved from that complication.

Eventually Lemieux had had enough. He told his officers to stop the search and set the room to rights.

"Now, if you're satisfied, I should like my passport back," Ryle said firmly.

"Not so fast, monsieur. I must ask you to get dressed and come with us to our offices in the Palais de Justice on the Quai des Orfèvres." Lemieux was equally firm.

"Why? You have found no drugs. There were none to find."

"There are questions to be asked. You will do as I request, monsieur—if you please. You are not being arrested. Shall we say that you are helping the police with their inquiries, as they put it in England, I believe."

Ryle hesitated. He hadn't expected this. Then, "I'm damned if I know why I should!" he said, but one glance at Lemieux's face convinced him that it was no use arguing; the Frenchman was undoubtedly in command of the situation.

The room was not uncomfortable. It even had a wall-to-wall carpet, though there was no doubt that it was intended as a cell. The window was narrow, high up one wall, and barred. The glass panel in the door was obviously of one-way glass: it was impossible to see out of it, and the only reason for its existence had to be to make it possible to see in. The single bed was fixed to the wall. Though it dispensed with a mattress, it was reasonably padded, and accompanied by a duvet and a pillow. The remaining furniture, all bolted to the floor, consisted of a wooden table and stool, and an armchair of some resilient plastic material, warm to the touch. The area of the main room was about three metres by four.

But there was an extension, which also—at least on the surface—provided an element of privacy. The alcove included a shower, with the shower-head flush with the ceiling, a toilet, and a washbasin. A box of tissues, soap, a towel, and an electric razor had been provided. Assuming that meals were forthcoming, the whole arrangement gave the impression of a cell in which a slightly sybaritic monk might well have been prepared to spend most of his time.

But Mark Ryle was not interested in the contemplative life. Lemieux and his two minions had taken him from his hotel room to a windowless van, blindfolded him during a short journey, and not removed the blindfold until they had helped him from the van into a building and guided him into this room. Left alone, he had given his surroundings a cursory examination. Then he had used the lavatory, washed his hands, used the razor, and waited. His wait had been brief. A man whom he had never seen before arrived with a loaded tray.

"Full English breakfast, monsieur," he said with a broad smile.

Ryle ignored the smile. "Tell Lemieux I want to see him," he said.

The man shook his head, put the tray on the table, and retired, but not before Ryle had caught a glimpse of a second man—clearly a guard—outside the door. So what? Ryle thought, and decided to eat. It seemed a long time since he and Jeanne had had supper together on the way back from Dinan, and the food looked good. In addition to the coffee and croissants, there were bacon, eggs and a sausage. Ryle ate hungrily but, having enjoyed his breakfast, found nothing to do except lie on the bed and wait again.

Lemieux and his men hadn't removed his watch, so that he was able to see the seconds and minutes tick away. After half an hour the monotony became overwhelming; he got to his feet and tried banging on the door. There was no response, and he retreated to the bed, wondering if he had been a fool to accompany Lemieux so tamely. Perhaps he had misread the situation, but when they had insisted on taking him in even though they had found no drugs, he had become convinced that Pierre Avaine was somewhere behind the set-up.

Now he was intimidated by doubts. It even occurred to him that Lemieux and his men might have been phoneys, Lemieux's papers forged, but he quickly dismissed the thought; there had been a professionalism about the men from the *Sûreté* that wouldn't have been easy to counterfeit.

Restless again, Ryle got up and started to pace up and down his small prison. What particularly irritated him was that he had no idea where he was. To judge from the time he had been in the closed van, he was fairly certain that he was still in Paris, but he was equally certain that this was not the Palais de Justice.

It was noon before the door of the room opened again, and Pierre

Avaine came in. Ryle hid his relief, and his anger. He regarded Avaine coldly.

"In England I could sue you for false arrest," he said.

"But you are in France, *mon cher,* and you are not under arrest. You are my guest."

"In that case I'll say thank you for your hospitality—and goodbye."

"Don't be petulant. You may not know it, but you do have reason to thank me."

Ryle looked sceptical, but said nothing. Avaine went to the door and gave some orders to the guard outside. Soon the man who had brought breakfast arrived with a bottle of wine and two glasses on a tray. Avaine poured the wine.

"Let us drink to our profession," he said.

"Not till you tell me why I'm here, and where 'here' is." Ryle was damned if he was going to be placated so easily.

Avaine sighed. "It was like this," he said. "Narcotics at the *Sûreté* received a tip-off that when you returned from your weekend away from Paris you would have drugs in your possession. Naturally, this had to be investigated."

"So Lemieux and his goons came round to my hotel room expecting to find the cocaine you'd planted there."

"Cocaine was it?" Avaine was interested. "And you got rid of it. Clever of you. What made you suspicious?" He seemed amused.

"What made you plant it on me?"

"Mon cher, it was not I who planted it. I swear it and you should believe me. The DST was not responsible." Avaine was speaking earnestly. "Just think. This drug could have been worth a hell of a lot of money. Could we have afforded to lose it?"

"You didn't expect to lose it. You expected Lemieux to collect it," Ryle said, though he was beginning to have some misgivings; Avaine had been convincing. "Okay!" Ryle went on. "Let's suppose that a Monsieur 'X' planted the dope on me, then tipped off the *Sûreté,* with the object of getting me arrested and out of the way. Tell me why, when they found nothing, did they go ahead and arrest me anyway?"

"On my order. Because, unfortunately, my object is the same as that of your mysterious Monsieur 'X'." Avaine shook his head sadly. "I may give orders, my friend, but I am also *under* orders, and I have to get rid of you."

Ryle looked up sharply, but Avaine grinned. "Not in any unpleasant way, *mon cher.* The point is that you are being a nuisance; I fear you don't appreciate how many very important feathers you are ruffling. After all, you know that our President—*le Président de la République*—was a personal friend of the late Viscount Mourne."

"Then maybe I should interview him," said Ryle. "All right," he added quickly before Avaine could begin to object. Ryle knew he must capitulate; he had no choice but to co-operate with Avaine for the moment. He held out his hand for the glass of wine. "So what happens now?"

"As you may have guessed, this is a secure house. Hence the comparative comfort of your—er—your present accommodation," said Avaine. "You'll be taken from here to the airport. A seat has been reserved for you on a mid-afternoon Air France flight to Heathrow. Your hotel bill's been paid. Your belongings have been packed, and I'll have them brought in after you've had lunch."

"What service!" Ryle was sarcastic. "I almost thanked you."

"So you should. If Lemieux had indeed found any narcotics in your room, you wouldn't be in such a happy position now, I assure you. Fair enough, everything would have been sorted out later, but in the meantime—"

"I appreciate that, but—"

"I hoped that an advertisement for a sale, addressed to you personally at the hotel, would make you think. As it obviously did." Avaine's meaning was obvious.

"You?"

Avaine nodded. "Lemieux is my trusted colleague, so my actions were somewhat restricted. But the right hand doesn't always know what the left hand does. Anyway, you owe me, *mon cher*. One day I expect I'll ask for the favour to be returned."

"And I trust I'll be in a position to return it," Ryle said truthfully.

The Frenchman stood up. "I'll leave you the wine. Your lunch will be arriving shortly, and I'll be back in good time to take you to the airport. It's a pity you have to cut short your visit to *La Belle France* like this, but alas you're unwelcome here, and will continue to be unwelcome here until this affair blows over."

As you've made perfectly clear, thought Ryle. "We can only hope that day will come soon," he said aloud, "though I'm not optimistic."

"Why not?" Avaine asked sharply.

"Just a funny internal feeling," Ryle said seriously, but he was grinning as the door closed behind the DST man. At least he had given Pierre Avaine something to worry about, he thought, but behind his amusement he too was worried—about who was on whose side.

CHAPTER SIXTEEN

On the same Monday morning that Mark Ryle had found himself an effective prisoner in a DST safe house in Paris, John Mourne, a few hundred miles away across the Channel in Hampstead, was having breakfast with his wife, Colette. As was usual when they were alone, they were eating in an alcove off the kitchen at the back of the house. Colette was reading a letter; John had a morning newspaper propped up in front of him.

"Jeanne says she's thinking of going to Spain," said Colette. "She'll stay with Hugh in Madrid, and if he can take some leave they might— John, are you listening?"

"Yes. Jeanne says she's going to Spain."

"You heard that? Good. Did you hear what I said before, about Mark Ryle?"

"No—no." John decided to tell the truth.

"He's in Paris. She's asked him to the cottage in Dinan for the weekend."

"Has she, by Jove?"

"Ah, at last you're showing some interest!"

"But of course, darling. Do you think there's any chance they might get together again?"

"I've no idea. It would be their business, wouldn't it?" Colette changed the subject abruptly. "John," she said, "you're *distrait*—you have been since last night. You're worried about something, I know. This business of Peter, I suppose. Tell me. Have there been any new developments?"

"Not that I know of. But you're right. Indirectly Peter has produced a problem." John Mourne smiled ruefully. He hadn't meant to bother Colette, but her perceptions were always so acute where he was concerned. "You've seen in the papers this story about the young civil servant who's accused of passing some Top Secret documents to her Czech lover? Well, I've been offered the brief by the girl's solicitor, and I can't decide whether to take it or not. The case is sure to attract a lot of publicity, and you can imagine the headlines— 'Late Viscount Mourne's brother to defend alleged spy'."

"Yes," said Colette, "I can." Then she went on, slowly and bitterly, "Damn Peter! I suppose it's not entirely fair to blame him, but this affair is affecting all our lives. Jeanne's broken engagement, and now this brief of yours—" Colette hadn't told him how hurt she had been when she and John had failed to receive an invitation to the wedding of a girl—the daughter of friends she had considered close—who was marrying someone important in the City; she could imagine their so-called friends' conversation as they decided that the Mournes must be deleted from their list.

"And those wretched abusive phone calls," she added. "At least they seem to have dried up."

She had scarcely finished speaking when the telephone rang. They exchanged glances.

"Oh, no!" said Colette, putting down her coffee cup.

"Don't be silly, darling. I'll get it. It's probably Helen or my Chambers or—or someone we know."

John hurried from the kitchen. In spite of himself he found that he hesitated for a moment when he reached his study and before he picked up the phone. Finally he grabbed the receiver and said firmly, "Hello. This is John Mourne."

"Great. I thought you'd still be at home, Mourne." It was a man's voice that John didn't recognize. Afterwards he came to believe that the intonation had not been English, though he couldn't be certain.

"Who's that?" he asked quickly.

"It doesn't matter. You haven't been outside this morning, cock?"

"No," answered John involuntarily.

"Then just go and take a quick gander at the front of your house."

"What do you mean?"

It was a foolish question, as John realized the moment he uttered it. For answer, the receiver at the other end of the line was banged down so sharply that he felt an acute pain in his ear. He swore under his breath. Then the man's last words hit him. He ran next door into the drawing-room at the front of the house, overlooking the semi-circular drive and the lawn it enclosed. Immediately he saw a group of people, nearly all men, standing on the grass and staring at the house. They were murmuring among themselves and jostling each other a little, as if somewhat uncertain what to do.

John went into the hall and flung open the front door. At his appearance there was a sudden silence. Then someone shouted, "Hold it!" Cameras clicked and whirred. The group surged forward. Microphones were thrust at him.

"What the hell do you think you're doing?" John demanded.

It was a girl who answered, her face vaguely familiar from television, though in person, dressed in jeans and a poncho, her hair pulled back in a ponytail, she looked much younger than she did on the screen. She repeated the phone caller's words. "Obviously you've not been outside this morning, Mr. Mourne. We got a tip-off that your house had been vandalized."

"And so it has," another voice added. "Come and look, Mr. Mourne, if you've not seen it already."

John Mourne would have liked to slam the door in their faces, but his curiosity was too strong. Besides, he had to know, and from where he was standing framed in the front door he could see nothing amiss. The drive and the front garden were neat and tidy, apart from the unwelcome guests, the trees and shrubs unharmed. He took half a dozen strides across the drive towards the grass and, as the group parted to let him through, turned to stare back.

The house itself was double-fronted, with the main door in the centre, bow-windows up and down on either side. Above and below the bottom windows, the beautiful mellow bricks had been defaced by capital letters painted from a spray-can of bright red enamel. It took John a few seconds to discern that the four groups of words, if the lines were read in the right order, constituted a kind of doggerel:

DON'T MOURN FOR MOURNE—
A JUDAS GUY.
FUCK BLOODY MOURNE—
A SOVIET SPY.

John's immediate, illogical reaction was admiration for the slick pun in the first line, and for the meticulous care with which the lettering had been done. His next was the realization that, though the verse could probably be cleaned off, he would never look at the house again without seeing it.

"What do you think, Mr. Mourne?"

"Any idea who did it?"

"It must be about your brother Peter, the late Viscount, sir. Any comment?"

Beset by the questions, and conscious that the cameras were once more at work, John Mourne said, "Sorry. No comment," and walked swiftly back into the house. As he shut the door he heard one of the newsmen say, "Poor devil. It's not his fault," but this was scant consolation.

Colette, wondering at John's long absence, had come into the hall in search of him. His grim expression was enough to tell her that something was wrong—very wrong. She hurried to him and put her arms round him.

"Darling, what is it? You went to answer the phone and—"

"Yes." John had almost forgotten the phone call. "There are reporters and cameramen outside. The house—our home—has been defaced. A filthy kind of poem's been sprayed on the front of it. The phone call was to tell me to go and look."

"Oh, John!" Colette clung to him, more to console him than for comfort. "I must go and look."

"No, not now, darling. The place is full of reporters and cameramen."

"Well, what does it say?"

John hesitated, then told her. To his surprise, she laughed.

"Quite clever," she said. "But you must call the police."

"I intend to, when I've checked the other walls. Not that they'll ever find the vandals. They never caught the girl who threw the red paint over Peter's coffin, or traced Simpson—that chap who went off with the silver from Fauvel." John Mourne was working off his anger. "In fact, they're useless."

"We've never asked for any protection," Colette said.

"Why should we? We've never needed it." John's temper was abating. "Come along. Let's inspect the rest of the house. We'll go out the back way and avoid those damned media men."

Fortunately the damage was restricted to the front walls. There was no sign that anyone had trespassed in the rear or elsewhere. John telephoned the police, who promised to come around immediately. This further placated him, as did the builder who said he would be along that afternoon to see what could be done about the paint. It then occurred to him to phone his sister to make sure that she was all right, and that her building had not received similar treatment. But, though he let the phone ring for some time, there was no answer from Helen's number.

John and Colette retreated to the kitchen, and another cup of coffee. As they were drinking it, a thought struck John's legal mind. He said, "You know, when you come to think of it, this is very odd. In the circumstances it's a bit over the top, even for an extremist left-wing group. There's no reason on earth for them to add to the accusations against Peter, especially if he *were* a spy. You'd think they'd keep quiet, unless they just want to make the Establishment, as they'd call it, unhappy."

"And unless there's a good deal more to the affair than we appreciate," said Colette.

Helen Mourne had had little sleep. The previous evening she had gone to have Sunday supper with a couple of old friends in Richmond. They told her that as usual they had invited Robert Carew to make a fourth. Carew was a retired civil servant and a widower; he lived not far from Helen, and she had known him a long time and had slept with him occasionally, though not for some while.

Because Carew's car was in dock she had offered him a lift to Richmond, and on their return to Kensington he had insisted they should drive to her flat, saying that from there he would walk home. Helen was not ungrateful. It was late and she had no garage, but only a resident's parking permit, which meant she might have to leave the car some distance away from her flat. She had no wish to hurry alone through the streets of London by night.

But I shouldn't have asked him in for a nightcap, she thought miserably, and I damned well shouldn't have taken him into my bed. I'm too old for that kind of lark any more.

This morning she had a hangover; her head ached and her stomach felt queasy. Thankful that Robert Carew had at least had the sense to leave in the small hours, so that she hadn't woken to find him beside her, she put on a robe and went along to the kitchen. Black coffee was what she needed, and perhaps a piece of dry toast.

The percolator was beginning to burp when an awful idea struck her. She remembered that she had let Robert drive the car back from Richmond, and she recalled how lucky they had been to find a parking space directly outside her building. She had got out and opened the front door. What had Robert done? Had he locked the car? If so, where were the keys? If someone had pinched it—

Helen found the keys immediately in the first place she looked—on the hall table, where Carew had sensibly left them. At once she was reassured. Robert was a reliable man and was certain to have locked the car. Nevertheless, just to be sure, she went into the sitting-room; she had been lucky with parking last night, and from the window she should be able to see the car easily.

And there it was, the red Escort that she had bought three months ago after taking a large profit on a parcel of shares she had owned for ages. She sighed with relief, and told herself she had been stupid to worry. Then, as she was about to turn away from the window, she paused. A man, walking along the pavement with a girl, had pointed to the Escort. They stopped, glanced at the building, saw her at the window of her ground-floor flat, and hurried on. When a middle-aged man acted in a similar fashion, Helen's doubts returned with a rush. The car was there, but something was wrong with it.

She stared through the glass. The Escort looked normal. What was the trouble? Had someone let down the tyres—or, worse, slashed them? She hated vandals. If only she had a garage . . .

Regardless of the fact that she was wearing only a thin robe over a flimsy nightdress, that her feet were bare, her hair dishevelled, and her face a revelation of age and dissipation, Helen ran to her door and out into the street. She was not a woman who loved possessions for their own sake, but she didn't have an excess of money and the car was almost new. If it had been badly damaged . . .

But as soon as she got close and had a clear view of the Escort, she knew that vandals were not responsible—at least no ordinary vandals. Deeply incised in the near-side door panel were the words: MOURNE—RED SPY. She walked quickly around to the other side of the car, not even noticing that her gown was trailing in the dust. On the off-side door the words were: MOURNE—RED TRAITOR.

Helen hurried back to her flat. Illogically she felt dirty—almost dishonoured. Her head was throbbing, and she was shaking, though she managed to pour herself a mug of coffee and find some aspirin. Then she sank down in a chair by the kitchen table, the mug clutched in both hands.

The telephone rang, but she ignored it. At the moment she didn't want to speak to anyone. But in a few minutes she grew calmer; her normal sanity reasserted itself. She finished her coffee, ate a piece of toast, and considered her next move. She could not, she decided, drive the Escort in its present state. She telephoned the garage she always used and said that during the night her car had been damaged by vandals.

"Is it drivable, Miss Mourne? We're very busy this morning. If you could bring the car over yourself it would be a big help."

"It's drivable, yes, but *I* can't drive it. You'll have to fetch it."

"If you say so, miss. I'll send someone along, but it won't be before noon. I'm sorry. That's the best I can do."

Helen took a deep breath. She thought of the car sitting outside for her neighbours to see as they went shopping later in the morning, and of how the news would spread. And she thought of herself driving the car. Perhaps while it was in motion the words wouldn't be so legible. She changed her mind.

"All right," she said. "I'll bring it along myself."

Helen wasted no time. Fifteen minutes later she was ready to leave. She was out on the pavement before she realized that several people were standing around, and one of them was taking photographs of the Escort. For a moment she paused, then her temper exploded.

"What the hell do you think you're doing?" she demanded.

She advanced on the photographer. Afterwards she was to swear that she never meant to hit the man, but merely to seize his camera. Unhappily, as she reached for it, one of the solid gold bracelets that she affected caught him under the eye, and its serpent's head ripped his skin and bruised him. It was a gift for the media. The arrival of a police officer only added to the interest of the scene—and ensured its sequel in the local magistrate's court.

Ironically Carmela, Viscountess Mourne, was aloof from all these events. She lived a sheltered, almost regal, existence, behind a hedge of security on which the authorities had insisted. Her telephone calls were intercepted before she was allowed to receive them. Her letters were opened— and read. The house and grounds were heavily guarded, night and day. This spared her a great deal of unpleasantness, but not, of course, all.

She read newspapers, though not the tabloids or the more popular press. She listened to the radio. She watched a certain amount of television. And she waited.

She had never relished waiting, had always preferred action, but what else was she to do? The days dragged. By now she was fully recovered from the overdose of barbiturates that she was presumed to have taken by accident, but she still refused such invitations as she received. They were few in number and, in her opinion, came only from the curious. She preferred to stay at Fauvel Hall, where she felt reasonably safe.

But time passed slowly. She was worried and lonely. She guessed that developments were taking place of which she knew nothing, and that inquiries were under way which might produce unwanted answers. Irrationally she wished she could have discussed the situation with Peter. She missed him profoundly, even more than she had expected, and found a strange consolation in taking Charlie, Peter's Cairn, for walks in the grounds. These days, she admitted to herself, as she watched the dog running ahead of her, the courage which had never failed her in the past, whatever the circumstances, seemed to be seeping away. She was desperately afraid.

CHAPTER SEVENTEEN

For the Mournes and those who were close to them this was a distressing time.

The front of John and Colette Mourne's house in Hampstead was swathed in scaffolding and plastic sheeting, as workmen sand-blasted the bricks to erase the offending painted words; experiment had shown that this was the only practicable method to rid the building of the outrage. It would be an expensive operation, and there remained a question as to the liability of the insurance company.

Helen Mourne's car remained in the garage to which, head held high, she had eventually driven it. The insults had been gouged deep into the paintwork and the metal beneath, and it was doubtful if a simple respray would hide all traces of them. The garage proprietor had suggested new door panels, but until the parts arrived Helen was without transport. To add to her annoyance, she had received a summons to appear in court to answer a charge of breaching the peace, because of her unwise attack upon the cameraman. She knew there were plenty of witnesses to the assault; she was advised to plead guilty and accept a fine. The trouble was that the case would undoubtedly give rise to yet more publicity for the Mournes.

And there had already been too much in the media—about the daubing of the Hampstead house and the vandalized Escort. Unluckily for the Mournes there had been no further developments in the horrific murder case that had monopolized most of the headlines the previous week, and the scare of massive food poisoning seemed to have disappeared without a trace. The result was a dearth of sensational news, and any incidents connected with the late Viscount Mourne or his family made good copy.

The more respectable newspapers expressed regret that "innocent people" should be victimized because they were related to Peter Mourne, who, it was pointed out, should also be presumed innocent until proof of any wrongdoing was forthcoming. Nevertheless, even the quality papers didn't hesitate to publish pictures of John Mourne striding from his front door to survey the façade of his house, or of Helen, barefoot in her night-dress, staring at her car. When she saw the photograph, Helen wept. And as for the less restrained tabloids—

"So much for British decency," Mark Ryle said angrily to Maggie, as he stormed into his Cork Street office the following Friday morning. "Some crowd of bloody creeps start a rumour, and the man's condemned. If he kills himself—if he's found dead and it looks like suicide—then there's no legal redress, and his poor unfortunate relatives become fair game."

Maggie regarded Ryle with some concern. "You're losing your objectivity," she said. "You're too involved with that damned family. I sympathize but— It's no good, Mark. It's not getting you anywhere."

Ryle regarded his secretary sourly. "Words of wisdom I don't need," he said. "Don't preach, Maggie. Keep to your own job. Just try to contact Viscountess Mourne and make an appointment for me to see her about the biography over the weekend or early next week. Incidentally, I plan to pay a surprise call on Chariber's girlfriend later this morning."

"You won't get any more out of her than I did." Maggie was indignant.

"Maybe not, but a follow-up's always a good thing. You should know that by now."

Maggie shrugged. "Mark, not everyone's against the Mournes, you know," she said placatingly. "Have you read the piece in this morning's *Telegraph*? It almost amounts to a eulogy of Peter Mourne." She paused, then couldn't prevent herself from adding, "That is, if you like right-wing autocrats." She continued more lightly, "There have been several letters in *The Times,* too, speaking up for him and quoting his record as a politician and a statesman. You must have seen them."

Ryle grunted, and went into his office. He knew it wasn't fair to take his irritation out on Maggie. He couldn't have hoped for a more efficient personal assistant, or one more agreeable and likeable. The trouble was his own frustration. Maggie was certainly right about one aspect of the inquiry. He was not getting anywhere, though it was a moot point whether his lack of progress was due to his personal involvement with the Mournes.

For the next couple of hours Ryle worked at his desk. He went through the day's press. The Mournes still occupied a good deal of space, though the incidents of the previous Monday no longer rated the front pages, and it was true that a certain amount of sympathy was expressed for John and Helen. He prepared a short report for General Bannol, went through his in-tray and made a few phone calls.

Maggie came in, and he said, "Sorry I was so unpleasant when I arrived this morning. I must have got out of bed the wrong side."

Maggie had regained her own equanimity, and nodded understandingly, though Ryle hadn't explained that the real reason for his earlier annoyance was a phone call he had made to Jeanne before leaving for Cork Street. Not wanting to appear to be taking their relationship for granted after the weekend, he had resisted the temptation to phone her earlier. And to his consternation, when she answered his call, he sensed that she was exceptionally distressed. It was only to be expected that she should be worried about her parents and her Aunt Helen, but Ryle guessed that there was something more, something new.

Eventually, after some meaningless chatter, she had told him. "I'm perfectly aware it's stupid," she had said, clearly furious with herself, "but I had a call from Simon. He wanted to know if I'd kept any of his letters and, if I had, would I please return them. I asked him if he thought I intended to blackmail him. Believe it or not, he took the question quite seriously and said no, but it wouldn't do if the wrong people got hold of them. Of course what he meant was that he's still dreading the thought of being involved any more with the Mournes, even though the whole world must know that we were engaged. God! How I ever thought I could be in love with the man! I—"

By the time she had rung off Jeanne had been able to laugh at Simon Maufant's stupidity. Ryle's own anger had taken longer to subside. In fact, he was still seething.

But there was work to be done. He grinned at Maggie. "Any luck with the appointment?"

"No. Viscountess Mourne relayed a message through whoever it was that answered the phone. It was a politely worded refusal. She regrets that she's not yet well enough to discuss a biography of her late husband. Perhaps in a few months—"

"A few months?" Ryle shook his head in mock despair. "Ah well, I'd better be off to see Chariber's popsy."

"She's not exactly a popsy," said Maggie. "She's in her late thirties and she's a sensible, practical woman, though as I reported she's been badly shaken by Chariber's death, especially the nature of it."

"What you're saying in your usual tactful fashion is that I should treat her kindly. That right?" Ryle was amused. And when Maggie nodded, "Okay. I promise," he said.

But it was a promise that Ryle was not to keep. When he arrived at Nottingham Place off Marylebone High Street and found the small block of flats in which Anna Ridley lived, he discovered a police car parked outside. His heart sank.

"I've come to see Miss Ridley," he said to the officer who was standing by the front door talking to a man whom Ryle guessed to be the porter.

"Then I'm afraid you're too late, sir. She's gone."

"Gone?"

The officer realized he might have been tactless. "Are you a relative, sir?"

"No. But it's important I see her." Ryle spoke authoritatively.

"Is that so, sir?" said the policeman. "Then can I have your name and address in case we want to get in touch with you."

"Sure, though I can't think why." Ryle gave his name and his home address.

The police officer said, "Miss Ridley is dead, I regret to say, sir."

"Dead? How?"

The officer hesitated. Then he said, "That's a matter for the inquest, sir. But the papers'll make it clear it looks like suicide. Apparently she took an overdose, and left a note saying she was sorry but she didn't want to live no more."

"She lost her boyfriend a week or so back—killed by a car, he was, one of those hit-and-run jobs," put in the porter. "She was very depressed. Sad. They were a nice couple, though he was a lot older than what she was."

Ryle nodded. "Thanks for the information," he said, and thought, so much for Maggie's "sensible, practical woman."

In the afternoon General Bannol sent for Ryle, and without a word handed him an envelope. In it was a photograph showing three men having drinks in a restaurant, at a corner table in front of what looked like heavy velvet curtains. Two of them were holding up their glasses to the third, a younger man. On the back was written: "Burgess, Maclean and Mourne. Moscow 1953."

"Dear God," said Ryle softly. "You recognize them, sir? All three of them?"

For a moment Bannol was silent. Then slowly he nodded. "Yes," he said. "I'm certain of Burgess and Maclean. As for Mourne, perhaps I'm not so sure. Or is that wishful thinking, Mark?" He turned the photograph over. "1953. After the duo had defected, but even if it's misdated it's still pretty damning."

"Providing it's not a fake, sir. We'll need an expert opinion."

"Yes, yes, of course." Bannol smiled wryly as he heard the hope in his own voice. "You know, Mark," he said. "I'm an old cynic—it goes with the job, I suppose—but I can't convince myself that Peter Mourne was a traitor. And that's a confession I should keep to myself, so I hope you won't mention it. I'm always preaching that in our profession a man with an *idée fixe* can't do a credible job."

Ryle remained silent, and General Bannol continued as if he were talk-

ing to himself. "In the early 1950s Peter Mourne could be said to have had
everything—an excellent wife, a fine house, money, an impeccable family
background, and a career that held great promise. Why should he have
risked all that to become an agent of a foreign power. As far as I can see
there are only two reasons—almost justifications, if you like—for such an
action in circumstances where material gain isn't a factor. First, there's
blackmail. Secondly, there's ideology—the convinced communist, to
whom communism is a faith for which he or she is prepared if necessary
to suffer martyrdom. I don't believe either reason could have applied to
Peter Mourne, and I'll tell you why, Mark."

The General rose slowly from his chair and walked about the office,
easing the aches and pains in his body. Ryle waited. He had a great
respect for Bannol's ability to analyse a situation and assess an individual's
character, an ability that at times had seemed almost uncanny, but had
often led to unexpected but irrefutable conclusions. It was a flair—or
perhaps faculty or talent would better describe it—that Ryle envied.

"I know this is largely subjective," Bannol continued, "but in my opinion Peter Mourne was a cold, unresponsive man. 'Laid-back', I suppose
we'd say today. But he was also clever, ambitious, determined to get to the
top, and even ruthless in his efforts to do so. I can't believe he had the
capacity, the heart—the concern or compassion—to devote himself to a
cause, any cause, and certainly not one that involved the risk of self-
sacrifice."

"That leaves blackmail, if your logic is accurate, sir."

"And how do people become subjects for blackmail?" Bannol continued as if Ryle hadn't spoken. "Sex? Mourne was happily married, and I
never heard a breath of sexual scandal about him. Money matters, as
opposed to money itself? We know he inherited plenty. I'm not sure of the
details, but it's common knowledge that he got most of the Mourne money
as he was the eldest son and his mother was an heiress in her own right.
Corruption of some kind, perhaps concerning money? There was once a
rumour that he was mixed up in some shady business in one of the
offshore islands, but I know for a fact that that wasn't true."

Bannol paused, and Ryle said, "So you've proved your point, sir."

"Not a hundred per cent, Mark." Bannol was quick to correct him.
"You'd have to know a man very well indeed to be completely sure of him,
to bet your life on him, as it were, and I would never do that for Peter
Mourne, vettings and investigations notwithstanding. He was too intro-
spective for my taste. He wasn't unpopular, but I don't think he had any
close friends. If he did, I wasn't one of them. Nevertheless, as I say, in
spite of that picture we've acquired, I can't really see him as a traitor."

"Let's hope the photograph can be shown to be a fake, sir—and, fake or not, that it's not going to be splashed all over the Sunday papers. Incidentally, where did it come from?"

Bannol smiled. "From a responsible journalist who owed me a favour. He'd received it anonymously. There may be more prints, but anyway I'll use my authority to make absolutely certain it doesn't leak further."

"Right," said Ryle, glad that this responsibility was not his.

During the next several days Mark Ryle's private life was far more satisfactory than his work. On the Sunday, thankful that the photograph, faked or genuine, did not appear in any of the press, he had telephoned Brigadier Ryle and his wife, Penny, and said that he would be coming down for the day. He felt that he had been neglecting them, and anyway he needed a little time to relax, to cease speculating about Peter Mourne.

"Lovely, darling," had said Penny Ryle. "We'll be quite a party."

"You have guests?"

"Just John and Colette Mourne. They're here for the weekend. Dick persuaded them. He thought they needed a change, considering all the dire happenings. No one else."

So after all he was to fail to escape from the Mournes, Mark reflected as he drove down to Sussex. He wasn't intensely disappointed. He liked John and Colette, and they would have the latest news of Jeanne—and possibly of Carmela. He reached The Willows as Dick was pouring pre-lunch drinks.

"We've been to church," Penny said, kissing him. "If you'd arrived earlier you could have come with us."

"And prayed for our enemies," said Colette.

"That they should suffer the woes of Job," said John. "I find it impossible to feel charitable towards them. I hope they get a damned stiff sentence, but I don't suppose they will."

"They've been caught?" For a moment Mark was nonplussed. "Oh, you mean your painting gang?" he said. "I hadn't heard."

"Yes," said Colette, "the painting gang, as you call them. They were arrested in the small hours of Saturday morning. We told Helen we'd be here for the weekend and she phoned to tell us."

"Helen? How does she come into it?"

John explained. "Two youths and a girl climbed over the wall into her garden. The doctor who lives above had just returned from a night-call and had gone to open his bedroom window at the very moment the moon came out from behind a cloud. He saw one head appear, and then another. He was sensible enough not to attempt to stop them by himself. He simply phoned the police and luckily there was a squad car nearby, so they were caught."

"Literally red-handed," Penny laughed. "Not that it's funny."

"No. It's not funny." John was bitter. "They had two spray-cans full of that red paint they're so keen on, and one can guess what they'd have done with them if it hadn't been for the lucky chance that the doctor looked out of his window."

"Did they manage to do any damage?" Mark asked.

"They destroyed a couple of bushes, more by accident than design, I gather, as they were desperately trying to get out of the garden," said John, "but they didn't have time for any real damage. No bloody art work."

"And thank goodness Helen's beloved *Manneken Pis* was unharmed," Colette said.

"What I don't understand," said Penny, "is why three young people should set out to—to terrorize the Mournes like this. It's such an absurd and improbable thing to do, even if they believed that these rumours about Peter were true."

"I've wondered about what's behind it all," Dick said.

"So have I," John admitted. "As far as I know there were never any attacks on the families of Philby or Blake or Percy Dart—and they were confessed or convicted traitors. Why single out the Mournes when there's not a shred of evidence against Peter?"

"What do you think, Mark?" Dick asked with seeming innocence. "You've not said much."

Mark shrugged. "I expect the little sods will be only too happy to explain when they come to court," he said, "and that'll mean a lot more unfortunate publicity."

"Oh God!" said Colette. "Let's talk about something else, something pleasant." Pointedly she changed the subject. "Jeanne's coming home on Tuesday. Then she's off to Madrid, to visit Hugh and have a bit of a holiday."

"Right away?" Mark asked.

It had been apparent for some time that sooner or later he would be going to Spain himself. Marie-Antoinette Corbet had intrigued him with her story that Carmela Drelano and Peter Mourne had brought back from that country some secret they were determined to hide, though General Bannol thought that the supposed secret was probably irrelevant. Nevertheless, the point needed to be followed up, if possible. Unfortunately, by now the Spanish Civil War was history, and they had no such leads as had existed in France. Carmela had always maintained that she had no living relatives. Mark didn't like the idea of using Jeanne, but she could at least provide him with an excellent cover for his visit.

"Yes, she leaves for Madrid on Thursday," Colette remarked.

"Really? It's a pure coincidence, but I expect to be there myself at the end of the week." Mark hoped that he didn't sound too disingenuous.

Colette hesitated, but John said at once, "Come and have supper with us on Wednesday, if you're free, Mark. You and Jeanne can talk about Spain. Have you told Hugh you're going?"

"No, not yet. I will. I'll phone tomorrow," Mark promised. "And I'd love to have supper with you on Wednesday, as long as you're sure it's not inconvenient." He glanced at Colette.

"Of course it won't be inconvenient," she replied at once. "We've invited Helen too. She'll have a chance to tell you all about how the doctor saved her garden—and the walls of her flat. You can imagine how grateful she is. It was bad enough having her car damaged, but this—"

"Maybe by then we'll know who the vandals are, and what their motive is," Dick Ryle said. "Let's hope so, anyway."

In court the three accused, all unemployed, were prepared to name themselves and plead guilty to the charges. This was highly unsatisfactory, because no evidence had to be given. However, in mitigation of sentence, their lawyer claimed that they had met a man in a pub who had paid them handsomely to do what he called the "four jobs." Because they were in need of money they had accepted the assignment. They were totally ignorant about and indifferent to the Peter Mourne affair and, their lawyer had the audacity to claim, it was to their credit that they had continued their efforts, even though they had been paid in advance.

General Bannol arranged for Ryle to interview them, but they stuck to this story with a cold determination. Reluctantly Ryle had to admit that, much as he disliked the trio, he believed them. As a lead they were a dead end.

The other disappointment was the technical examination of the photograph. With the best will in the world, the experts refused to commit themselves, merely saying that if it was a composite it was technically a magnificent job.

Nevertheless, as he set off for Hampstead to have supper with the Mournes on the Wednesday evening, Mark Ryle was not discontented. He had an airline ticket to Madrid for the next day in his pocket, and he was looking forward to Spain—and a new background for his inquiries.

CHAPTER EIGHTEEN

On Thursday afternoon Colette Mourne drove her daughter Jeanne to Gatwick, and picked up Mark Ryle on the way. It had been Jeanne's suggestion that she and Ryle should travel to Spain together. Ryle had intended to catch an earlier flight from Heathrow, but was fully prepared to change his plans, especially when Jeanne pointed out that her brother, Hugh, had promised to meet her at Barajas, the international airport fourteen kilometres east of Madrid.

"Do you really have work to do in Madrid, Mark?" Jeanne asked as the aircraft levelled out at its cruising altitude. "You're not merely coming on a swan?"

"No. Jeanne, I'd like to tell you I was just coming for your company, but it wouldn't be true. Spain is an important country, but somewhat neglected politically, and we're hoping to run a series of articles on the subject." Ryle lied fluently. "There are one or two people I want to interview, and I may have to make a few trips out of Madrid. But I certainly expect to have some free time."

"I'm glad. Now, how long did you say you were staying?"

"It depends how the work goes, and—" Ryle hesitated. "And I've got to admit that while I'm there I'm curious to see if I can trace any of Carmela's family."

"For your book on Peter?" Jeanne made no effort to hide her amusement. "You know perfectly well she says that all her relations were killed in the Civil War, though I suppose there could be an odd cousin or someone somewhere. But how would you set about finding him—or her?"

"I've a friend in the newspaper business. He might help." Ryle was intentionally vague.

For a while the two of them sat in companionable silence. The drinks trolley came along the aisle. Jeanne said it was too early for alcohol, but Ryle overrode her objection. He asked for champagne for them both.

"After all, Jeanne," he said, "you're on holiday, and I firmly intend to mix pleasure with business."

Jeanne laughed, but, when the trolley had passed on, she said, "Mark, do you think there could be any truth in that theory Helen produced last night—that Carmela didn't take an overdose, but that the houseman tried to kill her? True or not, it was a pretty ghastly outburst of Helen's, wasn't it?"

"Helen was tight," Ryle said bluntly—and not entirely truthfully. "I suspect she was letting her hair down for the first time. What with the damage to her car and the attack on her beloved garden, it's no wonder she's fraught." He didn't add that Carmela must also have been fraught to have reacted as Helen claimed she had done.

It seemed that, for no obvious reason, Helen had suddenly decided to pay Carmela a visit. She had borrowed Colette's car and driven herself to Fauvel Hall. Though she was unexpected Carmela hadn't refused to see her; after all, they were sisters-in-law. But when Helen had begun to probe about Carmela's accident, remarking that she was sure that by now Carmela must recall what had happened, Carmela had become extremely angry.

She had completely lost her temper, according to Helen, and shouted, "You're mad! Why should Simpson have wanted to kill us? You don't know! Of course you don't. All you're doing is starting yet another rumour, making more trouble!"

Helen had protested that she hadn't mentioned Simpson and had demanded to know what Carmela had meant by "us," since Peter had taken his own life. This was the end of the conversation. Carmela had told Helen to get out, had called for the security man and told him that Miss Mourne was leaving.

"Helen may have been tight, but she knew what she was saying, Mark," Jeanne persisted as a light meal was served to them. "And it's certainly true that no would-be suicide is likely to set an alarm clock to wake him— or her—the next morning."

Ryle made the same non-committal comment he had made when Helen had first told him about the clock: Carmela might easily have set the alarm from habit. "It's the mention of Simpson that's intriguing," he went on. "Why should Carmela have dragged him into the argument? For that matter, how could he have hanged Peter? Peter wasn't a big man, but neither was Simpson. And why the hell should Simpson want to kill either of them? That's the crux of the matter. If anyone can produce a credible explanation as to that 'why,' Jeanne, I might start to take the idea seriously. As it is—" He shook his head.

Ryle had no alternative but to dissemble. General Bannol was still not entirely convinced, but Mark was sure that Peter Mourne had been killed, and that Carmela knew it—and knew also that an attempt had been made on her own life. As for Simpson, his part in the saga remained a subject for speculation. And speculation was something Ryle was not prepared to share with Jeanne at this stage.

The aircraft landed at Barajas on time. Their bags arrived with surprising speed, and they had no trouble with immigration or customs. Very soon they were walking out into the concourse of the modern international terminal to find Hugh waiting for them. He embraced Jeanne warmly and shook Mark Ryle by the hand.

"Welcome to Madrid," he said. "It's great to have you both here. I was so glad to hear from you, Jeanne, and to get your call, Mark. I only wish you could be staying with me, but it simply isn't possible. We have a wonderful woman who does her best to keep us in order, but with three bachelors living together the place is chaotic, as you can imagine."

"Where are we staying?" Jeanne asked as Hugh led the way to his car, and piled their luggage into the boot.

"In a small hotel on the Calle Elena, which is a street close to my apartment and within walking distance of our Embassy on Calle Fernando el Santo. It's all very central, and the hotel's friendly and comfortable, and not full of tourists. We often put people up there. I've booked you both in for a week, though that can be changed."

"It sounds marvellous," said Jeanne.

Hugh said, "I've arranged to hire you some transport, Mark, as you asked. All they could manage at such short notice was a Séat—that's a small Spanish car, you know."

"That's very efficient of you," said Mark. "Many thanks."

"Anyway," Hugh went on, "it'll be delivered to the hotel tomorrow morning, but I don't advise you to use it in the city. Traffic here is hell— worse than Rome, I think. I've bought you some non-residents' parking tickets. You can get more from any local tobacconist's. But park with care, or the *grúa* will come and haul the car away—and fines are damned heavy. And the *Guardia Civil* are fierce, so be warned."

By now Hugh had negotiated the exit from the airport, and they were speeding down the broad Avenida de America towards the city. As Hugh had said, once they had crossed the Avenida de la Paz and got closer to the centre, traffic was heavy, and it took them about half an hour to reach Calle Elena. Hugh drew up in front of a non-descript building, presenting a typically-Spanish blank face to the narrow street, and announced that this was the Hotel de Claudio.

"It's a family concern, and the owner's name really is Claudio," Hugh said. "Mark, you do speak Spanish?"

"Enough to get by."

"Knowing you, that will be an understatement." Hugh succeeded in making this remark sound vaguely uncomplimentary. "Okay. In that case, you'll forgive me if I just help you into the place with your bags and introduce you. Then I'll leave you to cope with Señor Claudio and the formalities. I have to go back to the Embassy for a few minutes." Hugh glanced at his watch. "I'll pick you both up at nine-thirty. You'll have eaten on the plane, but I hope you'll be hungry again by then. Is that all right? News re family and so on when we meet?"

"That'll be fine," Jeanne said, but Ryle noticed that she was frowning as they carried their bags into the small foyer of the hotel and were greeted by Señor Claudio himself.

They filled in the registration forms and handed in their passports, receiving a promise they would be returned in the morning. A youth, who from his appearance was obviously a son of the owner, showed them up to their rooms. These were pleasant, looking out over a small but attractive courtyard, simply furnished but scrupulously clean—and connecting, as Jeanne soon discovered by releasing two bolts on her side of a door.

This amused them both. But later, as they were waiting for Hugh to meet them, Ryle became aware that once more Jeanne was frowning as if worried.

"Is something bothering you?" he asked tentatively. "It's not the rooms? I didn't—"

Jeanne responded without hesitation. "Don't be silly, Mark. It's Hugh. Didn't it strike you that he was awfully uptight and tense? He hardly stopped talking while he was driving us here, though he had the traffic to contend with."

"Yes, I must admit I thought he was a bit edgy," Ryle agreed. "It's probably something connected with his work. Anyway, you can ask him over supper."

"I suppose so." Jeanne sounded reluctant. "I expect I'm being stupid and you're right, Mark; it could be his work. But these days I'm always scared that any signs of trouble will turn out to be connected with this horrid business of the Mournes."

"This is a typical Castilian restaurant," Hugh said as they sipped their aperitifs. "Four forks, the equivalent of our four stars, which means it's fairly expensive, but it's well worth it because the food's excellent. Incidentally, it's my treat tonight, Mark."

"Many thanks, Hugh. It'll be my turn next time you join us."

"Why not? I had thought of taking you to a *tasca* first, but it's your first evening in Madrid and—"

"What's a *tasca?*" interrupted Jeanne.

Hugh grinned. "A place where you eat *tapas,* my dear sister. It's a bar where they serve the most delectable small snacks. They used to be truly Spanish, but those that remain have largely become noisy tourist traps, and I thought we'd want to talk."

Seeing the sudden flick of anxiety across Jeanne's face at the thought of what the coming conversation might include, Ryle attempted to intervene with a casual remark. "You forget that Jeanne's a Parisienne, Hugh. She's not familiar with this city of yours and its habits."

Further comment was interrupted by the arrival of the maître d' offering menus, and Hugh's need to advise his guests on their choices. As Ryle considered whether to eat *bacalao*—cod—in one of its many Spanish forms, or *fabada,* a pork and bean stew, he accepted that Jeanne had been right and that something was very wrong with Hugh. Anyway, he made his choice and waited while the others followed suit. Hugh ordered wine, and apparently decided to change the subject.

"Tell me how the family is," he said at length. "I spoke to maman on the phone yesterday, but obviously she was trying to make light of the latest attacks on us."

"Everyone's really all right, as far as one can tell," said Jeanne. "Helen seems to be taking things the worst."

"Poor old Helen. What about Carmela?"

Jeanne shrugged. "Who knows? She's such a secretive woman. She shuts herself up in Fauvel Hall and doesn't seem to care a damn about us. So why should we care about her?"

Hugh didn't answer at once. He finished his aperitif and tasted the wine the waiter had produced. He nodded his approval and waited while it was poured. When the man had left them he said suddenly, "Something rather odd happened here, too. There was an advertisement in a Spanish national newspaper—*El País*—about ten days ago asking that any relation of Carmela Isabella Drelano should get in touch with a box number. It's a very reputable paper, something like *The Times* or *Le Monde,* and I answered the advert. I wrote to them explaining who I was."

"You never mentioned this before," Jeanne said reproachfully.

"I wanted to see what kind of reply I'd get." Hugh shook his head ruefully. "All I received was a typed statement thanking me for answering but saying that the Carmela Isabella Drelano referred to in the advertisement was unfortunately not my relation but another Doña Drelano."

"How extraordinary," said Jeanne. "Would it be a common name in Spain?"

"I wouldn't have thought so," Hugh replied. "Not all three names together. What do you make of it, Mark?"

"It could be coincidence, I suppose. At any rate, I don't believe it's anything for you to worry about, Hugh."

"Why not?" Jeanne, in her turn, was aggressive. "Remember what's happened to maman and papa—"

"Jeanne, anyone who was seriously interested in the Mourne family must know by now of Hugh's relationship to Peter and the former Carmela Drelano. They wouldn't need to advertise to discover that, or to find him. This isn't what's worrying you, is it, Hugh?"

If Hugh Mourne thought the question abrupt or tendentious, all he said was, "I think it's damned odd!"

Their first course arrived and they began to eat. Then their conversation took a happier turn. They discussed the food and late Spanish dining hours, which accounted for the fact that the restaurant was still three-quarters empty. They considered their next day's programme.

"I intend to be a tourist," Jeanne said. "I'm going to the Prado. So no one need worry about me. I expect you both have work to do."

"Unfortunately, yes," said Hugh, "but I'll be free in the evening and over the weekend." He looked at Ryle. "And you, Mark?"

"I'll certainly be busy tomorrow. There's a man I have to see in the morning, and after that I'm not sure. It all depends on what this chap's got to say."

"About Peter and Carmela?" Hugh asked blandly and, when Mark made no immediate response, he went on, "About your biography of our famous or infamous relative?"

"Definitely not—nothing to do with any book," Ryle said truthfully. "I'm here for my magazine. That means their interests have to come first, and at the moment I really can't commit myself. But I intend to steal some spare time if it's at all possible."

"Good," said Hugh. "Tomorrow night there's a reception at the opening of an exhibition of modern Spanish paintings at the Palacio de Cristal in El Retiro. I've got to be there, to show the flag for the Embassy, and I thought you might find it interesting, Mark."

"Did you? I'm not terribly keen on diplomatic parties—or on modern Spanish art."

"They can be useful—the parties, I mean."

"I dare say."

"What on earth are you talking about?" Jeanne demanded, sensing that all this was merely verbal fencing. "Why are you going round in circles? What is this Palacio and where is El Retiro, as you call it?"

"I thought you'd been reading the guide books," said Hugh. "The Parque del Retiro, which dates back to 1625, is the most important park in Madrid. You must have heard of it. It's absolutely fabulous—wide avenues, splendid trees, and flowerbeds, an unbelievable rose garden, statues, a lake—and the so-called Palacio de Cristal, which is a wonderful building made of iron and glass, a bit like the old Crystal Palace in London. The *Madrileños* use it for exhibitions and receptions."

"You sound like a public relations officer. You know—come to fabulous whatever," said Jeanne. "Anyway, it would be dark by the time we got there, wouldn't it? We shouldn't see much."

"My dear sister, don't come if you don't want to." Hugh's voice was unusually grating. "But the invitation specifically included you—and Mark —so the Spanish would consider it a grave discourtesy if you couldn't be bothered to turn up."

"How on earth did they know—" began Jeanne, but Mark intervened.

"Of course we'll both come," he said. "I'll make sure I'm available, and afterwards I'll take us out to dinner. You decide where, Hugh—and as many forks as you like."

But later, when Jeanne had gone to the cloakroom and the two men were drinking Spanish brandy, Ryle said, "Tell me, Hugh, is there something special about this reception tomorrow?"

"I honestly don't know." Hugh Mourne frowned. "I hope not, but—I didn't want to talk about it in front of Jeanne. Of course, there could be nothing, but a chap who gave his name as Señor Don Pedro De Solina— there is a man of that name who's well known in Madrid, influential, with private means, a collector of art—telephoned me at the Embassy. He said he understood that my friend, Mark Ryle, was coming to Madrid, and he was very eager to meet him, quite informally. He would send us an invitation to this opening. When I mentioned Jeanne he said that of course she must accompany us. And that's all I know, Mark, but—"

"When was this call?"

"Tuesday."

"Really," said Mark. "I only decided to come to Spain on Monday."

Hugh grinned sardonically. "So how did this high-powered character know about your sudden decision? And why involve me? Mark, it must be something to do with Peter Mourne. What with that Drelano advert and now this—I don't like it."

Mark Ryle shrugged. "Here's Jeanne," he said, putting an end to further speculation.

CHAPTER NINETEEN

"Drelano? Yes, I saw the advertisement. Why are you interested in it?"

"I'd like to know how many answers there were."

"Would you? It's a bit irregular, but—"

Before he left London, Ryle had made sure to get an introduction to a senior journalist on the staff of *El País,* the Spanish national newspaper published in Madrid. The foreign editor, one Juan De Costa, had seemed ideal, though Ryle's informant could or would say little about the man, except that he was to be trusted, and knew a great deal more than he printed. In any case, on his arrival in Madrid, Ryle had phoned for an appointment and had discovered that Calle Miguel Juste, where the paper's offices and plant were located, was quite close to Barajas airport, in an industrial zone to the east of the city. Defying Hugh's advice, he had taken the rented car, and had found Madrid traffic relatively simple to negotiate.

Now he was in De Costa's modern office, trying to assess the Spaniard, whose swarthy face gave nothing away as he concluded his sentence, "— with your introduction, I don't see why I shouldn't make a simple inquiry." Then, shoulders hunched and dark head bent forward, he muttered into the phone.

At last he said, *"Gracias"* and put down the instrument. He turned to Ryle. "There was only one reply."

"Only one?" That would have been from Hugh Mourne, Ryle reflected. "Isn't that curious?"

De Costa shrugged. "It's hard to tell. It's not a common name. Two given names were mentioned, which should have narrowed the possibilities, and no reward was offered. Then the advertisement might have been missed, or someone who could reply reads another paper—or perhaps no one was eager to claim a relationship with Viscountess Mourne."

Touché, thought Ryle, as amused brown eyes regarded him. He grinned in response. Clearly he must not underestimate De Costa. Ryle hesitated a moment, but there seemed to be no alternative but to admit his interest, and stress that he was acting on behalf of John Mourne and his immediate family. Whether De Costa believed this partial truth he couldn't guess, but the point was immaterial.

"It's a nasty business," Ryle said. "Peter Mourne seems to have been accused, judged, and condemned, all on the basis of rumour, and his relations are suffering as a result. It's difficult to prove a negative in these circumstances."

De Costa nodded his understanding. "More than relations are affected when an ex-British Foreign Secretary is believed to be a foreign agent. Your Government must be wetting its communal pants, and no one in the West can be happy about the situation—as I'm sure you're aware, Señor Ryle."

"Of course," Ryle agreed. "So for any help—*muchas gracias.*"

They had been speaking English, and De Costa grinned as Ryle emphasized the last words. Then he put a hand to his forehead as if a thought had just struck him. He lifted his telephone receiver and tapped out a number he must have known well. There followed a flood of Spanish, not easy to follow, as De Costa spoke softly and very fast, keeping his lips close to the instrument. Nevertheless, Ryle heard his name mentioned once or twice, and managed to catch the gist of what was being said.

"I'm quite prepared to help you—but on a personal basis," De Costa said as he put down the telephone. "I've been speaking to an old friend of my father. He's in his late seventies and pretty infirm, but his mind is in good shape and, like so many people of that age, the past is sometimes more vivid to him than recent events. Certainly, he seems to remember the Civil War only too clearly, and often speaks of it."

De Costa paused. He drew a memo pad towards him, scribbled on it, tore off the sheet, and passed it across the desk to Ryle. "That's his name and address—Fernández Grado of Segovia, as you see. I'm sure you know that Segovia's about eighty kilometres the other side of the Sierra de Guadarrama, itself famous for Civil War battles."

Ryle glanced at the memo sheet. "This is very good of you. You think he may recall something of interest?" he asked.

"It's possible. He was a journalist. He may well have met Peter Mourne. That's all I can say, except that you can rely on him for first-hand background information. He's worth a try."

"Indeed. Thank you very much." Ryle folded the slip of paper into his wallet. "What did you tell him about me?"

"Merely that you would like to talk to him about the Civil War, and that I vouched for you. I didn't mention Mourne. He said he'd be glad to have a chat with you. He's usually at home these days but, if not, his housekeeper will point you to the nearest bar, and he wouldn't refuse a drink."

Ryle laughed. "I won't forget. I'll go to Segovia tomorrow."

"Now, is there anything else I can do for you?" asked De Costa.

"There is one point," said Ryle. "What do you know of Señor Don Pedro De Solina?"

There was an appreciable pause before De Costa replied. Then he said slowly, "He is a man of great influence and he has powerful friends—in a country where influence and powerful friends count for a great deal. If I were to say that I know little good of him, it would mislead you. Besides, it wouldn't be true. He goes to Mass on Sundays and Holy Days. He gives generously to charities. He helps to support and encourage the arts. He has a wife and an attractive family, and his *relaciones íntimas*—you understand?—are always conducted with the utmost discretion, which is more than can be said of some men in Madrid, or elsewhere for that matter. But—"

Ryle said, "Yes. After that eulogy, I thought there'd be a 'but.' "

"The fact is that there really isn't anything against him, Señor Ryle." De Costa opened his arms wide in a gesture of hopelessness. "Many newspapers in Madrid wish there were something they could print. Nevertheless, he is the last person—had the possibility ever arisen—that I would have wished my daughter to marry. Call it instinct or what you will, but I don't believe Pedro De Solina is an entirely admirable character."

"He is to be mistrusted?"

"He prides himself on his sense of honour—but so do all Spaniards. If he makes a bargain and gives you his word, he won't break it, but between ourselves it's my opinion he'd make a bargain with the devil if it amused him. He's—he's arrogant—that's the English word I was searching for. He's convinced he can play with fire without coming to any harm. I can't be more explicit because I don't have any facts, but, if you must have dealings with him, Señor Ryle, be careful. He is a dangerous man."

"I'll remember your advice, Señor De Costa, and I'll respect your confidence. I'm most grateful to you. *Se lo agradezco mucho.*"

"If you read Spanish you could look through our file on him, but it's curiously empty of anything except routine social events and so on; it would tell you nothing more about him. In the meantime—" De Costa smiled broadly. "I suppose you wouldn't like to satisfy a newspaperman's curiosity and tell me why you're interested in De Solina? Off the record, of course. Is there some connection with the late Viscount Mourne?"

"Frankly, I don't know of any connection. Might there be one?"

"There could be, I suppose. De Solina has many friends in the *Cortes,* so some kind of political link is not impossible, and he travels widely. He could easily have met Mourne in London, for example. They would both move in much the same high-powered circles."

"I see," said Ryle thoughtfully. He decided there was no harm in taking

De Costa further into his confidence. "Maybe I'll know more this evening. The great man has asked to meet me—no reason given—at a reception tonight."

"That should be safe enough," De Costa assented. "But treat him with circumspection, as I say."

"I will," Ryle promised. It was a promise he had every intention of keeping.

By the time Mark Ryle had returned to his hotel the *Madrileños* were enjoying their siestas. The *conserje,* nodding at his desk, gave Ryle a reproachful look when he asked for his room key. He was half asleep again before Ryle had reached the foot of the stairs, which he preferred to the rickety lift.

Anticipating with pleasure a cool shower and an hour spent dozing on top of his bed, Ryle opened the door of his room. He took two steps inside and stopped short. He laughed aloud.

"Hello, Mark," a sleepy voice said.

Jeanne was lying under the duvet. As she pushed herself up on the pillows the duvet slipped, exposing her breasts and making it obvious that she was naked. She held out her arms to him.

"I thought you'd never come back, Mark, so I went to sleep."

"Aren't you meant to be at the Prado?"

"I was, but there's a limit to art appreciation, however great the pictures may be."

"And there are better things to do of an afternoon?"

"When in Rome— Isn't this how Spanish men spend the time from two till four?"

"Definitely. That's what *macho* means."

Ryle kicked off his shoes and pulled off his clothes, letting them drop to the floor where he stood. His desire for a shower and an hour of lethargy had disappeared, replaced by healthy lust. He threw back the duvet that half-covered Jeanne and slid into the bed beside her. He entered her almost at once. They hadn't made love the night before, remaining in their separate rooms, and it was all the sweeter now, at first passionate, then slow and gentle.

"That," said Jeanne some while later, "was a good loving."

"I'm glad I pleasured you, ma'am."

"You were pleasured too?"

"Infinitely."

They lay on their backs, side by side, just touching. Their bodies were satisfied and relaxed. At last Jeanne broke the silence.

"You know I was never really in love with Simon Maufant," she said unexpectedly. "I got engaged to him on the rebound from you, Mark. He seemed to be all the things that you aren't—dependable, reasonable, not secretive, always there when and where he said he would be. He wasn't forever breaking dates at the last minute. He remembered my birthday. His secretary never phoned just as I was getting into my dress or doing my face to say that Mr. Maufant was terribly sorry, but he'd been called away suddenly. He didn't disappear for weeks on end without warning, and then reappear just as suddenly. He didn't call me or send me a cable from God knows where when I was expecting to meet him in Paris. He—"

Jeanne ran out of words. Mark said nothing in reply. And she dug him viciously in the ribs with her elbow; still sore from the attack in Senlis, he cried out loud. Then he propped himself up on one elbow and looked down at her.

"You know perfectly well that Maufant is a dull, orthodox oaf," he said, spacing his words to emphasize them. "If you'd married him you'd have been bored and unhappy. You'd have jibbed at the third Conservative fête you were expected to open. And, as you love me rather than him, you wouldn't even have remained faithful to him for very long."

Jeanne glared. "Damn you!" she said, and burst into tears. "Damn you!"

Mark put his arms around her and drew her to him. Gradually her sobs grew less and eased. He rocked her gently, as if she had been a child. "What is it?" he asked. "What is it, darling?"

"I'm sorry," she said. "I'm tired. I've been working hard and—and it's this bloody Mourne affair. It gets worse and worse. I thought Simon was being childish and I don't really care. But from his point of view he was right. It—it hit me when I got home this week and saw papa and maman and our poor house with the front all scoured, and Aunt Helen looking like a wraith. I thought I'd get away from it, coming to Spain, but of course I haven't. There's this Drelano advert Hugh never mentioned before, and now this arty party tonight. Why do you have to go to it?"

"Jeanne, I don't—"

Jeanne rolled off the bed and stood, looking down at him. She seemed unaware that she was naked. Her mouth was set and her eyes blazed with sudden anger. It was difficult to accept that such a short time ago they had been one body, lost in love. He could see the sweat between her breasts and the soft down on her thighs. He thought her beautiful. He put out a hand to pull her towards him, then let it drop as she started to speak again.

"I hoped it would be different this time," she said bitterly, "but it's just like before. The same lies and half lies. The same deceits. The same little mysteries that you refuse to explain. Anyone would think you were in some kind of secret service and not merely a glorified journalist. I wouldn't be in the least surprised if you decided to leave Madrid tomorrow and go off somewhere by yourself."

"In fact I'm going to Segovia tomorrow."

"To see a man about a dog?"

"To talk to an elderly newspaperman about the Spanish Civil War. He may or may not remember Peter Mourne. Does that satisfy you?"

"It might, if I were sure it was the truth. But I never know with you, Mark. I simply can't rely on you."

Jeanne picked up the robe she had thrown over a chair, but didn't bother to put it on. Trailing it behind her, she stepped carefully over the heap of Mark's clothes on the floor, as if they were distasteful to her. She didn't look back as she walked through the connecting door to her own room.

CHAPTER TWENTY

Mark Ryle and Hugh Mourne went alone to the opening of the exhibition of contemporary Spanish painting at the Palacio de Cristal. In spite of her brother's exhortations and eventually his ill-concealed irritation, Jeanne had refused to accompany them. Mark had taken no part in the increasingly acerbic argument between the two Mournes; he was in no mood to be helpful.

Now the two men stood in the main gallery of the Palacio, before a large canvas entitled *El Apocalipsis,* and regarded it sombrely. The exhibition had been declared open and the lengthy patriotic speeches, extolling the place of Spain in the world of art, were over. Everyone was at last free to make his or her own critical appreciation of the exhibits, though few of those who had been invited seemed anxious to take advantage of the opportunity. Most preferred to greet friends and acquaintances, drink, exchange gossip, and arrange future meetings. The atmosphere was that of a cocktail party, the paintings and sculpture an irrelevance.

"*¡Salud!*" said Mark, raising his champagne glass and gesturing towards the canvas. "What's your opinion of that?"

"It reminds me of a nightmare—a recurring one I had as a child," said Hugh, grinning. He looked at his watch. "Time's getting on."

"Yes. I'm not sure that your chum's going to appear."

"De Solina's no chum of mine, Mark, but from what I know of him he doesn't play silly games. He'll be here."

"Maybe. But I don't intend to make myself conspicuous by waiting till everyone else has gone."

They had been among the first guests to arrive. They had been greeted by a small receiving line and accepted glasses of champagne. They had wandered desultorily around the gallery. They had listened to the opening ceremony, and duly applauded at appropriate moments. They had spoken to one or two fellow-guests with whom Hugh was acquainted.

They were still waiting for De Solina to arrive, and the situation was becoming slightly embarrassing. The majority of the guests had already left. Others were beginning to make a move. The waiters had started to clear away the glasses. It was quite clear that the reception was reaching its conclusion.

"Let's go, Hugh."

"Okay," Hugh agreed, though somewhat reluctantly.

They thanked their hosts, expressing admiration for the exhibition, and said goodbye. They had left the gallery, and were about to descend the stairs, when a man who had been standing outside the door approached them hurriedly. He was young, in his early twenties, and was clearly nervous.

"Señor Ryle?"

"Yes. My name's Ryle," said Mark.

"Please would you come with me. We have something that might interest you." The young man spoke English with a very fair accent. Then he looked doubtfully at Hugh.

The two Englishmen exchanged glances. The young man had waved Mark ahead, and so placed himself that it was apparent that Hugh was not included in the invitation.

"Shall I—" Hugh began.

"No. I'll meet you at the car," Ryle said quickly.

"Okay." Hugh was hesitant, but finally he turned away and started down the stairs.

The young man led Mark Ryle along a corridor, through two small galleries where Mark caught glimpses of paintings that he would have liked to inspect quietly, by himself, undisturbed by a background of clinking glasses, explosive laughter, and brittle conversation. At the end of the second gallery they were faced by double doors, which the young man flung open.

"Señor Ryle," he announced, and stood back to allow the señor to enter.

The room was not large, but was furnished as a luxurious office, or possibly a rich man's study. There was a Chinese rug on the marble floor and the curtains were of heavy silk. The furniture managed to combine practicality with elegance. Books lined two walls, and on the third was a magnificent Vicente López, though Mark Ryle was given no time to admire it. As the doors closed behind him, excluding the man who had been his escort, he was aware only of the strong personality of Señor Don Pedro De Solina.

"*¡Qué amable en venir a verme, Señor Ryle!*" De Solina said affably. He then offered his hand and repeated his opening sentence in effortless English, "How kind of you to meet me, Señor Ryle. I know you speak Spanish, but I think there is less chance of misunderstanding if we continue in English."

You know I speak Spanish, do you? thought Ryle. I wonder how many other inquiries you've made about me. But De Solina was continuing.

"I apologize for boring you with the exhibition which, I'm afraid, is less than first-class, but the Director of the Palacio has been good enough to lend me his office for an hour or so, and it seemed a convenient place for us to arrange a private encounter."

De Solina was a big man, well over six feet, his stature emphasized by his military bearing. About fifty, his dark hair was worn long and just tinged with grey. He was handsome in a raffish kind of way, so that it was easy to imagine him as the hero of one of Hollywood's more exotic costume dramas, complete with ruffled shirt, breeches, and sword. In fact, he was in normal evening dress, with the ribbon of some decoration around his neck. Ryle wondered if it was being worn to impress him.

"Please sit down, Señor Ryle." De Solina gestured to an ornate chair. "May I offer you something to drink? Whisky? Brandy? Champagne?" He smiled, showing white even teeth, which probably owed more to the expertise of his dentist than to nature.

"Thank you, no." This was the first time Ryle had spoken. He refused the drink but took a seat in the brocaded chair. "I have a friend waiting for me."

"Ah yes, Señor Mourne, who was good enough to deliver my message to you. I'm sure he won't mind waiting a while—and he will be discreet if you tell him that it's best our meeting should not be mentioned to anyone."

"Why not?"

"Señor Ryle, you are not stupid."

"I might return the compliment, Señor De Solina, if I understood the need for this encounter, as you call it." Ryle refused to be intimidated by the forceful Spaniard. "So may I remind you that it was you who expressed a wish to speak to me, not vice versa. Perhaps you would now explain."

"Very well. But first I must stress the fact that I am only a—a *medianero* —a go-between is perhaps the best translation. Personally, I cannot help you or your country, much as I might like to. I can only do what I have been asked to do—that is to put to you a certain proposition, and return your answer to the gentlemen who approached me, and whom for the moment I represent. Do I make myself clear?"

As clear as muck, thought Ryle, but he said carefully, "I understand what you are saying, señor—as far as it goes."

"I take your point, señor, so I'll proceed." De Solina leant back in his chair, and crossed one neatly tailored leg over the other. He regarded the tip of his Gucci evening shoe. "At present, as you are aware, Señor Ryle, the United Kingdom, together with her many allies, including Spain of course, is extremely embarrassed by the spate of rumours that the late Viscount Mourne, your ex-Secretary of State for Foreign Affairs, was a communist agent and a traitor. Now, it is possible that these rumours could be quashed, and Peter Mourne completely exonerated. If that could be accomplished, your Government would be grateful, Señor Ryle?"

"I assume they would, Señor De Solina, but naturally I can't speak for them."

"You could, however, relay what I have to say—what I am empowered to say—to the right quarters. Please, señor, do not pretend otherwise. It will only waste time and, as you said, you are keeping your friend waiting."

"What are you empowered to say, señor? As I see the situation, a man's reputation has been destroyed by a pack of lies. How can such a wrong be redressed?" Ryle had no intention of discussing his own situation.

"Suppose that an individual were to confess he had started these rumours, and had then paid some louts to spray red paint around, in order to generate and retain the interest of the media?"

Ryle didn't ask why anyone should make such a confession; the communists never found it difficult to "persuade" someone to confess. He took his time before replying. "An intriguing hypothesis," he said eventually. "One can hardly ask that this individual should be reputable, but at the very least he must be able to demonstrate a credible motive."

"Of course. That would be arranged."

"You have someone in mind?"

"Not I, señor. It is not for me to arrange such matters. As I told you, I am merely a go-between. But I would venture to guess that there *is* someone who is prepared—"

"A volunteer?" Ryle couldn't resist the sarcasm.

"You care to joke, Señor Ryle?" De Solina was suddenly cold, menacing. "This is a serious proposition which your Prime Minister should be happy to consider. It could be the salvation of the Government and solve what may otherwise become an insoluble problem for your country and its allies. To be blunt, it represents what is almost certainly the only solution that is likely to present itself in the near future."

"I see," Ryle said slowly. "And in return? I assume the gentlemen you represent and for whom you speak will require a *quid pro quo.*"

"Certainly. That is only reasonable, is it not?" De Solina was affable once more.

"Yes, indeed." Ryle wondered idly what De Solina hoped to get for himself out of any deal. "Providing the *quid* and the *quo* are equally balanced."

De Solina laughed. "You are cleverer than you pretend, Señor Ryle, if you will forgive me for saying so," he remarked a little patronizingly. "In this case I suspect your masters will consider it a very fair balance. In return for getting them off the hook, as it were—Sir Percival Dart!"

Mark Ryle thought quickly. The KGB and the GRU had always had a reputation for doing their best to help or retrieve their agents if they were caught, and certainly Percy Dart, who had served them well during an apparently distinguished career, deserved their best efforts now. They would not hesitate deliberately to ruin the reputation of an honourable man, regardless of the consequences, in order to rescue a despicable character like Dart. But it was going a bit far, even for the Soviet authorities, to murder the man in question to add credence to their innuendoes.

"Anything else, Señor De Solina?" Ryle asked at last, his voice steady and emotionless.

"Apart from details—assurances, length of time to complete arrangements, ways and means, and so on—which will obviously have to be discussed if your people take up the offer, there is one point. Moscow would be prepared to issue a flat denial that Peter Mourne was ever, at any period, an agent for any communist country or organization. It may or may not be believed, but in combination with the confession of another, it should at least help to calm the fears of our American allies," De Solina concluded.

"If, as you say, the offer is taken up." Ryle was not encouraging. Deliberately he consulted his watch, then rose to his feet. "I will pass on everything you've said, Señor De Solina, as best I can, but I feel certain that your proposition will have to pass through many channels, and any decision will probably take some time."

"*Esto, lo entiendo.* That, I understand. Probably a second meeting between us will be necessary—here, or I could come to London. At any rate, I shall be at your service, señor." He passed a small piece of pasteboard across to Ryle. "I can always be traced through that telephone number. It is unlisted, and I trust you to keep it to yourself." By now De Solina had also risen. He went to the doors, opened them, and bowed to Ryle with some ceremony.

"*¡Hasta la próxima vez!* Señor Ryle, and thank you for listening to my offer," he said with grave courtesy, as if they had merely been discussing the purchase of a painting by some internationally renowned artist. "My secretary will see you out of the Palacio."

"Goodbye, Señor De Solina." Hiding his reluctance, Ryle shook the Spaniard's proffered hand.

CHAPTER TWENTY-ONE

Breakfast had arrived on the dot of eight and Mark Ryle was on his second cup of *café con leche* when he heard a slight scuffling sound at the door communicating with Jeanne's room. The door, however, remained shut, and it was not until Ryle stood up to investigate that he saw the folded sheet of hotel notepaper that had been pushed underneath it and lay, a neat white rectangle, on the green carpet. He stooped and picked it up.

The note was short. "I'm very sorry. I was a bitch. Forgive me. Love, J."

Ryle grinned ruefully. Damn her, he thought. And damn the dilemma in which she's placed me. He loved her. He didn't want anyone else. But she had to accept him on his terms, or it would be no use. He liked his job and was good at it, and he considered it worth doing. He was not prepared to give it up, not even for Jeanne.

He tried the communicating door, but it was firmly bolted and he could hear the water running in Jeanne's shower stall. Useless to telephone. The answer, since she obviously had no wish to see him at the moment, was to find paper and pen and send back a message by the same route. Childish, perhaps, but—

He wrote, "Mutual forgiveness. I'm off to Segovia. See you and Hugh tonight. Love, M."

Ryle finished his coffee, thrust the note under Jeanne's door, and left his room. He walked to the British Embassy in the Calle Fernando el Santo, glad of the exercise. Maggie had done her work well. Though the Embassy was officially shut on Saturdays—fortunately, for it meant there was little likelihood of his meeting Hugh on the premises—he pressed the bell, and found the SIS Head of Station awaiting him, with his communications officer.

"Hello, Ryle," said the Head of Station. "Good to see you again, though we wish you hadn't chosen a weekend."

"I apologize, but it's rather important."

"So I assumed. I also assumed you wouldn't tell me what it was about."

"You were right, I'm afraid."

"Okay, okay. I understand." In spite of the banter, there was no lack of efficiency. Ryle had already drafted his long cable to General Bannol. The communications officer let him key it into the cipher machine himself. He received an acknowledgement, and was told to await a reply.

Ryle waited, drinking more coffee and chatting. He hoped that his instructions would not prevent him from visiting Segovia. The message, when it arrived and he had snatched it from the teleprinter, was brief and uninformative. It merely told Ryle to get in touch with his contact again, express interest and ask for further details; he was not to make any commitments. In fact, get everything he could and give nothing, he thought cynically, knowing that De Solina would have other ideas.

He decided to leave the Spaniard until the evening. There was no point in appearing over-eager, and who knew what he might learn in Segovia. He thanked the communications officer, and started back to the Hotel de Claudio to collect his car. Once again he walked fast. He had hoped to leave Madrid earlier and arrive well before De Costa's ancient newspaperman had sampled his first drink of the day, so that they might talk while the old man's mind was still clear. This now seemed unlikely.

As De Costa had said, it was only eighty kilometres to Segovia and, once clear of the centre of Madrid, Ryle made good time along the dual carriageway across the Castilian Plain. But after he turned north at Collado-Villado to cross the Sierra de Guadarrama, he was forced to slow, and it was already noon before Segovia's magnificent skyline came into view. As he drove across the Sierra he thought of the bloody fighting that had taken place in the area all those years ago, and wondered if Peter Mourne had been there—perhaps at the same time as Fernández Grado, the long-retired journalist whom he was about to meet.

As he had expected, when he reached the medieval city and had located Grado's apartment in the Calle San Juan, close to the twelfth-century Romanesque church of San Martín, the old man was not at home. A smiling housekeeper informed him that Señor Grado could be found at his usual bar fifty metres along the street.

"You can't miss him, señor," she said. "You have only to ask anyone there. Everyone knows Señor Grado."

This proved to be true. In fact, when Ryle inquired of the man behind the bar counter, it was Grado himself, standing beside him and just finishing a tall glass of *cerveza,* light Spanish beer, who answered.

"Buenos días, señor. Me llamo Fernández Grado." He broke into slow and accented English. "You—you must be Señor Ryle. My young friend, Juan De Costa, told me to expect your visit."

Ryle replied in Spanish, and they shook hands. Grado gave Ryle a look of keen interest from brown eyes the colour of horse chestnuts. He was short and fat, with a beer belly and a great deal of grey hair, but there was little sign of age in his demeanour. Ryle was relieved as the Spaniard gave him a twinkling smile and glanced suggestively at the empty glass that stood before him on the bar.

Ryle took the hint, then followed the old man to a wooden bench against a wall, where another man, who might have been Grado's twin, sat waiting. Grado introduced him as his brother, Miguel. Ryle bought him a drink, too.

"¡Salud!" They exchanged compliments, and chatted for some time, as Ryle answered casual questions about himself and his impressions of Spain. Ryle was wondering how to introduce the subject of the Civil War, when Miguel Grado suddenly stood up and said that his wife would be waiting for him. He departed after leisurely farewells.

Left alone on the bench, Grado regarded Ryle quizzically. "You wish to know about our war, señor?" he said. "It is a long, sad story—much too long to tell in half an hour. What part are you especially interested in?" He put down his empty glass on the floor beside him.

"Let me refill that before I answer you, Señor Grado," said Ryle.

By now the bar was fairly full. There was much shaking of hands as new arrivals came in. Clearly this was a place for habitués, and several curious glances were cast at Ryle, the stranger, as he went up to the bar, but the fact that he was with Fernández Grado seemed to make him acceptable. A space was at once cleared for him, and he was served before his turn.

Returning with the glasses, he said, "You are well known here, señor. Have you lived in Castile all your life?"

"No. I was born right here in Segovia, and I worked in Madrid before our war. When that was over I was a foreign correspondent during the big war of 1939. Afterwards I went to America for some years, but in the end I was happy to come home. I realized that, as dictators went, Generalissimo Franco was not too bad. Under his rule, life was reasonable—even bearable—as long as one kept one's nose clean."

"Your sympathies had been with the Republicans during your own war?"

"If you had seen what the Huns' Condor Legion did to Guernica you wouldn't ask me that, señor. Oh, there were atrocities on both sides, of course—there always are in civil wars—but that sort of bombing was new in those days."

The old man seemed glad to talk, and Ryle was content to listen. As De Costa had promised, Ryle learnt a lot about the Civil War and the strength of feeling it had engendered among the Spanish people. But issues such as these were not really his concern. He realized that he would have to ask more direct questions if he were to obtain any relevant and worthwhile information.

To lead the conversation in the right direction, he remarked, "A fair number of Englishmen came to Spain to fight for the Republicans, didn't they?"

"*Sí.* It was seen as a great cause, and many died for it." Grado was suddenly sad. "On the other hand, there were some who supported Franco."

"Did you ever come across an English journalist, very young—in fact, straight from school—called Peter Mourne?"

Ryle had done his best to sound casual, but there was no way to avoid mentioning Mourne. Waiting for the reply, he almost held his breath. Grado had mentioned some names and dates, and recalled the details of many incidents. There seemed to be nothing wrong with his memory, but at his age it was probably not entirely dependable. Grado frowned, but almost at once his face cleared and he answered without hesitation.

"I do remember him, yes. And the other boy. What was his name? Steve. Steve—Midvale? Midhurst? Something like that."

"They were friends, these two?" Grado's answer had been unexpected.

"*¡Amigos? ¡No! ¡No!* On the contrary. They hated each other's guts—and all because of a girl!" Grado laughed. "Who would have guessed the cold English could be so passionate?"

Carmela, Ryle thought. If he could trace this other man—this Steve—he might learn all he needed to know about Carmela and Peter Mourne. In the meantime, he asked, "Any idea what happened?"

"None whatsoever," said Grado. Then he corrected himself. "That is, I did hear that Steve had been badly wounded and had died of his wounds. This may or may not have been true. You must appreciate, señor, that I am in my eightieth year. If I were to meet any of these people now the age difference would not matter, but then I was the wise, experienced man and—to me at any rate—they were just kids. There were many like them. It was only the fight that made me remember them so well."

"They fought—over the girl?"

"*Sí*. Carmela. That is what she was called. I've forgotten her last name. I didn't see the actual fight, but she came dashing into the bar where we were billeted, holding something. Incredible as it may seem, what she was holding was Peter's finger. Steve—"

"What?" Ryle almost shouted the word, failing to hide his surprise and shock.

"*¡Sí! ¡Sí!* I remember it clearly. Steve had chopped it off!" The old man grinned, enjoying his reminiscences and the obvious bewilderment they were causing. "Carmela said it was an accident, and Steve pretended to be contrite, but I had my doubts. At any rate, the mutilation ended the fight, as you can imagine, though I doubt if Steve and Peter ever grew to love each other!"

"Señor—" Ryle had no desire to contradict the old man, but the story was patently untrue, or at least muddled. "Señor, I'm a little confused. You see, I've met Peter Mourne, Viscount Mourne, the former British Foreign Secretary, and I assure you he is *not* missing a finger."

"But—but— You misunderstand, Señor Ryle. As I said I remember the occasion clearly. Who would not—even in the middle of the war? But I am talking about a young and inexperienced journalist, not your well-known politician. The two men must just happen to have the same name."

"No, Señor Grado, they are the same person. At least, they were. Viscount Mourne has died recently."

Fernández Grado shook his head slowly. "Amazing!" he said. "It never occurred to me. Why should it? By the time I heard of your Mourne yet another war was over, and there was no reason for me to make the connection."

Ryle had recovered from his initial surprise, but was unsure whether or not to place any credence in Grado's story. The man was no peasant who didn't give a damn what went on outside his village; he was intelligent and had been a competent and travelled journalist. But by his own admission he had left Spain after the Civil War and had later spent some time in the United States. It had been a long and troubled gap which, in spite of all the evidence to the contrary, could have affected his memory for details. Or, just conceivably, he might be lying. But why should he do that? Or, again, was it possible that Viscount Mourne had had a false finger, a prosthesis of some kind? But no! Surely his wife and family would have known, and the post-mortem report would have mentioned it.

Grado was speaking again. "Señor Ryle, you say there was nothing wrong with Peter's—Viscount Mourne's—hand? Ah, dear God! I must be getting old. Too many years and too many—" He gestured towards his empty glass.

The old man leant forward and put his hands to his head before he continued. "Señor, I could have sworn to what I told you, though I suppose I must have been wrong. But I can see the girl now. She was wearing a dirty white blouse, but the blood on it was bright. And the finger—it was like a—a penis." He wrinkled up his nose in disgust. "I suppose it must have been Peter who chopped off Steve's finger, and not the other way. I'm sorry, Señor Ryle. Sometimes I expect I get confused."

Suddenly the old man was looking his age and Mark Ryle felt sorry for him. He offered him another drink, but Grado refused and said he must be going home; he no longer had a wife, but his housekeeper—a relation—was a martinet.

Ryle hid his amusement—he had thought her a pleasant, motherly woman—and agreed to walk Grado to his apartment. There were at least a couple of further questions he wanted to ask, but it was obvious that, almost in an instant, the old man had become very tired.

They were at Grado's house when the Spaniard said, "I wish I could be sure of Steve's second name, but I can't."

"It doesn't matter, señor," Ryle lied. "I expect there's someone else I can ask. Someone who was in the bar with you when Carmela burst in with the finger, perhaps?"

But Grado shook his head. "No. The bar was pretty empty then, and the next day the bloody Boche bombed the place. Everyone was killed. It was pure chance that I was out on a story and wasn't there myself."

So much for that, Ryle thought as, having said goodbye and thanked Fernández Grado, he decided to make his way on foot to the Plaza Mayor, the main square of Segovia. He found a café in the bustling Plaza, and a table outside where he could sit, facing the fine seventeenth-century Town

Hall, and watch the Segovians pass by. He hadn't matched Grado beer for beer, but he wasn't hungry. He ordered coffee and satisfied himself with a plate of *tapas,* which made a more than adequate meal.

He was extremely disappointed. He couldn't blame Grado, who was trying to recall events that had taken place over fifty years ago, and much that the old man had revealed had been fascinating. Unfortunately, Ryle decided, it could not be considered altogether reliable evidence; the story of the finger suggested—or proved—that. And the references to this Steve, who had been close to Peter and Carmela, only succeeded in tantalizing. Even if he were still alive—and he would be in his seventies by now—the chances of tracing him without his surname were remote. Of course Carmela Mourne should remember his name, but—

For the second day running Ryle returned to the Hotel de Claudio during siesta and disturbed the dozing *conserje,* who resentfully produced his room key. Half hoping that he would once again find Jeanne in his bed, he went upstairs. But today she was missing, and the room was tidied and impersonal. Ryle threw himself on top of the duvet and reached for the telephone.

He tapped out the number that De Solina had given him, and after a while a woman's voice, heavy with sleep, answered him. He asked to speak to the Spaniard.

"Señor De Solina does not live here," she said.

"One moment!" said Ryle quickly, afraid that she was about to cut him off. He repeated the number and gave his name. "Señor De Solina wrote this number down for me himself and asked me to call him," he said firmly.

"Ah!" This remark was greeted by a rippling laugh. "Of course, of course, Señor Ryle," the voice said. "Here he is."

De Solina came on the line. "Señor Ryle, I'm delighted to hear from you. Your people are interested?"

"Oh yes, señor. At least, they're interested enough to want to know more details. You would be prepared to discuss the matter further?"

"Certainly. But not today—or tomorrow. Today I have no time, and Sundays I reserve for my Church and my family." In the background there was a sound of smothered amusement, instantly hushed, and Ryle had time to grin to himself before De Solina continued, "Monday morning. Ten o'clock at an address I will give you. It is near the University and you will have no trouble finding it. Is that convenient?"

"Yes, that's fine," Ryle agreed.

He had scarcely taken down the address and said goodbye to De Solina when there was a rap at the door. It was the *conserje,* more disgruntled than ever. He was holding out an envelope.

"For you, señor. The man who has just delivered it by hand demanded that it be brought to you immediately."

Ryle expressed his thanks and found a suitable tip, though he guessed the *conserje* had been rewarded in advance. Alone, he regarded the envelope, which was addressed in a hand he did not recognize. He slit it open.

The envelope contained a press pass for a *barrara* seat at the bullfight to be held the next day at the Plaza de Toros in Carabanchel, the smaller of the two bullrings in Madrid, together with an advance programme. There was a note on the programme, in English: "Hope you enjoy the bulls. Hire a cushion. The seats are hard. J. De C."

Why the foreign editor of *El País* should have arranged for him to visit a *corrida* was at once self-evident. De Costa had crossed out the surname of the matador who was due to open the proceedings as a curtain-raiser, and had replaced it with "Drelano." Ryle couldn't hazard a guess as to the significance of this substitution, but he was grateful to De Costa. Sunday promised to be an interesting day.

CHAPTER TWENTY-TWO

The atmosphere in the Plaza de Toros was almost tangible. The excitement of the crowd—and every seat was taken this Sunday afternoon—hit Mark Ryle like a physical blow as he stumbled towards his seat. Voices were loud, laughter shrill, as the *aficionados* anticipated the passion of the *corrida,* in the knowledge that soon, very soon, all emotional restraint would be thrown to the winds and pure exhilaration would take its place. But the crowd knew, too, that the violence on the sand below them would be tempered with discipline and grace as the nearly religious art form proceeded inevitably on its traditional path.

Not quite everyone shared these sentiments, and Ryle was among those who didn't. He had no fervent objection to bullfights for those who appreciated them, but several years ago he had been taken to the Plaza Monumental, the larger and more prestigious bullring at Las Ventas on the other side of Madrid, and had been sickened by the spectacle.

And there were other reasons for his current malaise. He was tired and he was worried. He was tired, because he had had little sleep the night before. He had taken Hugh and Jeanne to an excellent dinner at one of Madrid's most glittering restaurants, and from there they had gone to a flamenco nightclub. He could still hear the throbbing guitars, the stamping heels, and the passionate, wailing singing. And he was worried because he was now certain that, as in Paris, his movements were under observation. He had noticed the two men for the first time at Barajas airport, as he and Jeanne were loading their bags into Hugh's car, and he had seen them twice since, though not together. One had been nearby as he left the British Embassy yesterday morning, and one had sat at a table in a different café in the Plaza Mayor in Segovia. This afternoon he had decided, partly because of probable difficulties with parking, to come to the bullfight on the Metro as far as Vista Allegre and then walk; one of the men had got into the same carriage, and had shadowed him to his destination.

His thoughts were interrupted by his neighbour, who had dropped his spectacle case and was trying to retrieve it from under his seat. Ryle picked it up for him.

"Thanks a lot," the stranger said, with an American drawl.

"Don't mention it."

The American grinned. "Dave Crowe," he said, offering a hand.

"Mark Ryle."

"You new here? You must be a newsman to have a seat in this section, but I've not seen you before. Who do you file for?"

"Me? Oh, I'm freelance—just visiting, and taking the opportunity to get some material for a book. A friend gave me—"

The American turned and regarded Ryle sceptically over the top of his heavy horn-rimmed spectacles. He was about fifty, Ryle judged, with an ugly, intelligent face. "After Hemingway and Condon," he said sadly, "there's precious little left to be written about the *fiesta brava.*"

"No, I suppose not," said Ryle, and after a moment added casually, "but I was told the matador who opens the proceedings, Julio Del Sol, might be worth watching."

"Really?" Crowe was amused. "I guess someone was having you on. He's a nobody, straight from the provinces. He'll probably get a mediocre bull, and won't even be awarded an ear, unless—"

The rest of the American's words were drowned in a great roar of noise as those taking part in the afternoon's *corrida* entered the sanded ring and paraded around it. Soon the ring cleared and the first bull of the afternoon came charging into it to face the first matador. The bull stopped, snuffled, and skittered suspiciously towards the surrounding wooden barrier, pawing the ground. Even to Ryle's inexpert eyes the bull, as the American had suspected, did not appear particularly fierce. The matador—Julio Del Sol, whose real name, Ryle hoped, was Drelano—eyed the animal carefully. He was young and slim, and if he were nervous in front of the demanding and knowledgeable *Madrileños* he didn't show it.

In fact, as far as Ryle could tell, Del Sol worked the bull well, taunting him with the big red and yellow *capote,* so that the animal charged again and again at the cape. Ryle enjoyed these preliminaries but, unlike most of those present, took no pleasure in watching the *picador* in his Sancho Panza costume lancing the bull's shoulder muscles, or the *banderilleros* stabbing long coloured darts into the poor brute.

By the third *tercio,* when the matador returned to run the tiring bull through yet more passes, now using his small dark-red *muleta* cape, the contest was already decided. In spite of the efforts of Del Sol and the vociferous encouragement of the spectators, this particular bull had lost all interest in the proceedings. He stood, apparently aware of and thankful for his approaching death, as the *torero* thrust for the kill.

There was clapping, stamping, a few cries of *¡Olé!* and some boos, but on the whole the crowd was generous. Young Del Sol was awarded an ear.

"Not bad!" Crowe shouted to Ryle. "If the little ray of sunshine doesn't get himself killed he may turn into a fine bullfighter one of these days."

Ryle nodded, accepting the judgement. "I'll tell him what you say. I'm going to interview him now."

The American raised an eyebrow, but made no comment. "Nice to have met you," he said. "Go down the steps and through there." He pointed. "Wave your press pass and I guess someone'll take you to him."

"Thanks."

Ryle was indeed grateful. It was not the way he would have thought of going, but the advice was sensible. Although he was accosted immediately, the press pass proved an open sesame, and once he had explained his ostensible mission he was escorted along an echoing concrete corridor to the matador's dressing-room, where, with a brief apology, he was asked to wait outside. He loitered in the passage, unable to hear the muted conversation within the room. Then the door was flung open.

"Don Julio will see you now," he was informed, somewhat pompously.

At close quarters Julio Del Sol was less impressive than he had seemed while he was flirting his cape in the bullring. He was excessively thin. His hair, presumably due to his recent exertions, was dark with sweat. His complexion was sallow and he looked as if he could do with a fresh shave. Nevertheless, it was with an air of condescension—almost arrogance— that he offered Ryle his hand and indicated a chair.

"What paper do you represent, señor?" he asked after he had accepted Ryle's congratulations on his performance.

"I am from London. My articles are syndicated in various magazines," Ryle lied glibly. "Don Julio, I need not tell you how interested our readers would be to learn more about you, to hear of your early life, your family, why you decided to fight the bulls." He wondered how much more flattery the young man would take.

Ryle need not have worried. "Yes, I understand," replied Del Sol. "I have had other articles written concerning me," he added with satisfaction, "but always for a suitable fee."

"Of course. That must be arranged between us." Ryle attempted to show respect by giving a small bow of his head. He was beginning to dislike Del Sol. "Perhaps we might begin with where you were born, señor." He produced a notebook and pen from his pocket.

"In Chinchón, which is an old medieval town. In reality, it is not far from Madrid, but in most ways it could be a million kilometres away. My family has lived there for many, many years . . ."

Ryle let the man talk, and liked him less as he spoke disparagingly of his birthplace and his relations, who seemed to work in the clay quarries near Chinchón, or in the aniseed liqueur business. It was clear that Madrid had always been Del Sol's Mecca, and at last he had achieved it—and the place in it he prized above all others, the bullring.

"I fought my first bull in the plaza at Chinchón—there is no proper Plaza de Toros there, and fights take place in the town square. But here I am now," he said with pride. Then suddenly he added with surprising modesty, "But I'm still far from being the main attraction in the great Plaza Monumental de las Ventas."

Ryle grinned his sympathy. "I'm told on good authority that you will reach your goal," he said. "Let us hope the name of Del Sol will become a part of the history of the *corrida*. Of course, that is how you are known professionally. What is your family name?"

"Drelano, but it is of no importance." Del Sol was scornful.

"Drelano? How strange! Did you see that advertisement in *El País,* señor?"

"Yes, I did, and I told my brother and my mother that it was of no consequence to us, so there was no point in replying. None of us had ever heard of a Carmela Isabella in our family. If there ever were one, it must have been many years ago."

"A coincidence, obviously," Ryle said. He made a dismissive gesture, as if the mention of Drelano had been unimportant, and returned to questions about Del Sol's career and ambitions. For five minutes more he listened, putting the occasional query and taking notes. Then, having agreed upon the matter of payment, he brought the interview to an end. He thanked Del Sol, wished him luck, and said goodbye.

On the surface, he reflected, there was little possibility of any connection between Julio Del Sol and Carmela Mourne. Nevertheless, Carmela had arrived in France a refugee, without papers of any kind, and it was her marriage to Peter Mourne that had given her status and enabled her to enter the United Kingdom as a British citizen. Her claim to have been born in Madrid and to have lost all her family and possessions during the Civil War was based on her word alone. So was the name Drelano. But Chinchón was the only lead Ryle had, and he would have to follow it, if only because of the minute possibility that it might lead to some understanding of the "secret" that old Marie-Antoinette Corbet had overheard Peter and Carmela mention when they were first in the De Chantals' house in Paris. To Chinchón, therefore, he would go in the morning, unless the result of his meeting with Pedro De Solina forced him to change his plans.

The Metro journey back to the centre of the city was hot and uncomfortable, and Mark Ryle was glad to reach the shelter of the Hotel de Claudio. On the whole, his afternoon had been less than enjoyable, but he was grateful to De Costa for having arranged it. He reminded himself to send a thank-you gift—a bottle of Scotch, perhaps—to the offices of *El País* before he left Madrid. And, apart from what he might or might not have learnt from young Drelano, he had another satisfaction, albeit minor; inadvertently, because he hadn't bothered, he seemed to have succeeded in losing the men who had been tailing him.

He had no doubt they would reappear, but he had arranged to spend the evening with Hugh and Jeanne in the harmless pursuit of a good dinner and a further sampling of Madrid's nightlife. His watchers were welcome to follow if they wished. But tomorrow, he felt, would be different. He had no wish for company when he met De Solina or visited Chinchón.

Lying on his bed, he considered the problem. The morning, he concluded, would present few difficulties. The address De Solina had given him was, as the Spaniard had said, near the Ciudad Universitaria. It was not De Solina's home which, Ryle had learnt from the Madrid telephone directory, was in the elegant area near the *Cortes*—the Spanish Parliament. From the voice of the woman who had answered the phone and the background noises he had heard, Ryle guessed the number he had been given was that of De Solina's mistress, and she might not appreciate being under observation. But it should be simple enough to lose the men by taking a taxi to one of the big department stores—El Corte Inglés or the Galerías Preciados, perhaps—and dodging out of another door to find a new cab.

What happened later would depend on his talk with De Solina, but Ryle was fairly sure that he would have to go to the Embassy to send another cable to London, and he might have to wait for a reply. It was almost certain that Chinchón would have to be left to the afternoon, and he would need his car—or preferably *a* car, one that wasn't instantly recognizable by the opposition. If only Maggie had been with him—

There was a tap on the communicating door, and "Jeanne!" he exclaimed as she came in.

"You sound surprised, Mark. Were you expecting someone else?"

"On the contrary. I was thinking about you," he lied. Why not Jeanne? he thought. A sightseeing trip to Chinchón? He could say there was something wrong with the car he had rented, and ask her to hire another one during the morning and meet him somewhere for lunch. With a minimal pause he continued, "I was wondering if you'd like to come on a trip with me tomorrow afternoon. I assume Hugh will be hard at work, and—"

"It's an offer I can't refuse," Jeanne said, laughing.

CHAPTER TWENTY-THREE

It was a modern block of apartments and, unusually for Madrid, it was rectangular and uninteresting from the outside, though it overlooked a pleasant expanse of parkland. There was no *conserje,* but instead an intercom system with no names against the numbers of the flats. When Mark Ryle had pressed the number he had been given as part of the address, a voice answered and he was able to identify himself and gain admittance to an inner hall.

Pedro De Solina was waiting for him when eventually Ryle emerged from the lift on the third floor. There was no sign of the woman who had spoken to him on the telephone on Saturday. But, having shaken hands and preceded De Solina into the salon, he was immediately aware that the apartment was not a male preserve. Only an exceptional man would have scattered such a profusion of multi-coloured cushions around, or bothered with so many flowers and plants, or managed to create the general impres-

sion of carefree comfort that pervaded the place. There was also a lingering scent of some perfume that Ryle couldn't identify.

"May I offer you coffee?" De Solina asked. "It's a little early for anything
else—even in Spain."

"Thank you. I'd like coffee."

Ryle accepted more out of curiosity to see who would serve the coffee,
rather than from any desire to drink it. But he was disappointed. De
Solina, waving him to a chair, disappeared towards what was presumably
the kitchen. Minutes later he reappeared, carrying a tray covered with an
embroidered linen cloth. Together with a silver coffee pot and two cups, it
held a plate of extremely small and elegant pastries.

"I prepared it in advance," De Solina said. Then he added, "You
wouldn't have expected me to be so domesticated, would you, señor?" His
expression was bland.

Ryle shrugged. "You are a married man, señor," he said, as if this
remark constituted an answer to De Solina's question.

"¡Sí!" De Solina bit off the monosyllable.

Ryle had regretted his remark almost as he made it, but it was too late to
take back his words. De Solina had lied about the coffee. He knew that,
and De Solina knew that he knew it. De Solina's question had been
intended as an opening gambit, to test his mettle, as it were, or perhaps to
measure the extent of understanding that might come to exist between
them. In return, Ryle realized that he had, in De Solina's eyes, shown
himself to be gauche, unsophisticated, and very British. This, Ryle realized, was no way in which to commence delicate negotiations with a
subtle Spaniard whose insight and intelligence must not be underrated.

Ryle took the cup of coffee that was being offered to him, and quickly
chose a small cake. *"Gracias, señor,"* he said, and then he thought it best
immediately to tackle the subject of his visit, before De Solina had an
opportunity to ask further equivocal questions. "My principals were very
interested in the proposition you asked me to put to them," he said
quickly. "But, as I'm sure you expected, they would like more details."

De Solina took his own coffee cup, and himself became business-like.
"Could you be more precise, señor?" he inquired.

"I was hoping that *you* would be more precise, señor."

De Solina, his good temper seemingly restored, laughed aloud. "We
could go on like this for the rest of the morning," he said. "Let's call a
truce, Señor Ryle. As I believe that I—or rather those for whom I speak on
this occasion—are in the stronger bargaining position, I am prepared to
begin. However," he continued without a pause, "first, tell me something.

Did you not enjoy the *corrida* yesterday? You left after the preliminary bull."

Ryle bit the tip of his tongue to help him control his temper. In this battle of wits, De Solina had worsted him again—and with great ease. He felt like an amateur playing against a professional, like a young inexperienced bull against a seasoned and veteran matador. What was more, he knew that this was exactly how the Spaniard wanted him to feel. But what really angered him was the unnecessary trouble he had taken earlier that morning not to lead his watchers to his present meeting place with De Solina.

Conscious that he had already let the silence last too long, he did his best to appear blasé, and said casually, "It was an experience, señor—an experience I have had before. It's not one I would go out of my way to repeat. I prefer golf."

Again De Solina laughed aloud. "Ah, you play golf, do you, Señor Ryle? So do I, when I can find the time. Perhaps we could manage a round when I come to England."

"You intend to visit the UK, señor?" Ryle asked innocently.

De Solina hesitated before replying. "I assume so. If our negotiations proceed smoothly, as I sincerely hope they will—for everyone's sake." The Spaniard stopped abruptly, then went on again. "Now, let's get down to business. Offer and counter-offer—that's what we're about, is it not? And we are just at the beginning."

"You volunteered to commence, Señor De Solina," Ryle reminded him. "And so I shall."

De Solina gestured towards the coffee pot and proffered the plate of little cakes. When Ryle shook his head he helped himself. Ryle waited for the Spaniard to lead the conversation into another apparently irrelevant cul-de-sac, but found he had misjudged his opponent.

"Señor Ryle," said De Solina, leaning forward as if to emphasize the momentous nature of his words. "When we spoke before, you made two points. Your principals, you told me, would need assurances that the man who would admit to having made these allegations against Viscount Mourne—false allegations, as he would insist—should be a credible character himself, and show himself to have a credible motive for his actions."

"Yes," Ryle agreed. "Those points are quite obvious. Otherwise the entire operation would be useless—from the point of view of *my* principals."

"Of course. Well, I am not at present at liberty to give you the name of the man in question, but I am authorized to tell you that he would be a Soviet diplomat *en poste* in London. He's not one of the very senior members of the staff, but he is of middle rank, and you can take my word for it that his statements would be credible and convincing."

"And this—this individual has volunteered for the job?" Ryle made no attempt to hide his scepticism.

De Solina smiled briefly. "Yes—and no. The proposition has been put to him, and he has accepted. Shall we say that, given a choice, he preferred it to the alternative."

Ryle didn't ask what the alternative had been. "You said this—er—volunteer was a diplomat. What about immunity?"

"Yes. He'll claim immunity, if any attempt is made to bring charges against him—for slander, say, or any one of a number of indictments. That will be part of the deal, señor. There should be no question of his immunity being challenged. And when he has made a public declaration of his guilt, he will be flown back to the USSR, and the Soviet Government will offer formal apologies."

"Interesting," said Ryle, wondering what would happen to the unfortunate diplomat on his return to Moscow. "I would imagine that something on those lines would be acceptable, but only if he could be shown to have a valid private motive. Otherwise, many people—and commentators—in England might argue that the whole thing was a ploy organized by Moscow to protect the posthumous reputation of a man who had been one of theirs all along."

"Quite. This man was chosen, señor, because he has a valid motive or, to be more precise, can appear to have one. You see, although he has a wife and children, he is homosexual."

Ryle stared at the Spaniard. He understood now why the wretched diplomat could be persuaded to perjure himself. Homosexuality, even between consenting adults and however widely practised in reality, was still officially considered monstrous and illegal in the Soviet Union. The man would be severely punished, especially if he had become involved with a foreigner. But did he have to return home? If he had a "friend" in London, couldn't he—? And, in any event, how the hell could any of this provide any kind of motive for his operations against Peter Mourne?

As these thoughts sped through Ryle's mind, he said coldly, "I appreciate this man's position, but I fail to understand its relevance. My principals will have no wish to exchange one scandal for another—or perhaps to add one to another. There has never been the slightest suggestion that Mourne was inclined to homosexuality. Indeed, he seems to have a singularly unblemished reputation in sexual matters."

"Exactly. I fully understand your objection. But suppose that—let's call him Ivan, which is not his name—suppose that Ivan had made advances to Mourne—advances which had been repulsed with scorn and derision. Would it not be in the nature of such a character to seek a form of revenge? And, Señor Ryle, what better revenge could he plan on an eminent politician, an elder statesman, than to attempt to ruin his reputation?"

It's a bit far-fetched—and disgusting—but it might work, Ryle thought with grudging admiration. It just might work. He could imagine the vituperative outcry in the media against the despicable Ivan, the reinstatement of Viscount Mourne with a shiny new halo, the denials that the ludicrous accusations against him had been believed for thirty seconds.

But how far could the Soviet Union—presumably in the shape of the KGB—be trusted? They were good at rewriting history when such a process suited them, but they could prove equally good at "un-rewriting" it, as it were. Having secured Dart's release, what was to prevent them announcing that their "Ivan" was totally innocent, and that Mourne had been—

Ryle gave up this fruitless speculation for the moment. "This Ivan," he said, as if his thoughts had all along been concentrated on the Soviet diplomat and his role. "A great deal would depend on him. Supposing he were to break down under interrogation, or seize the opportunity to ask for asylum?"

"That possibility has been considered. He is at present under house arrest in his Embassy. His wife and two children—a son and a daughter —have already returned to Moscow." De Solina smiled sadly. "He is said to be devoted to his offspring, if not to his wife. An emotion which I believe many married men share."

"I wouldn't know, señor. I'm not married."

"A pleasure to come, no doubt—perhaps when the most charming Señorita Mourne makes up her mind."

At that moment Ryle would happily have hit the Spaniard, who seemed to have an uncanny ability to goad him—just as the *banderilleros* goad the bull, Ryle couldn't help thinking. But Ryle's real anger was reserved for General Sir Walter Bannol, who, knowing of his relationship with Jeanne, had deliberately involved him in the affair of Peter Mourne. And once again he realized that De Solina had shown himself to be in charge of the situation, directing the conversation as it suited him.

"Do you have any more questions, Señor Ryle?" De Solina didn't wait for a response. "Because if not, perhaps we might consider the case of Sir Percival Dart."

"I'll certainly listen to anything you have to say, señor, but I have no authority at present to make any commitment concerning him." Ryle was definite. "My principals have merely decided to commence preliminary negotiations, as I'm sure you realize—as I told you myself, in fact."

"Oh yes, but I'm quite sure our negotiations will continue to a happy conclusion," De Solina said confidently. "In which case the order of events will be of prime importance. Obviously no connection must be made between Dart's departure and the establishment of Mourne's innocence. As I said, I hope to be in London myself to assist with such matters. However, a new factor has arisen. Dart has been taken ill."

This was news to Ryle, but he didn't doubt its accuracy. A lie would have no purpose. Silently he cursed Maggie for not having let him know. Ignorance could be a liability, and when it wasn't necessary it was unforgivable.

"You see that as relevant, señor?" he said.

"It introduces a time element. At present Dart is under observation, but if he does have to have his gall bladder removed, which seems likely, he will be in hospital for some days at least, and it would be simpler to spirit him away from there than from the prison proper—a fact your principals will appreciate."

"I'll inform them," Ryle said drily, "and make inquiries about the timing of any surgery." He thought that Dart's illness, if genuine, was singularly opportune.

The interview—or encounter, if that were a more appropriate term—with De Solina had taken longer than Ryle had expected, and he then had to call at the Embassy and spend further time drafting a lengthy telegram to Bannol and waiting for a reply. The reply, when it came, merely ordered him to take no action until he received further instructions. As a result of all this, he was late meeting Jeanne, and was conscious that he had taken few precautions against being followed.

"I've brought some food and wine," Jeanne said. "I thought we might have a picnic *en route,* or perhaps we could find a spot when we get to Chinchón."

"Good idea," Ryle said, doubtfully regarding the car to which Jeanne was leading him.

"What's the matter?" she asked sharply. "I did what you told me, Mark. I rented another car."

"Yes. It's fine," he said, unable to tell her that, apart from the licence number, it was identical to the one his followers had already spotted, and she need hardly have bothered. "And the picnic's a great idea. I don't like two huge meals a day. Bad for the waistline."

They chatted casually and amicably. Jeanne drove, and at first Mark tried to watch surreptitiously for any vehicle that might conceivably be tailing them. But on the main highway south from Madrid it was impossible to be certain, and he abandoned the attempt, until after some thirty kilometres they turned eastwards on a secondary road to Chinchón. Then, breasting a hill, Jeanne saw ahead what promised to be an ideal place to draw off the road and eat. Traffic passed, but no one showed any interest in them, and they shared a pleasant, relaxed meal.

As they were tidying up the remains of their picnic, Jeanne said suddenly, "Why are we going to this place, Mark? I don't believe it's to buy their liqueur—I'm not fond of aniseed—or their garlic, and I really don't want a huge earthenware jar."

Mark laughed. "You've been reading those guide books again," he said. "Didn't they tell you what an attractive small town Chinchón is? I'm sure they used some such phrase as 'redolent of old Spain and a must for all visitors to Castile'."

"Sure. But they didn't tell me why you'd developed a sudden yen to visit it," Jeanne said firmly.

"To visit the Drelanos."

"What!"

Slightly twisting the truth, Mark told her that he had learnt by chance at the bullfight the previous day that the real name of the first *torero*, Del Sol, was in fact Drelano, and that his family came from Chinchón. He stressed the fact that there might be no connection with Carmela Mourne, but Jeanne was excited.

"What fun!" she said. "I do hope they turn out to be relatives, though Carmela might not be so keen on having them traced. What do we do? Have you an address for them?"

"No, but it's only a little place. I'll ask at a bar or the *Guardia* station. There's sure to be one, however small. It shouldn't be a problem."

Nor was it. In the event it proved perfectly simple to locate the Drelano family. They were not numerous, but they were well known, mainly because of their relationship with the great matador, of which the whole town seemed to be aware. Ryle learnt that Del Sol's parents, two younger brothers, a sister, and a widowed aunt all lived in a white stucco house overlooking the wooden arcaded central Plaza—the town square where Del Sol had fought his first bulls.

Once they had found her, they discovered that Del Sol's mother, though middle-aged and a typical Castilian peasant, had her wits about her. At first she appeared uneasy about answering questions concerning her family but, assured that no harm could come of it, she still vigorously denied that they were related to anyone called Carmela Isabella. They had been

shown the advertisement in *El País,* and had discussed it at length, wondering if perhaps money was involved, but had decided it would be a
waste of time to reply as the woman mentioned was clearly nothing to do
with them.

"But who is she—this Carmela Drelano, señor? Why is she important
to you?" Señora Drelano inquired at last.

It was a question Ryle had been expecting. "She is an old lady in her
seventies," he said. "She is a widow now, living in England. She left Spain
many years ago, and married an Englishman—a relation of Señorita
Mourne here." He gestured towards Jeanne, who, unable to follow the
flow of Spanish, smiled vaguely. "As we were in Madrid we thought we
might take the opportunity to trace some of the family with whom she has
lost touch."

Señora Drelano was shaking her head. "I see," she said. "And I'm
sorry," she said. "Family connections are important to Spaniards." Then
suddenly she brightened. "An old lady, you say. My parents' generation? I
wonder—"

"You have thought of something, señora?"

"My husband had an uncle of that kind of age but— During the Civil
War he was buried under the rubble when Madrid was bombed, and it
affected his poor mind. He is—" She tapped her temple. "But not all of
the time, you understand, señor, though it's not possible to be sure when
he is with you or when he is far away. Perhaps it would have been better if
he had been killed like so many others. War is a terrible thing," she ended
sadly.

"No luck, I gather?" said Jeanne as they left the house and started to walk
around the Plaza. "I couldn't understand a quarter of what she was saying,
but I guessed some of it from her expressions."

"No luck," Mark agreed. "They'd discussed the advertisement in *El País*
and agreed that none of them had ever heard of a Carmela Isabella. I
suppose it's not really surprising. It's over fifty years since Carmela left
Madrid, and anyone who might have known her seems to have been killed
in the war, or died since—except for some batty uncle of theirs, apparently. I don't think anyone's asked him anything, so far."

"Couldn't we, then? Or is he really batty—in an asylum?"

"No. He lives in Chinchón—quite near here. I have the address. But
don't expect too much, Jeanne."

Although it was true that Miguel Drelano didn't live far from the main
Plaza of Chinchón, they had some difficulty finding his narrow cobbled
lane. And when they found the small dark house, it proved impossible to

get at the door. An old man and a donkey, laden with bits of furniture, completely blocked the entrance. The old man grinned at them, showing a mouth full of discoloured teeth, but made no effort to move.

"Oiga, por favor, señor," Mark Ryle said. "Excuse me, but can you tell me if Señor Drelano lives here?"

"Miguel Drelano. *Me—me llamo Miguel Drelano,"* said the old man. *"Sí.* I live here. It's my friend who's moving. I'm helping him. Have you any sugar for the donkey? He likes sugar."

Mark translated, and he and Jeanne exchanged glances. It was clear why the Drelano family hadn't bothered to ask Miguel about Carmela. The old man's mind was obviously clouded.

"We're here now, Mark," Jeanne murmured. "We've nothing to lose. Ask him."

"Okay. Señor," Mark addressed Miguel, "do you remember many years ago a young girl called Carmela Drelano?"

The reply was startling. Miguel stopped pulling gently at the donkey's ears and gave his full attention to the visitors. "Of course," he said at once. "She was my sister, God rest her soul." He crossed himself slowly. "She was a bad girl. She deserted her family and her Church, and went away with her English lover—one of her lovers. She was a bad girl," he repeated. "When I was small I used to follow her sometimes and watch her at it."

"Señor, do you remember the name of the lover she went away with?" Ryle paused, thinking of Fernández Grado, the old journalist in Segovia, and the name he had mentioned. "Was he called Steve?"

"Steve. *¡Sí!* That was his name—Steve. She really loved him, that one, I think. Ah well!" Drelano returned to pulling the donkey's ears. "It was a long time ago. Perhaps she repented, like our cousin, the priest. He loved her too. I saw them together."

Miguel Drelano stopped speaking. He smiled at the donkey, seemingly lost in thought and memories. Jeanne, who had understood little that had been said, pulled impatiently at Mark's sleeve.

He shrugged away her hand. Instead he asked urgently, "Señor, what was Steve's second name?"

"Are you sure you've no sugar for the donkey?" Drelano said.

"Who's Steve?" Jeanne wanted to know.

"Supposedly one of Carmela's ex-boyfriends," said Mark in English. It was useless, he thought—and infuriating. They had got so far and no further. Miguel's mind was weak. He couldn't concentrate. He couldn't be considered reliable.

"You should be kind to dumb animals," Drelano said. "That's why I liked Padre Francisco. He wasn't Padre Francisco then, of course, when he was sniffing after Carmela. But then one shouldn't speak ill of the dead, should one?"

"Padre Francisco is dead?"

"*¡No! ¡No!* I told you, señor." Drelano was irritated. "He is a priest in Aranjuez. Priests never retire. It's my sister, Carmela, who's dead. That's the donkey's name, too, you know—Carmela. But she's alive. Aren't you, my love?" He kissed the beast on its nose.

"The poor old dear really is crazy, isn't he?" Jeanne said after Mark had explained the situation to her on the way back to their car, though without mentioning the priest in Aranjuez. He knew that tomorrow he would have to come south again to talk to this Padre Francisco, but he suspected that such a mission would be simpler without Jeanne's company.

"I'm afraid so," Mark agreed. "But he seems to be reasonably happy."

"It's hard to think of him as Viscountess Mourne's brother." Jeanne was thoughtful. "Or, for that matter, to imagine Carmela causing scandal to her family with a whole string of lovers."

"You just can't depend on what the old man says, Jeanne. It was a long time ago, as he said, and he's pretty confused about names. For one thing, I don't believe that miserable donkey is called Carmela."

Jeanne laughed. "Where to now, Mark?" she queried as they reached the car. "Back to Madrid and a—siesta?"

"Why not?" said Mark at once.

CHAPTER TWENTY-FOUR

The following morning Mark Ryle was again driving south from Madrid, this time alone. Hugh Mourne had taken the day off, and was escorting Jeanne—a great admirer of the paintings of El Greco—to Toledo. They had suggested that Mark should accompany them, but he had pleaded another commitment and, as soon as they had left, he had set out for Aranjuez.

He found somewhere to park—no easy matter in this crowded town, considerably larger than Chinchón—and walked into the huge rectangular main Plaza. The best place to start his search for Padre Francisco, cousin of Miguel Drelano and Carmela Mourne, seemed to be a church, and the Iglesia de San Antonio dominated the south side of the Plaza.

Ryle walked along the busy, jostling arcade to the porticoed entrance, and pushed open one of the heavy doors of San Antonio, to be greeted by the musty smell of old incense. He paused, letting his eyes adjust to the gloom of the interior, lit only by the flickering rows of candles in front of a variety of highly coloured statues and by the sunlight that managed to shine through the dusty stained-glass windows and create bejewelled patterns on the altar.

There were only a few people in the church. Two or three passed him on their way out, and he got the impression that a mass had recently ended. A woman left a confessional on his right, and shortly afterwards a priest emerged. He was an old man with grey hair on a head that looked too heavy for his slight body, but he walked swiftly. Ryle had to hurry after him.

"Padre!"

"Yes, my son. Can I help you?"

"I hope so, Padre," Ryle said. "I am trying to trace a priest who, I'm told, now lives in Aranjuez. All I know about him is that he's called Padre Francisco, and his family name is Drelano. It may sound improbable, but I am most anxious to speak to him."

"*¿Porqué?*"

The terse response startled Ryle, who had not expected such a direct question. He gave no direct reply, but said, "Do you know of such a priest, Padre?"

"*Sí.* You might say I know him well—or at least that I've known him for a great many years." The priest smiled broadly. "I am Francisco Drelano, señor." He stared at Ryle before adding, "And now I will repeat my question. Why are you anxious to speak to me in particular, rather than to any priest?"

"It's a personal matter, Padre—about your cousin. She was Carmela Drelano. She married an Englishman called Peter Mourne, who has recently died. You remember her?"

The priest was shaking his head in disbelief. "How absolutely extraordinary! I nearly asked if you were sure of your facts, but I presume you are. You are English too, are you not?"

"Yes. My name is Mark Ryle." He spelt his surname.

"And I am Padre Francisco, as I've told you, Señor Ryle." He offered his hand. "Let us go and sit in the Chapel of Our Lady. No one will disturb us there. I can give you fifteen, perhaps twenty minutes. Then I must get ready to say my Mass."

The priest led the way to a side chapel where, as in the church proper, the seating consisted of separate chairs with seats of woven straw. He pulled two of these close together, so that he and Ryle sat more or less opposite each other and it was easy for them to converse quietly.

"Tell me about Carmela," said Padre Francisco. "I haven't seen her for years and years, more than half a century. In fact, I thought she must be dead by now, though I had no reason for this belief since she was younger than I am." He shrugged. "But she disappeared, like so many others, during our Civil War. I heard she had gone to France."

"She did go to France, to Paris, Padre—and then to England."

The priest was shaking his head again. "What surprises me most is that she should have married Peter Mourne."

"Padre, this is important. Obviously you knew Peter Mourne. Why should the marriage surprise you?"

"Because—because she was not in the least in love with Peter, señor. Oh, he was in love with her—desperately in love, as I was myself at that time." He smiled wryly. "I was not a priest then, you understand. But she had no more thought of marrying me than—than Peter Mourne."

"Padre, you have to believe me. She did marry Peter Mourne, in France in 1939," Ryle said earnestly. "Perhaps it was a marriage of convenience, so that she could get a British passport—but they remained a devoted couple until his death this year."

"*Lo siento,* Señor Ryle. I'm sorry. I'm not doubting you, but it remains a surprise. It's hard to explain. You see—Peter was a nice boy, a pleasant English schoolboy, with rigid ideas. He claimed to be a journalist, a free-lance, and he got around. He was accepted. He always had plenty of money, which was useful because most of us had none. So we put up with him when he tried to convert us to his right-wing beliefs. And, I'm ashamed to say, we laughed at him behind his back.

"Don't misunderstand me, señor," the priest continued. "You have heard of the International Brigade, of course. There were many foreigners who came to Spain to fight for their beliefs—as I myself was doing in my homeland, before the Republicans also sickened me. They saw the battle against Fascism as a cause worth dying for. No one laughed at them. They were respected, honoured. But—poor Peter!" Father Francisco ceased speaking, seemingly unwilling to explain his last comment.

"What would you say was Carmela's attitude to Peter then, Padre?" Ryle asked, in an effort to persuade the priest to go on with his reminiscences.

"She tolerated him, but she loved neither him nor his politics. I have heard her say he was 'a stuffed shirt with empty trousers.' I suspect that

whatever favours she granted him were to make her other admirers jealous
—especially Steve."

"Steve?" Ryle queried at once, his interest now fully aroused.

"Steve Midvale," Padre Francisco said, and smiled reflectively. "Is it not
strange, señor? Those two, Steve and Peter, were fellow-countrymen of
about the same age, and indeed so similar in appearance that they were
sometimes taken for brothers, but yet they couldn't have been more different in character. Steve—he was a man, strong, forceful, ardent. Peter was a
boy, and in many ways a pathetic figure. Now, if you'd told me that
Carmela had married Steve, I wouldn't have been in the least surprised.
He was always her favourite."

"Do you know what happened to this Steve, Padre?"

"No." The priest shook his head. "I did hear that he had been very
badly wounded. Someone told me that he had died, but I cannot vouch for
that." Padre Francisco glanced at his watch. "Señor Ryle, I've not much
more time to spare."

"I'm researching the life of Viscount Mourne, Padre, and naturally his
wife is of interest to—"

"Viscount Mourne? The politician? The man who's suspected of treason
in England? I read the papers, Señor Ryle. But what has Peter got to do
with him? Señor Ryle, are you suggesting that the Peter Mourne I knew
became—Well, I'm blessed! That's the second shock of the day. So Carmela became Countess—"

"Viscountess Mourne, to be precise, Padre."

"Dear God! Who would have imagined it? I had no idea. I never dreamt
of connecting the poor Peter I'd known with the famous character I sometimes read about in the newspapers. A relation, perhaps—but nothing
more—"

Padre Francisco stopped as if an idea had suddenly struck him. "I
suppose it was you who put that advertisement in *El País*. I didn't answer
it because it seemed pointless. It was so long since I'd even thought of
Carmela. I'm sorry."

Ryle didn't contradict him. "It's not important, Padre, especially now
we've met."

Father Francisco stood up. "I'm sorry, but I must go now. *¡Adios y tenga
cuidado!* Take care and God go with you."

"Just one more question, Padre," Ryle said hastily. "About Steve Midvale." Remembering what the ex-journalist Grado had said, he worded his
question carefully. "Since Steve and Peter were rivals for Carmela's affec-
tions, did they quarrel?"

"Oh, they quarrelled. Fiercely." Padre Francisco spoke without hesita-

tion. "Peter was jealous because he knew in his heart that Carmela loved
only Steve, and Steve was envious of Peter because he had money and was
better educated, and obviously came from a quite different background.
Steve, for instance, never knew his father, who was killed in the first
German War a few months after he was born, and his mother had had a
hard time and had eventually died of tuberculosis, leaving the boy to be
brought up by his aunt. A sad story, but not uncommon."

The priest was moving off, and Ryle caught at the sleeve of his soutane.
"When you say they quarrelled fiercely, Padre, do you mean they actually
fought each other?"

"Yes, on occasion." Suddenly Padre Francisco gave a low laugh. "Are
you thinking of Peter's missing finger, señor? What story did he and
Carmela devise to explain that? Did they claim he lost it fighting for
Generalissimo Franco? Whatever they said, I'm sure it wasn't the truth—
that Steve caught him in bed with Carmela and went for him with a
knife."

Mark Ryle sat in a chair in the far rear corner of the church. He was in
shadow, his head bent, and he might have been deep in prayer. No one
would have thought of interrupting him, which was fortunate because he
needed to concentrate, though his meditation was not on religious matters.

He had delayed the priest as long as was possible, though, apart from
reiterating what he had said already, there was little that Padre Francisco
was able to add to his tale. But he was adamant that he had made no
mistake. He had not been present when the fight between Steve Midvale
and Peter Mourne took place. The only actual witness had been Carmela,
but she herself had described it to him, and he had seen both Steve and
Peter a few days later.

Peter Mourne's little finger on his left hand had been severed at the
second joint. Carmela had insisted on calling it his war wound, and had
made a great fuss of him. Steve had sulked; he had professed regret and
distress, but no one had believed him.

"What does it matter now, Señor Ryle?" Padre Francisco had demanded
at last. "It was all so long ago."

Yes—so long ago, Ryle thought, but of vital importance for the present
and the future. He hadn't believed Fernández Grado; he had assumed that
the old man was confused by his age and an excess of Spanish beer. But
the priest confirmed his story.

The fact must be faced. Viscount Mourne, the man whom everyone,
including his own family, had accepted as Peter Mourne, elder son of

David Mourne and his first wife, Sophia, was in fact an imposter called Steve Midvale.

Abruptly Mark Ryle rose to his feet. He had wasted enough time. The sooner he could get back to London and talk to General Bannol the better.

CHAPTER TWENTY-FIVE

General Bannol received Mark Ryle's information with some scepticism. "Mark, as I see it the situation is that we've got the word of an ancient, drunken journalist and a slightly less elderly Roman Catholic priest, both Spanish, that during the Civil War Peter Mourne had most of the little finger of his left hand chopped off in a fight with some character called Steve Midvale."

"That's correct, sir—as far as it goes," said Ryle, who had flown in from Madrid a couple of hours ago.

The General paid him no attention. "And from these bits of hearsay you've concluded that at some point in 1939—certainly before one of them arrived in Paris with Carmela—Steve Midvale and Peter Mourne changed identities. If you're right, where on earth do you suppose the real Peter Mourne is now?"

"Not on earth, sir. Dead, obviously!" Ryle was tired, but he spoke without hesitation. "A skeleton by this time, possibly somewhere in Spain in an unknown grave, buried as an unidentifiable victim of the last few months of the war, or perhaps—if he started the journey to France with the other two—in a crevice in the Pyrenees. I suspect that the latter possibility is the more likely. If he'd gone missing as a journalist while the war was still on, I might well have learnt of it from my Spanish informants. On the other hand, when the Republican front in Catalonia collapsed and Barcelona fell to the Nationalists, half a million refugees fled the country. Many of them went north-east to Port-Bou, which was the crossing point through the mountains to south-west France. Not all of them made it. Peter Mourne might have been one who didn't. Whether his death was accidental or not remains to be seen."

"But you must admit that's all supposition on your part, Mark. Mourne wasn't a refugee," the General protested, getting up from his chair to ease his aching limbs and walking slowly to the window.

"True, sir, but he was besotted with Carmela Drelano—and it's more than possible that he'd have gone with her—alone or with this Steve Midvale."

Bannol nodded slowly, and Ryle pressed home what seemed to be an advantage. "The one thing we do know for certain is that—for whatever reason—only two of the three of them reached the De Chantals' in Paris. And there's also the evidence of the De Chantals' maid, Marie-Antoinette Corbet. You recall her insistence that Carmela and the presumed Peter had some secret they were determined to conceal?"

The General grunted, and suddenly returned to his chair and swivelled it around to stare at Ryle.

"So you really do put credence in this theory of yours, Mark? You don't consider it somewhat unrealistic—fanciful, even?"

Ryle hesitated, loath to give way on even the smallest point. "Maybe," he said at length. "But it's certainly worth checking on, isn't it, sir?"

It was typical of the Director that, having made up his mind, he dealt with the problem firmly and swiftly. "Of course it is, Mark, and we're going to check on it thoroughly. But there must have been innumerable problems with any such impersonation. What about Peter's family, for instance? His friends? Wouldn't they have suspected a deception?"

"I don't know that he had any close friends, sir. Everyone agrees that he was a solitary person." Ryle paused, then spoke more slowly, arranging his thoughts. "As for his family, none of them had seen him since he was eighteen, and he was bound to have changed. He had taken part in a foreign war and he'd been ill for some months before he reached home. People would have expected him to be different, and look different."

Bannol was nodding again in apparent agreement. "Of course, by the time he returned to England his father was dead, and his half-brother and sister would have been too young to remember him well. But what about his stepmother?"

"Padre Francisco said that Peter and Steve could have been taken for brothers," Ryle replied. "Besides, we must bear in mind that Peter and Carmela didn't get back to England until Hitler had invaded Poland and we were at war. Elizabeth Mourne had her own problems by then, with Fauvel close to London in the vulnerable south-east of the country. And Peter was still far from well. That in itself could have helped to cover any dissimilarity—in voice, say—or any gaffe he might make."

"They were taking an unholy risk," Bannol commented.

"They must have considered it worth while, sir—as it proved to be," Ryle said. "And there's another point that's just occurred to me. Why did they go to Paris? Why not straight to a Channel port? If Peter had been alive he could have telegraphed or phoned Elizabeth Mourne for money once they were in France. No, instead the two of them went to Paris where they could try out the imposture on the De Chantals first."

"It was probably easier to get to Paris than to somewhere like Calais," Bannol commented mildly. "But all right, Mark!" General Bannol again eased his limbs out of his chair. "You've made your case for the moment. Now what we need is definite proof that we can lay before the PM. If we're right, it shouldn't be hard to find, now we know what we're looking for. There are dental records and fingerprints, for a start. Handwriting's less useful; the experts tend to disagree, and one's hand changes with age. It's too late to do anything today, but first thing tomorrow—" General Bannol sighed. "Until we're sure of our ground on this one, Mark, we'll have to move very carefully—very carefully indeed."

The next morning Ryle telephoned Jeanne early to apologize for his sudden departure from Madrid, but the *conserje* said that she had already paid her bill and left the hotel. She had given the British Embassy, care of Señor Hugh Mourne, as a forwarding address. Ryle tried the Embassy, only to be told that Hugh was in a meeting. Disgruntled, he set off for work.

He spent some time with Maggie and, with General Bannol's permission, briefed her on the situation, and gave her the task of investigating what could be discovered of Steve Midvale's early life. He himself would try to verify Peter Mourne's identity. In some ways his task was simpler, but it was hard to know how to approach it without arousing curiosity and awkward questions. However, the matter was urgent, and finally he was forced to compromise.

With the help of Special Branch, he was able both to establish that the pre-war dental records and X-rays of Peter Mourne had been preserved and to obtain them; the records of the late Viscount were of course readily available. The expert comparison took ten minutes. It proved beyond reasonable doubt that a substitution must have taken place.

By nine o'clock that evening the Prime Minister had been made aware that the late Peter Mourne, long-time Member of Parliament, former distinguished Secretary of State for Foreign Affairs, who had been honoured by Her Majesty the Queen with a peerage and created Viscount Mourne, had in fact been one Steven Philip Midvale, an impostor—and presumably a Soviet agent.

The implications were shocking—appalling. There was little doubt that the Government would fall, and the damage to relations between the British intelligence and security communities and those of the cousins—

the Americans—and the rest of the Western alliance would be immense. The long-term consequences of the débâcle could be foreseen only dimly.

Besides, as General Sir Walter Bannol was forced to admit to the PM, they had not yet reached the bottom of the affair. There remained the question of the Viscountess, and the extent of her involvement. Was she herself an agent during the Spanish Civil War? Had she recruited Midvale, or had he recruited her? Or was it chance—and love—that had brought them together, to make an opportunistic profit from a situation that presented itself?

And there was more. Why had the Russians—assuming it was the Russians who were responsible—started these rumours about Mourne while he was still alive? It was out of character for the KGB to act in such a fashion. As a rule they were insistent on protecting their own, and however much they might want to rescue Percival Dart and bring him "home" to Moscow, there seemed no reason why they should have sacrificed another highly placed agent—Mourne—to this end, and apparently left Carmela Mourne totally vulnerable. It would be useless for her to plead innocence.

The PM, Bannol and Ryle mulled over these questions urgently. They could reach no conclusions, except on the next step. Two hours later a large black chauffeur-driven limousine drove through the gates of Fauvel Hall and up to the front door. Inside it were General Bannol, Mark Ryle, and Maggie—dragged from her bed at short notice. The General had insisted that in the circumstance the party must include a woman.

There was a long pause before Mrs. Compton opened the door to them. She was not welcoming. "Lady Mourne has retired," she said at once in response to their request. "She cannot be disturbed."

The General took charge, and spoke formally. "Show us to a room where we can wait, and then tell your mistress that the matter is of the utmost importance. Mrs. Stewart here"—he indicated Maggie—"will accompany you."

The housekeeper seemed about to protest further, but the General's manner clearly over-awed her. With some hesitation she showed them into the drawing-room, and departed with Maggie. Ten, twenty minutes went by while the two men sat in almost total silence, busy with their speculations.

Quite suddenly Carmela Mourne came into the room, followed by Maggie. She was pale, with dark circles under her eyes, but she carried herself proudly, her head upright, her mouth firm. She was fully dressed in a black velvet skirt and a bright-red silk shirt, which immediately made Ryle think of a matador, and she was carrying a handbag. Ryle glanced at the bag, his thoughts obvious, and looked at Maggie, who nodded reassuringly. Carmela bowed her head in acknowledgement as the two men rose, then chose a chair and sat, staring at them. She uttered one word.

"So?"

"Madam," General Bannol began, "it is our duty to ask you questions, personal questions, relating to both the public and the private life of your late husband and yourself. I hope you will co-operate with us to the best of your ability, and give us straightforward and truthful answers."

"I am not in the habit of telling lies," Carmela replied coldly, "and I'm quite prepared to co-operate with you. But before we begin this—this interrogation, if that is what it is—I must make one thing clear. My husband was at no time in his life in the service of a foreign power. He was no spy—no traitor to his country."

"I'll bear your statement in mind, madam." Bannol remained seemingly unmoved.

"Then please do me the courtesy to remember my title. I am Viscountess Mourne, unless or until Her Majesty decides to deprive me of an honour that she was happy to bestow on my husband."

General Bannol sighed, but made no direct comment on this. It was a poor start, he reflected. It was clear that Carmela Mourne had every intention of continuing the game for as long as possible. It was also clear that she was unaware of their knowledge of Steve Midvale and the part he had played in her life. The General decided on shock tactics.

"Your late husband was Peter Mourne, eldest son of David Mourne and his first wife, Sophia. Is that correct, Viscountess Mourne?"

"Yes, of course," she answered impatiently.

Slowly Bannol shook his head. "No, Viscountess Mourne. My statement was not correct, as you well know. Your late husband was in fact Steven Philip Midvale who, with your knowledge and co-operation, has been masquerading as Peter Mourne since 1939."

"What utter nonsense!"

"It's the truth, and it is futile for you to deny it."

"It's another of those vicious Russian rumours like suggesting Peter was a—a traitor. He was—"

"Please, Viscountess Mourne." The General spoke sharply. "You are wasting our time. There is irrefutable evidence—records which do not lie. Think! You're an intelligent woman. If you help us, we will help you. If you're stubborn and stick to your absurd story that the late Viscount *was* Peter Mourne, then you're likely to spend the rest of your days in gaol. You have a choice. Which is it to be?"

There was silence until suddenly Carmela shrugged, and said, "I'm an old woman. My life is almost over—though it's strange how one clings to the last remnants. It may surprise you, but I've no regrets, except—"

"Except?" Bannol repeated quietly.

"Perhaps if we had come to you or, more practically, to John Mourne, who is a kind and good man, and told him of the imposture, I might have saved my husband's life. But maybe not. Considering all those dreadful rumours, who would have believed us?"

"I don't understand."

"No. I'm sure you don't." Carmela smiled sadly. "I see I must explain."

The General nodded to Ryle, who took his recorder from his pocket and switched it on. He murmured into it for a moment or two and placed it on a table between them.

"Now," said Bannol. "First would you tell us what happened to Peter Mourne?"

"He died in January 1939. Steve and I had decided that there was nothing left for us in Spain. The war was all but over, and Franco had won. It was a dreadful time. The weather was cold and wet and we couldn't have been more miserable." Carmela hugged herself, as if even here she could still feel the chill penetrating her bones. "Peter had a bad cold, and we tried to persuade him not to come with us over the mountains into France—after all, he was a non-combatant—but he insisted. On the way he became worse and died, possibly of pneumonia."

Carmela stopped speaking. She now looked small, shrunken and pathetic. But only Maggie showed any pity for her.

"So you tossed him into the nearest hole—the nearest crevasse or the nearest ditch," Bannol said brutally.

"Yes! That's just what we did do. And you'd have done the same in our place." Carmela grew in stature and replied in kind. "But first we swapped his good warm clothes and boots for Steve's things, which were thin and offered almost no protection. Then we set off again, but the leader of our party had come back for us. He saw Steve in Peter's clothes and assumed he was Peter. They were very much alike; they'd been taken for each other before, and Steve was ill just like Peter—though Steve was suffering from a battle wound, a bullet wound," she concluded almost proudly.

"Anyway, that was what gave us the idea," she continued after a pause, "especially as Peter's passport and papers were in the pockets of his clothes. And Peter had often spoken of his home and his relations, in considerable detail. I think he liked to boast, to show his superiority to Steve when, in fact"—Carmela Mourne hesitated, then exclaimed, "Oh, poor Peter! In any case, without meaning to do so, we had gathered a great deal of information about his family and his background. So here was a chance. Remember, we had nothing except what we stood up in, and that was mostly 'stolen' from Peter, and we had no prospects whatsoever. It was a chance worth taking. In the beginning we thought only of finding a breathing-space with the De Chantals, so that Steve could recover from his wound, but—"

"The temptation was too great for you both," Ryle said, his voice louder than he had intended.

Carmela turned her head to give him a wintry smile. "Yes, Mr. Ryle, you're quite right. It was all so simple. We had almost no trouble. Monsieur and Madame De Chantal accepted us without question. Oddly enough, the only person who seemed to harbour any suspicion of us—or rather of Steve—was the manager of the De Chantals' vineyards, to whom we were sent. I can't remember his name. He must be dead by now."

"Monsieur Brecquou," said Ryle, thinking of Chantilly and the fire-bombing of the old Frenchman's house there. "Oh yes, he's dead all right. He died a few weeks ago."

Carmela glanced at him questioningly, but merely said, "He must have been very old. As to why he suspected Steve, I don't know, but Peter had spent a holiday in the vineyards not long before going to Spain, and perhaps Steve showed that he didn't remember something he should have. However, Brecquou can't have told anyone, because we had no trouble in France, or when we got to England. By then, of course, we were man and wife. It goes without saying that we had various alarms. I'm not pretending that life wasn't nerve-racking, especially to start with, but it was easier than one might have imagined. And as time went on we really became Peter and Carmela Mourne. We no longer expected to be caught out."

"So all was well until the Soviet authorities discovered your secret, and you were approached by the KGB—or was it the GRU?" General Bannol said quietly. "Do you know how they came into possession of the facts?"

Carmela hesitated again. "It was the KGB—of that I'm sure. As for how they knew, I'm not sure. You must remember that Spain—and the France of the refugees—was at the time in question a place of plots and counter-plots, of spies and counter-spies, of eyes and ears. Someone might have guessed our secret and passed it on later for their own reasons."

"You may be right," said General Bannol.

Carmela resumed. "Anyway, as you say, it happened. It was a dreadful blow."

"You can scarcely expect sympathy," said Bannol. Then, abruptly, "Exactly when and how did the KGB approach you?"

"Fifteen months ago."

"What! Are you seriously telling me the approach was as recent as that?" The General made no effort to hide his incredulity.

"Yes," Carmela said calmly. "I could give you the exact date if I looked it up, though at first we didn't realize what was happening. It was at one of those large, amorphous parties the Government gives for visiting VIPs. There was a Spaniard. His name is Don Pedro De Solina. I suppose he was some sort of go-between. He called Peter 'Señor Midvale' and when Peter corrected him he laughed and said, 'I could have sworn you were Steve Midvale.' Naturally, we were worried, but nothing more happened for a fortnight. Then De Solina invited Peter to lunch, and made it clear the invitation couldn't be refused."

Carmela paused and sighed. Her voice had grown hoarse. Her small tongue came out, and wetted her lips. Unasked, Maggie rose, went to a table that served as a bar at the side of the room, and poured her a glass of Perrier. Carmela sipped at it gratefully.

"Thank you." She directed herself to Bannol again. "I'll be brief. There was a third man at that luncheon. A Muscovite from the Soviet Embassy, known to Peter as a KGB officer. When the Spaniard had left them alone together he didn't mince words. It was either become a Soviet agent—or face exposure and denunciation. Peter prevaricated, said it had been a shock—which was true—and generally played stupid. The Russian was *very* understanding, and before they all parted De Solina said he would be in touch.

"Peter came home—to Fauvel—and collapsed, but he wouldn't see a doctor. We were desperate. We had no idea what to do. Peter thought of going to the Prime Minister, but the PM isn't a sympathetic character— could one expect a PM to be sympathetic in these extraordinary circumstances? Then—"

"Then?" Bannol prompted.

"Well, then Peter had his heart attack. We played it up. Made it seem more serious than it was. It was a God-given opportunity to resign from political life. We hoped that perhaps—but it was wishful thinking."

Again Carmela paused and sipped the Perrier. She looked from one intent face to another. She had no worries about holding the interest of her audience, but she could read little from their expressions.

"The next thing," she went on, "was that the Spaniard, De Solina, did get in touch—he phoned to accept an invitation to lunch at Fauvel—an invitation he'd not received, naturally. He came. And by now the offer had changed in character. They accepted that Peter must retire from public life, but what he knew was still of importance. In return for their silence, De Solina said, we must go to Moscow—which would shake the British Government—but we would be well-treated while Peter was being questioned, and afterwards. Peter told the man to go to hell—that he'd rather be dead."

"Did De Solina seem to know about the imposture? Did he understand the alternative to your obeying instructions and going to Moscow?" Bannol asked suddenly.

"No, I'm sure he didn't," Carmela said after a moment's thought. She frowned. "It was a strange meeting. De Solina showed no surprise at Peter's attitude, and he didn't try to persuade us. But it was after that episode that these hideous rumours began. You know as much about them as I do, General, and probably a good deal more. To us they seemed pointless—a stupid revenge because Peter wouldn't do as they asked. But there must have been more to it than that, because they were prepared to kill Peter to make it look as if he were guilty, and couldn't face the consequences."

"What makes you think it wasn't suicide?" asked Bannol. "That was the verdict."

"Two reasons," Carmela said quickly. "Peter would never have chosen that way to die, and if he had decided to take his own life he would have left me a letter. I searched everywhere. There wasn't one. You must understand that my Peter and I were very close. Even after all these years we loved each other." Her voice broke, and she added without bitterness, "We had no one else."

She smiled sadly, and then added, "Actually, there is another reason. Much as I was upset by Peter's death, I didn't want to die myself, and I did not take that overdose, as everyone believed. The houseman, Simpson, must have spiked my milk. Though I can't prove it, I suspect he was responsible for killing Peter, too. And, if they killed Peter and made one attempt on me, why not another? Apart from avoiding publicity, that's why I've co-operated with the authorities and hidden myself in Fauvel all these weeks—I was fearful. Do you blame me?" She paused, and made a visible effort to regain her composure. "Now," she said, "I expect you want to ask questions."

"Yes," said Bannol non-committally. "First, if we are to believe your story, you and Peter—let us continue to call him Peter for simplicity—at some point ceased to be communists. When was this?"

"We were *never* communists—*never* members of the Party, nor fellow-travellers, as they used to be called," Carmela stated firmly. "We fought with the Republicans, yes. What we wanted was to save Spain from the dictatorship of El Caudillo. To achieve that end we were fully prepared to accept the Soviet Union as our ally, as you did in the Second World War.

Oh, lots of Republicans were Reds—true communists—as you know quite well; but not us. Peter—I mean Steve—was too intelligent. He said communism merely ended in another form of dictatorship. For heaven's sake, you must know what a clever man he was. After all, he did become British Foreign Secretary and an internationally respected statesman, in a very real sense on his own merits. General Bannol, I'm talking about Steve Midvale, who *earned* the title of Viscount Mourne. It's ironical, I know, but if it had been Peter Mourne who had survived, he would have achieved nothing of that kind. He was a nice enough boy, but he lacked ambition, flair, true intelligence."

It was a lengthy declaration, and at the end Carmela looked exhausted. Her face was white, tinged with grey. Her lips were bloodless, and there was a faint sheen of sweat around them. Bannol was afraid that she was about to collapse. He eased his limbs out of his chair and stood.

"Enough for now," he said. "There will be more later, of course—but enough for now. Thank you, Lady Mourne."

"Thank you," Carmela responded. She had opened her handbag, and was busy fumbling inside it. "In a sense I had anticipated an interview of this kind, and I want you to take these. This is a letter to my bank manager, authorizing you to remove everything from my safe deposit box, and here is the key. In the box you'll find a collection of diaries written by Peter over the years. They'll tell you all you want to know and will prove —prove beyond doubt—that my husband and I were never traitors to this country."

CHAPTER TWENTY-SIX

"More coffee?" Maggie asked.

Ryle stared at her sourly. "At the moment I'd be prepared to swear off coffee for life," he replied.

He had been at the bank the moment it opened that morning. There had been no difficulty about collecting the diaries of the man who had become Viscount Mourne and, sustained by cups of coffee and plates of sandwiches, Ryle had read solidly throughout the day. He had finished over an hour ago and made his report to the General, who had himself pored over some of the books and skimmed through others. Now even after he had bestirred himself to wash and shave and put on the clean shirt that he always kept in a drawer of his desk, Ryle felt tired and tense.

"Cheer up," Maggie said. "Viscount Mourne may have been an impostor, but at least we can be sure he wasn't a foreign agent. You said yourself that no one could have written diaries so consistently over all those years unless they were genuine. We've just got to accept them and everything they imply. Personally, I can't help feeling sorry for the poor man. He served the country so well—and yet his life was founded on a basic fraud."

"I doubt if the Prime Minister will share your sympathy for Mourne—or Midvale—or whoever he was," said Ryle. "The situation could be worse, I agree, but it's still appalling."

This was confirmed by General Sir Walter Bannol on his return to Cork Street later that night from a hastily arranged interview with the Prime Minister at Number Ten. The Director was looking old and very tired. He eased himself into his chair slowly and carefully.

"A decision has been reached," he said. "We are to bargain with the KGB. There really is no option, though the PM believes the diaries put us in a somewhat stronger position. There's no getting away from the fact that our Foreign Secretary was a liar, a cheat, a phoney. Even though the diaries prove to our satisfaction that he wasn't a traitor too, they won't necessarily convince anyone else without the Russians' co-operation. I can see the headlines: 'Mourne Diaries a Government Fake, say Opposition.' "

The General sighed. The PM, unjustifiably in Bannol's opinion, had given him a most unpleasant hour. "There's rarely a clear-cut victory in this business—as you both know quite well—and, if you're not absolutely certain of a win, the name of the game changes. It becomes compromise."

"Yes, sir." Ryle knew that the Director was speaking the truth and knew that he was equally irked by the inevitable pragmatism. "So, what do we do now?"

"I shall arrange for Dart to be removed from the hospital where he had his surgery. I'm told he's sufficiently recovered to be taken to one of our safe houses. Then, at the right moment, it will be announced that he has died suddenly during his convalescence. It's been established that he's got no close relations, so no one's likely to claim kinship with him. The bureaucrats and their niceties will be squared." General Bannol paused and stretched himself.

"Meanwhile you, Mark, will get hold of Señor De Solina. You'll tell him the truth. Say we know precisely what the KGB has been planning, and why. Quote chapter and verse—including the murder of that old man at Chantilly. Which reminds me—" He broke off for a moment, "I must have a word with the DST about those French types—Le Rougetel and that restaurateur on the Île de la Cité."

"What about Simpson, the houseman at Fauvel Hall, sir?" Maggie asked.

"We forget him," Bannol said at once. "He could never be charged with murder or even attempted murder, only theft perhaps. Anyway, there's been no sign of him yet, even from Interpol, and he won't resurface this side of the Iron Curtain."

"Sir—" Ryle prompted as the General lapsed into silence. "Anything more for De Solina?"

Bannol spoke slowly and carefully. "Tell him that we're convinced that Viscount Mourne was not an agent—you can mention the diaries—and that we're quite aware of the Midvale angle."

There was a pause before the General continued. "Say that if we have to we'll go public, but for obvious reasons we don't want to do that except as a last resort—De Solina's bright enough to see the point. So, if our instructions are followed, the KGB can have Dart. But—but if they try to double-cross us, Percy Dart, who will by that time be officially dead, will become a corpse in reality."

"Would the KGB mind if he did?"

"Certainly. They were prepared to murder in order to spread the word among their people that they never forget them."

"Of course, sir. And these instructions—our instructions for them?"

"When we give the word—and not before—their unfortunate diplomat will confess to his plot against Viscount Mourne. The Soviet Ambassador will apologize, and . . ."

The operation proceeded smoothly, both sides, as was typical of such "exchanges," having a good deal to gain and a lot to lose. The "death" of Percival Dart, who was heavily guarded in the safe house to which he had been removed, caused a spate of publicity in the media. Minor legal problems were fairly readily overcome. But his life was rehashed on television, a new biography was promised and various pundits—on and off the air—analysed the reasons for his treachery.

Inevitably, with Dart once more a centre of interest, attention turned again to the rumours about Viscount Mourne. It wasn't necessary to plant a question in the House at PM's question time. The Opposition kindly obliged, and the PM was able not only to reaffirm complete faith in the former Foreign Secretary, but also to state that Mourne's diaries, admittedly edited for security reasons, would be published within eighteen months. Naturally, as Ryle had foreseen, this declaration was met with expressions of distrust and even ribald comment, but these were inhibited as the scenario unfolded.

Two days later several leading newspapers received a letter from a Soviet diplomat *en poste* in London. He declared that he had made homosexual advances to Viscount Mourne, which had been angrily and scornfully rebuffed, and because of this he had embarked on a programme of spreading baseless rumours that Mourne was—and had been for many years—a traitor and a Soviet agent. He had also bribed three young people to commit acts of vandalism against the Mourne family in order to keep these rumours alive. He concluded by asserting that his conscience had been distressing him, and he had finally decided that he must tell the truth, whatever the consequences.

Needless to say, this confession created a furore. There were demands for further explanations, for a statement from the Prime Minister; there were many who suggested that the revelation was extraordinarily opportune, if not too good to be true. There was even a suggestion that the whole thing was a joke. Some papers cried for the Soviet authorities to waive diplomatic immunity and allow the official in question to stand trial for libel, but the more responsible commentators were prepared to settle for the expulsion of the diplomat, on the assumption that the man would suffer more from Soviet law than from British justice.

The doubters were finally convinced when the Soviet Ambassador requested a meeting with the Foreign Secretary. At a press conference after the interview he admitted that the young man had made a similar and full confession to his own authorities, that he had been vigorously interrogated, and that the truth of his statement could not be doubted. He was to be flown back to Moscow immediately, and there he would be severely punished.

The Ambassador made a handsome apology for what had happened, to the Foreign Secretary in person, and to the British nation on television. He made special mention of the Mourne family, and repeated his affirmation that at no time in his life had Viscount Mourne been a Soviet agent, or worked in any way for the Soviet Union or any of its allies. The Ambassador was totally unequivocal, and his apparent candour in what was an unprecedented situation won him much favourable comment.

Even General Bannol was satisfied. "They can't go back on that," he said with pleasure. "There's bound to be a lingering whiff of brimstone, but to all intents and purposes Viscount Mourne is cleared."

"I wonder what they'll do with their wretched man," Maggie said.

The General remained silent. But the next day a Soviet Embassy spokesman regretfully announced that the diplomat had been found dead in his bedroom. Rather than pay the penalty for his crimes, he had cut his wrists with a broken glass.

"More likely forced to take a cyanide pill," Bannol commented, but he was not displeased; a weakness in the scheme had been eliminated. "Now we must keep our side of the bargain, and let them have Dart, whose sad demise happily seems to have slipped into oblivion, as far as the media are concerned."

"Then let's hope he's not given a civic reception and a press conference the moment he reaches Moscow," said Ryle. "I know it's part of the agreement that he'll stay incognito for at least six months, but the Kremlin will be tempted to vaunt its prize."

"But it's a temptation they'll resist." General Bannol spoke with complete confidence. "After all, there has to be some trust even among people in our line of work."

It was a remark that Mark Ryle was to remember.

The following evening, after a trying day of negotiation with De Solina, Mark Ryle set off for Hampstead and dinner with the Mournes.

He found that it was a family party. The De Chantals—Louis and Annette—had come over from Paris to visit John and Colette. Hugh was home on leave from Madrid. Helen was there, and Jeanne, whom Mark had seen only two or three times in the weeks since his return from Spain. He was the only non-relative present.

"You never minded knowing us when Mourne was a dirty word, Mark," said John, "so it's right you should be here with us now to celebrate the end of what has been a ghastly, abominable business. The publicity's dying down at last, and we've become an ordinary family again—which is certainly something to give thanks for."

"What's more, there's Fauvel," said Hugh.

"Fauvel?" inquired Mark.

They told him, though he already knew. Carmela, Viscountess Mourne, was retiring to a small house on the south coast with Mrs. Compton to look after her. Fauvel Hall was to be made over to Hugh and Jeanne with a large sum of money, ostensibly for its upkeep, during her lifetime, and her whole estate was to be shared by them when she died.

"There may be some tax problems, but I'm told we can cope with them," said John.

"It's very generous of Carmela," said Colette.

"Surprisingly so." As usual, Helen was slightly acerbic. "She must have had a sudden change of heart."

Jeanne said, "I can scarcely wait. I'm thrilled!"

"What? Why? Because you're moving to Fauvel? Surely—" This time Mark didn't know the answer to his question.

"Fauvel's much too big and expensive for either Hugh or me to live in as it is, but it'll divide splendidly into three or four parts. We'll keep the two best for ourselves, and rent the rest. But I shall redecorate the whole place. It'll be a wonderful job. That's why I'm thrilled."

"My enthusiastic sister," Hugh said, laughing.

"Who is now an heiress," said Jeanne. "Gentlemen will be queuing up for my hand. Do you know, Mark, Simon Maufant had the nerve to phone and congratulate me on the fact that the Mourne affair was over, and would I have dinner with him one evening? I told him about Fauvel, just to whet his appetite. Then I told him to go to hell."

"Good for you." Mark grinned at her.

"Incidentally, Mark, were you not writing a book about Peter Mourne?" asked Louis De Chantal in his precise English.

"Er—yes, I was. A biography."

"What's happened to it?" Hugh inquired.

"Oh, its format has changed somewhat," said Mark airily. "I've been commissioned to edit his diaries, with notes and commentary where necessary. It should be an extremely interesting project." He didn't mention that the idea had been suggested by the Prime Minister.

"What about your usual magazine job?" Jeanne asked.

"I'm taking a sabbatical, so I expect to be in London pretty steadily for a year."

"And after that? Oh, never mind! I'll expect you to visit me at Fauvel then, Mark."

"Jeanne, you won't be able to keep me away. There must be a lot of papers there I'll need to read," he teased her.

Jeanne laughed. "Good," she said. "It sounds like a very satisfactory arrangement."

But this was a lighter aspect of the affair. Some nights later Mark Ryle stood by himself in the rain on the tarmac of a military airfield near London, and wondered what the Mournes would have thought had they known the truth about the late Viscount. He hoped they would never know.

Ryle was awaiting the arrival of the aircraft that was to take Percival Dart and De Solina to the Soviet Union. De Solina—the eternal go-between—had been appointed by the Soviet authorities to escort Dart on his flight, and he and Dart were at that moment being given drinks and a meal in the building behind Ryle. Ryle himself could not bring himself to eat with them.

The small passenger jet with its Soviet markings duly landed. Dart and De Solina came out to the aircraft, accompanied by an RAF Squadron-Leader who had merely been told that this was a VIP departure. Dart made straight for the aircraft, where he was greeted by the Soviet aircrew and a doctor who had been sent from Moscow, but De Solina insisted on shaking hands with Ryle, expressing the wish that they might meet again.

It was with a sense of relief that Mark Ryle watched the jet as it taxied to the runway, lined up, and took off into the night sky. That, he thought as he turned away with the Squadron-Leader, was the end of the whole sordid business.

But he was wrong. It was some days before British Intelligence learnt what had happened as the jet cleared British airspace. Apparently Dart, who had at first been very tense, at last relaxed, especially when a plump stewardess offered Caucasian champagne.

"Not long now," said Dart.

And they were the last words he uttered. He gave a strangled cry—"No! No! *Nyet!*"—and slumped forward against the back of the seat in front of him.

Beside him, De Solina turned and shouted. The doctor came forward at once. He took one look at Dart and dashed for his bag. He tried an injection and emergency resuscitation, and the hostess ran with a portable oxygen mask. At last the doctor shook his head.

"Heart," he said. "Excitement, I suppose—even relief can do it. I gather he's been through a lot in the past few years."

De Solina was silent. Responsible for Dart, he had no alternative but to agree with the doctor. If there were any truth in his suspicion that the British never intended their traitor to reach Moscow, it meant that he—De Solina—had been outwitted. In such circumstances, it was best to keep quiet.

Surprisingly, Mark Ryle shared some of De Solina's emotions, though for very different reasons. Remembering General Bannol's confidence that Dart's arrival in Moscow would not be fêted, in his turn he decided that silence was expedient.

About the Author

Palma Harcourt was born and brought up on Jersey, one of the Channel Islands. She then read classics at St. Anne's College, Oxford University. After her graduation, she worked in various branches of British Intelligence, in one of which she met her husband. Since then she has edited magazines and taught at universities. Palma Harcourt has now returned to live on Jersey. She travels frequently in search of new settings for her books.